THE TAMING OF THE SCREWS

Bedridden Bluestocking Barony
Book 1

Jade Hendren

© Copyright 2026 by Jade Hendren
Text by Jade Hendren
Cover by Dar Albert

Dragonblade Publishing, Inc. is an imprint of Kathryn Le Veque Novels, Inc.
P.O. Box 23
Moreno Valley, CA 92556
ceo@dragonbladepublishing.com

Produced in the United States of America

First Edition May 2026
Trade Paperback Edition

Reproduction of any kind except where it pertains to short quotes in relation to advertising or promotion is strictly prohibited.

All Rights Reserved.

The characters and events portrayed in this book are fictitious. Any similarity to real persons, living or dead, is purely coincidental and not intended by the author.

AI Statement: No AI or ghostwriting was used in the creation of this story, or any story, published by Dragonblade Publishing. All text, structure, content, ideas, and concept are 100% human generated solely by the author whose name appears on the cover. It is prohibited to use this material, or any copyrighted material, for AI engine training.

ARE YOU SIGNED UP FOR DRAGONBLADE'S BLOG?

You'll get the latest news and information on exclusive giveaways, exclusive excerpts, coming releases, sales, free books, cover reveals and more.

Check out our complete list of authors, too!

No spam, no junk. That's a promise!

Sign Up Here

www.dragonbladepublishing.com

Dearest Reader;

Thank you for your support of a small press. At Dragonblade Publishing, we strive to bring you the highest quality Historical Romance from some of the best authors in the business. Without your support, there is no 'us', so we sincerely hope you adore these stories and find some new favorite authors along the way.

Happy Reading!

CEO, Dragonblade Publishing

Author's Note

This book's title comes from Regency era slang, where "the screws" was a phrase used to refer to what was more formally called rheumatism. And that was an umbrella term for what was likely many different conditions involving chronic joint pain, but the closest modern-day equivalent would be rheumatoid arthritis, an autoimmune disease that causes joint erosion and many other debilitating symptoms.

Each book in this series features a chronically ill main character, and their symptoms and diagnoses are based on my own experience. While I have the privilege of modern medical advancements, Della does not, and imagining how our journeys with the same disease would be different because of the hundreds of years between us was the inspiration for this novel and the Bedridden Bluestocking Barony series.

*For my grandmothers, who both loved reading.
One would devour this book, and it would make the other clutch her pearls. You know who is who. While you were alive, you fought over who could be prouder of me, and I'd like to think that you both still are.*

CHAPTER ONE

LADY ADELAIDE HARRIS was content. Strangely so, some might say. For the forever-ill daughter of a viscount to be content in her banishment to the country, most might think her mad. But Della enjoyed the days she was able to spend out in the gardens. The air was fresh after a new spring rain, and the damp grass was soaking through the wool blanket beneath her.

"You look at peace," said her lady's maid. Della had not heard Clara approach, as she often walked so silently because she was less than fond of shoes.

"Your feet will be muddied," Della admonished. Though she loved Clara's general lack of propriety, walking outdoors with bare feet seemed less improper and more foolish.

"I know how to bathe." Clara lowered herself to the ground less than gracefully, as she did most things. After so many years, Della was more than used to Clara's eccentricities, especially her untamable mouth.

Della tried to move, though it took considerable effort. She knew better than to lie flat like this for so long, but she'd been so relaxed lying there with the afternoon sun on her face. Her hips were now completely inflexible, and her knees were so swollen that she struggled to fully straighten her legs.

"Are you well enough to spend so long in the sun?" Clara asked. She crossed her own legs underneath her effortlessly, brushing a bit of grass off her knee. She wore men's riding breeches with no socks or boots and a flowing men's shirt with no cravat. Della dusted off her own seafoam green day gown. It was from several seasons ago, and more formal than she ever needed to be, but she felt like an afternoon in the gardens was an event for which to dress up.

"I am quite well, actually." Della leaned back on her aching elbows and looked up once again at the sun. It had drifted behind a cloud, basking them in shade. An odd chill ran through Della. She was well enough to spend the afternoon outdoors, but perhaps not well enough to continue sitting on the wet ground.

Della looked out at the expanse of verdant grass, at the land that made up her home. Little had changed about the landscape in the nearly eight years she'd spent here. Little had changed about her, either. Since the doctors had determined her rheumatism was a lifelong affliction, she'd gone from debutante to invalid in a matter of weeks. That was ages ago, and Della appreciated each of her life's moments, whether they be in the brightness of the sun or the darkness of the silk curtains that canopied her bed.

"Have you begun to teach Gwendoline her numbers?" Clara asked. She'd started to pick blades of grass out of the earth and tie them in knots.

"I have." Della tried to straighten her posture before her elbows refused to support her weight. "It seems I've taught you everything I know, so I've had to move on to someone else. She's a bright young girl."

"Oh, please." Clara laughed. "You act as if you are an old maid yourself. Gwendoline is only a few years younger than you and I."

Della moved again as her spine stiffened. Gwendoline was the daughter of their cook Mrs. Goldsmith, and she was indeed only four years her junior, but Della felt as if she had worlds of experiences Gwendoline hadn't had the chance to partake in. Before she fell ill, Della had received the best education a lady of noble birth could, and she'd spent her early years here at

Westfield Manor staving off the riotous emotions caused by her casting out from society by reading. Now, Della taught all she could to whoever she could.

"She is only one-and-twenty, and she still has her chance at a decent marriage, if that's what she wants. If she doesn't, she'll have at least some education to rely on."

Della had been prepared for her come out into London society when her body began to hurt, and it hadn't stopped yet. Even now, as she rose to her knees and stretched out her trembling arms, that pain still lingered. Today was a good day, but even good days were painful.

"And you?" Clara asked, supporting one of Della's arms with both of hers. "What of you and marriage?"

Della stood, with the help of Clara on one side and her walking stick on the other. Clara shook the blanket they'd been sitting on to free the grass clippings.

"I cannot believe you would even ask," she huffed.

"Why not? Is the notion of marriage at our age so impossible?"

They took several steps back toward the house. The terrain was uneven, and her feet felt like they were made out of stone. They were so heavy and ungraceful. Della looked toward the ground. She watched Clara's bare toes sink into the grass.

With Della nearing five-and-twenty, and Clara a few months older, they would be considered spinsters in London society, but they were not in London society.

"You know it is not my age," she murmured. Della didn't know why they were having this conversation. She was happy, as was Clara, as far as she knew. "Marriage is still very much a possibility for you."

This was her life. Days spent abed, nights dining at the table with her staff, and the extremely occasional afternoon in the gardens.

"Have you heard from your Mr. Lockhart lately?" Clara's words were nonchalant, but there was an implied undertone of deeper meaning. This was not just polite conversation. Clara simply did not make polite conversation.

"You know I have not, but I expect a letter in the next few days," Della allowed. It wasn't that Andrew was especially punctual in his correspondence with her, it was more that she always began to anticipate a letter just before it arrived. It was the best kind of premonition. Della sensed it, as she always did. It was like the rain or a particularly frigid winter—she had the innate power to see it before it happened.

Those letters were a part of her life, too. A particular joy she knew was improper, but an indulgence she could not deny. She was never more grateful for her distance from the *ton* than when she received one of those letters.

Clara had opened her mouth to speak when they heard a shout. It was a commanding tone, but one of urgency. Mr. Stanton, their butler, was standing near the doorway to the house, calling for Clara.

"Harry," Clara sighed. Della couldn't tell if it was a breath of fondness or frustration.

He called her name again. The shouting was rather rude, even by the relaxed standards Della held at Westfield Manor. There was no need for the formal etiquette loved by the rest of the nobility, but basic politeness was appreciated.

"Stay right here," Clara did not wait for a response before taking off. She nearly skipped to Mr. Stanton's side. Della should admonish him for shouting at Clara, but she had the notion that there was much deeper impropriety woven into that particular relationship. Even from this distance, Della could tell they stood much closer together than was acceptable. Clara's body swayed toward his. He, so much taller and so much more stern. She, small and boisterous and bright. They made a beautiful pair. Marriage was certainly in the cards for Clara, and Gwendoline too, if she was so inclined.

But not for Della. She had to remind herself of that, sometimes.

Clara did not skip back to her side, she ran. It was unladylike, even for her. Della knew there could only be one emergency that inspired this sudden rush of chaos. Harry did not shout, and Clara did not run. Unless . . . Clara reached her side with such force they both nearly toppled over into the grass. Della would not have been able to get back up.

"It's your parents, Miss Harris." Clara gripped Della's arms, already resorting to that sense of formality they both despised. "They're on their way here."

Clara sighed.

"Well, I suppose you had better find your shoes."

CHAPTER TWO

WHEN DELLA NEXT saw Clara, she was properly dressed. She was almost unrecognizable with her dark muslin dress and her hair pinned back. The clothing could be overlooked with a bit of effort, but the darkened nature of Clara's spirit could not.

"When are they to arrive?" Della asked. She was attempting to get out of bed and actually succeeding, which was a rare occurrence.

"The viscount and viscountess should arrive tomorrow, Miss Harris." Clara dipped into a curtsy, and Della wanted to roar.

"You know you needn't do all this for me." She gestured to Clara's appearance. Her behavior was off-putting like this. The person in front of her was not Della's best friend. She seemed to have been replaced by an imposter.

"I know." Clara shook her head. "But it is good practice."

Della stood up on her own, a feat not always possible first thing in the morning. She felt bad for summoning Clara; she really didn't need the help.

"Are you still feeling well?" Clara pulled a day gown out of the armoire without being asked. Della was not fond of the stiffness of the fabric, and she would often lounge about the house in her night rail and a dressing gown. Should her mother ever see such a thing, however, she'd drop dead on the spot.

"I am." Della put on the proper undergarments and let Clara tighten the stays that always hurt her ribs. Even if she wore a day gown, she never wore her stays unless she absolutely had to. The laces were horrible to deal with when your hands were irreparably damaged. "But I am sure this period of good health will end as soon as my family descends on the manor."

Lacing up the ties behind her back, Clara laughed.

"Undoubtedly so." Clara tied the bows, and they finished getting Della dressed. "Let's go down for breakfast."

"Surely a poor, ill woman should be exempt from the notion of socializing so early in the morning," Della grumbled. She'd woken up in a dour mood, and she didn't want to be removed from it. It was comfortable in this cocoon of her own disconsolate feelings.

"Oh, for heaven's sake." Clara huffed, grabbing Della by the arm and pulling her toward the door. She needed the help, truthfully. Her left hip was locked into place, and it just wouldn't allow the movement required to walk. "You are not some pitiful, helpless, sick woman. You are ill, yes, but there is nothing sad about you."

She spoke with such conviction that Della had to agree, even though she didn't want to. She felt pitiful, sometimes. Sitting alone in her chambers clinging to old letters. Relying on the domestics her parents employed for company. Avoiding the aforementioned parents even when their brief time in residence would be all she'd likely see of them this year.

Her illness was one thing. It was painful. It was relentless. It had irrevocably changed the course of her life, and it was something that would always be with her.

But her isolation was another thing entirely. Clara may think there was nothing sad about her, and Della appreciated her vigor, because she knew she really believed that. It was just difficult to reconcile that with her reality. It was nearly impossible to think she wasn't some pitiful creature when her own parents had sent her away as they had. When they kept her here nearly alone.

Nearly alone wasn't alone, though.

Clara kept hold of her arm until Della's hip stabilized. They both heard it crack like a tree limb breaking, and then everything felt the slightest bit better. For a second, Della wished she could do the same to her emotions—move a certain way, hear a sound arguably too loud for any stable body to make, and then feel magically improved. That was the thing, though. That magic improvement was temporary, and her pain was forever. Perhaps the same could be said for her sudden melancholy.

She felt wobbly today. That was unusual. Perhaps her down-trodden emotions were making her pain worse. She dismissed the thought as the kind of rubbish her mother believed. The kind of hearsay and pseudoscience that backed their logic to send her all the way out here, away from the chaos of London.

"Did they mention if David would be accompanying them?" Della asked of her brother, the future viscount. As much as Della did not want her parents to visit, she would do almost anything to avoid her brother. He was a few years younger, and to Della's memory, they'd been close as children. Now, she couldn't remember the last time they'd spoken. The last time she'd received a letter from him, even. It was as if, in her brother's eyes, her illness had killed her, and that distance made her doubt her own perception of their shared childhood. It made her believe they'd never been close at all.

"Their letter did not say. It was rather brief."

They left Della's chambers and descended the stairs at a slow pace. Della could've taken any of the chambers on the ground floor, but she rather liked the heightened view from the second story windows.

"At least they've sent a letter ahead this time. Every day, I'm fearful they'll surprise us."

At her right side, Clara laughed.

"Perhaps if your mother did not have specific requests for the menu that required advance preparation, we would have no warning at all."

Della was grateful for the advance notice of their arrival, but not for the strain it put on Mrs. Goldsmith and the rest of the house. Della was not even in the habit of planning a menu. Mrs. Goldsmith cooked whatever she liked. If the viscountess knew Della dined with her entire staff *en famille*, she would be apoplectic.

They reached the bottom of the stairs, and everyone was aflutter. Gwendoline dusted the curtains. Mrs. Goldsmith could be heard from the kitchens beating and banging. Silas, their lone footman, coachman, and stable boy, rearranged the furniture in the drawing room, returning it back to the way it had been the last time the home's true owners had been in residence. Della couldn't remember when that was, exactly. Her parents were so fond of town, they didn't even return to the country at the end of the season as most did.

Della's stomach turned at the sight of everyone she cared about in such a state. Her parents made them anxious, and that was an experience they all shared. It wasn't like this when it was just Della's house. It was calm and serene, and she hoped it was a nice place of employ. Now, it felt like a lion's den.

"Good morning, Harry," Clara hummed. Della thought she saw him blush. Mr. Stanton was the only person not moving about the house in a rush. He stood stalwart against the wall, wearing formal livery and fine white gloves.

"Good morning, Miss Fletcher." The formality in his voice was not new, and Della knew it was not only for her parents' sake. He did normally refer to Clara by her first name, though. Della thought she saw Clara blush.

"Please allow me to apologize in advance for everything, Mr. Stanton." Della would utter this apology to each of them, probably more than once. She didn't need to explain herself any further. They all knew what she meant.

"No apology necessary, Miss Harris. I'm sure the viscount and viscountess will have a splendid visit." Harry nodded, as if it would be so simply because he said so.

Della was sure it would indeed be a splendid visit for her parents. They'd go back to London and tell everyone how wonderful it was to see their poor daughter. They'd speak about how the fresh country air did them such good, and every second in their presence would be hell for Della and everyone she loved.

CHAPTER THREE

T HE VISCOUNT AND viscountess descended on Westfield Manor with a flourish of aristocratic indulgence, arriving just as evening settled. Della watched from the chaise longue in the corner of the front parlor as their carriages approached. She counted them by the lights illuminating their way. Three carriages was excessive, quite frankly. One carriage for the viscount and viscountess, another for their servants, and the last appeared to be exclusively for their belongings. Their note hadn't indicated how long they had planned to stay, or the reason for their rare visit to the country house. That bit of excess suggested a lengthy stay, and Della felt her spine tense up at the thought.

She sat alone, all of her household having been consumed by the fervor of her parents. It was not a particularly great day for her pain, and all of her joints felt fevered. She wore one of the day gowns her mother insisted on sending in the newest fashions each season. The fabric was starchy and uncomfortable, and the style restricted her movement. She supposed she didn't need to move much with her parents in residence. She'd be expected to ring for Clara should she need even the slightest thing, and her walks about the garden would be put on hold until they left. There was a stark dichotomy between the way Della lived and the way her parents thought she did. There were times where she was able to forget how fundamentally they misunderstood her, but today was not one of those times.

"Adelaide, my dear." Her mother entered the parlor with as much flare as they'd approached the manor. Her gown was more fit for the evening than for traveling, an abundance of bright-pink silk and garish gold trim, but Della would've expected nothing less.

Della blanched at the sound of her full name. She heard it so rarely, and it seemed so ill-suited. Della rose to her feet to greet them, the heavy skirts of her gown getting tangled around her legs. She hated the blasted thing, as pretty as it was. She might be a young lady, but she was a young lady in a great deal of pain, and she had no patience for the discomforts of the finery her mother preferred.

"Oh, don't get up." Her mother approached the chaise longue and waved her hands in Della's general direction.

Della braced for a hug or a kiss on the cheek in greeting, but nothing came. This was what hurt the most about her mother, that she'd loved her dearly as a child, and their mutual mission to see Della well married had provided common ground in her adolescence. When Della had fallen ill, Esther had exhausted herself in trying to make her better. She'd summoned doctors from all around. They'd tried experimental and downright harsh remedies. Her mother had even spent many nights sleeping in a chair beside her bed.

But one day, she'd come to the realization that Della's condition would never improve, and the beauty of their connection was lost forever. As was Esther's sense of compassion, it seemed. She'd become as harsh as the treatments they'd tried, and Della could hardly recognize the woman who sat in front of her now.

The viscountess lowered herself gracefully into an armchair opposite Della, and she looked around as if she'd never seen their front parlor before. It had once been a familiar place for her, when they were a young family. But they had made the journey out to the countryside less and less over the years, as her mother became more involved in the *ton*, and now Della wondered how the room appeared through her mother's eyes. Della knew she'd find something lacking. A speck of dust or a scuff in the gilded wallpaper. Perhaps a chair that was not placed at exactly the right angle in relation to the door. The dimming fire making the place too warm.

"I often forget why we do not travel to the country more often. I'm reminded now that the journey is simply exhausting," the viscountess said. She looked around once more. "And I rang for tea and cakes ages ago. Where could that cook be?"

Della wanted to rage. Mrs. Goldsmith was but one person, doing her best to meet the downright unreasonable expectations held by the lady of the house.

"I still find it quite unusual that the cook has her daughter here. A young lady of her station should be working in her own position."

Mrs. Goldsmith entered the parlor at that moment, delicately balancing a tray full of refreshments. Mr. Stanton opened and closed the door as she came and went. The formality of it all was so exhausting to Della. If she had to live out all of her days like this, those days would number very few.

"I've been teaching Gwendoline. We're starting with simpler things, like her numbers and letters. She's doing quite well." Della tried to defend them—all of them, Gwendoline, Mrs. Goldsmith, and herself.

"I'm so pleased to hear that." The viscountess's face pinched as she leaned over the cart to pour tea. Her words were achingly artificial, and her pink garnet necklace fell away from the skin at her throat as she hovered. "Your former governess would love to know there was some use for your education after all."

She handed Della a teacup and saucer, and Della thought her fragile hands might drop the delicate china and ruin the plush, green carpet. Behind that worry in her mind was a childish desire to drop the damn thing on purpose. If she thought she could do so effectively without some sort of skeletal malfunction, Della might make a scene, leaving the room and stomping her feet the entire way. She'd done things like that in the past. Her early days at Westfield Manor were rife with those kinds of tantrums, but they'd borne dire consequences. Clara wasn't her first maid. Back when Della had first been sent away, her mother had abruptly dismissed the lady's maid she'd brought with her from London. She'd always suspected her mother had done so just because Della liked her. It was a sign that rebellion wouldn't be tolerated, and Della had never forgotten. She couldn't risk anything like that happening now, not to the people who had since become the closest thing she had to family.

"Have you been quite well, dear?" her mother asked. Having returned to her own chair, she sat so close to the edge that Della thought she might tip over. This was in an effort to keep control of her skirts, even though there was no impropriety in accidentally baring an ankle to one's own daughter.

"I've been fine, thank you." Della nodded. With her mother, her manners were reflexive, as was the sentiment. Della wasn't sure what it meant to be well, in her case. Under the circumstances, sitting upright and enjoying tea in the parlor would be quite well indeed, if only she had better company.

She knew that the standards of politeness would have her ask the same question of her mother, but Della could not be bothered to do so. At certain times, the falseness of it all was more than Della could speak through. Silence reigned, and the only sounds were the movement of other people about the house and the light clanging of their teacups against their saucers.

Even in the stifling awkwardness, Della hoped. She hoped her mother would acknowledge the day's importance. She hoped someone would. It was foolish, that reckless faith Della still had in everyone around her.

"I should like to take a bath," her mother huffed, dusting invisible dirt off of her sleeve. "And I believe I'll take my dinner on a tray in my room. Goodnight, my dear."

The viscountess departed the room without another word,

only stopping in the doorway so Mr. Stanton could bow toward her feet. A mix of disappointment and relief sailed through Della. Relief that one evening with her mother was over. Disappointment that they'd shown up at all.

Della rose slowly, the aches traveling from her feet up to her shoulders, then back down her arms. She climbed the stairs with the aid of her walking stick and the banister, and she thanked the heavens that her mother preferred rooms in the home's other wing. She opened the door to her own chambers, and Clara was seated behind the writing desk in her sitting room.

"Clara." She startled at seeing her rooms already occupied. She would've toppled over without the stability of her walking stick. "Goodness me."

"Oh, do come in!" Clara stood, pulling back the desk chair and patting the padded back.

"I didn't know I needed an invitation." Della smiled. Clara's excitement was obvious, and she wondered what could have changed her mood so significantly. There was hardly much to be excited about with her parents in residence.

"I have a gift for you." Clara stood with her hands behind her back as Della sat behind the desk. This was all very ceremonious, and for absolutely no reason. "But first, I must apologize for today. We had plans to all have dinner together, and Mrs. Goldsmith was going to make your favorite chocolate cake, but—"

Someone had recognized today. Clara had. They had. Her entire household had planned to make today special for her, and her own parents could only be bothered to ruin it. There was no room on her mother's delicately selected menu for chocolate cake, and there was certainly no room at her mother's table for servants. Della felt the sting of tears in her eyes, and for a moment, she was completely without words.

"There is no need for apologies, Clara. I'd hoped you'd know that by now." Della looked at her, and she did seem almost unbearably apologetic. Her face was so earnest. She'd tried so hard, and it almost hurt Della how much Clara cared.

"In fact," Della grimaced, "have I apologized yet for the atrocious things my mother will surely do?"

Clara laughed. She nodded.

"I'll accept no apologies from you either. Though I did hear her warn poor Mrs. Goldsmith on her way in against over-sweetening the porridge for tomorrow's breakfast. She hasn't even been here for breakfast in a year, but of course, she remembered that the porridge was too sweet. She said they weren't wealthy enough to be eating in such splendor every day, and you don't need such rich food. It isn't good for your health, she said. As if they care about your health. As if they care about you at all."

Della flinched at the brutally honest statement. Life with her mother was full of little hurts like those, and nothing hurt worse than the truth.

Clara stepped forward, leaned against the solid wood desk. Her brown hair was escaping the pins she despised wearing. Della wondered if her head had started to ache yet. The gray, plain dress she wore was so uncharacteristically boring. She looked every bit the respectable lady's maid, but Della didn't want to be speaking with any respectable lady's maid. She wanted to speak with her best friend.

"This was delivered for you this afternoon, just after your parents arrived. I was able to convince Mr. Stanton to allow me to pass it along personally. I thought you'd rather he not present it on silver in front of your mother."

Della's cheeks flushed with warmth. She knew exactly what Clara held so tightly behind her back. Perhaps this day wasn't a lost cause after all. That instinct of hers never failed. That very morning, she'd unearthed some of Andrew's old letters, even some of her own early drafts she'd never sent. Andrew's were pristine and well-preserved, except for the natural wear and tear of being read over and over again. Hers were scribbled out, ripped in half, and occasionally stained with tears. There was no particular reason she was doing this, Della told herself. She was simply feeling nostalgic. Something about her milestone birthday, she assumed.

That the previous part of her life she felt most nostalgic for was her correspondence with Andrew was of little importance.

"Convinced him, did you?" Della arched one eyebrow. "I'll ask that you protect my delicate sensibilities and spare me the details."

Clara's exasperation was a fun thing to play with, but Della was getting a bit impatient herself.

"I assure you it was nothing untoward. Harry truly did not want to alert your mother to your correspondence."

For that, Della was immeasurably grateful. She hardly thought a series of chaste letters was anything to fret over, but society did so love to fret.

"Thank you, Clara." She meant it sincerely. "And please thank Mr. Stanton for me. But please do so discreetly. I know that he makes you giddy, and I would hate for my mother to witness it."

The viscountess had a sixth sense for other people's happiness. She knew how to find it, how to exploit it, and how to destroy it. Della couldn't bear it if she let that harm Clara or Harry or anyone in her home.

Clara simply nodded. Her eyes still held that strange excitement, but her face was composed. As if no secrets had been shared.

"I suppose I should leave you to your reading, unless you should need me for anything else?"

Clara handed over a letter. Della recognized the paper and the wafer and the scent wafting from it immediately. Her heart lurched in her chest, and she told herself it was simply a rebellion of her ribs after so much time spent in restrictive clothing.

"If you could return to assist me out of this infernal contraption some call clothing, that would be much appreciated." Della hated to ask. As much as she loved Clara's company, she despised relying on her help. She never wore gowns and undergarments like this that required delicate hands to take on and off.

"Of course," Clara glided toward the hallway with a smile, and Della heard the soft snick of the door close behind her.

She ran her fingers over the letter. It was a preposterous thing to cherish so fervently. How ridiculous that something as simple as a piece of paper could tempt her heart into such feeling. After holding back everything that made her herself today, most of all her deep emotions, it was such an indulgence just to feel. To touch the paper that he'd touched and run her fingers over the dried ink and imagine being this close to him somehow. Della broke the seal.

She'd kept them all, eight years' worth of correspondence sat at the bottom of a trunk in the corner of her rooms. She always kept the latest one within arm's reach. Many of them were creased and weathered from her fingers running over each line of script. That was how she savored them, how she kept their conversation going.

Today, that didn't feel like enough. Her fingertips and his words weren't enough to banish the loneliness that made her ache in a way her illness never could. Or maybe it had. Maybe her illness was an integral part of that loneliness.

Dear Della,

Thank God, she thought. Someone used her real name. It was a familiarity that she shouldn't allow, being that they hadn't seen each other since she'd come to Westfield Manor over eight years ago. She should be Miss Harris to anyone in her acquaintance. Her Christian name was perhaps even a step too far, but to shorten it even further was really far too casual.

If I've managed my timing, and the post has cooperated with my plan, this should arrive on the anniversary of your birth.

Oh, Andrew. He'd remembered.

I'm told it's a recently established tradition to celebrate the anniversary of one's birth like a holiday. The idea sounds rather fanciful and is perhaps better suited for the children of the world, but I do think you are always worth celebrating.

Della's breath clutched in her throat, and she could no longer pretend it was the fault of her stays. She ran her fingers over those last words before she kept reading. Just to remind herself that he thought she was worth something.

There is no other reason for my writing, I'm afraid. I've no meaningful new pieces of my life to share. My work in London continues to drag on. It does so whether I am mentally present or not, oddly enough. I've settled a bit more since my last letter. Returning to England after so long abroad was a shock to the senses, and I think perhaps I need a break from the fast pace of town. I know it to be impolite to assume an invitation for myself, especially to the home of an unmarried young lady, but our clandestine correspondence has always been on the wrong side of propriety. So, do you think you might have room for a guest at Westfield Manor?

Della gasped out loud, so taken aback at the mental image of him walking up to her front door. Sitting in her parlor for tea. She could barely picture it. It had been so long since she'd seen his face. He'd have changed so much over such time. She wondered if he'd still have that slightly long hair that curled at the ends. If his smile was still as breathtaking. If he still had those deep dimples on his cheeks she'd always wanted to kiss.

Della wondered if he was still the same man she'd always adored.

I'll stop my rambling, but please consider my terribly rude proposition. I do certainly miss you. I hope you've had a lovely birthday, Della.

Yours,
Andrew

She ran her thumb over those last words, just one more time. He hoped she'd had a lovely birthday. And suddenly, she had.

❧❧❧

CHAPTER FOUR

DELLA HAD RETIRED early. Each day spent with her parents was more agonizing than the last, and they'd nearly turned her into the recluse they thought her to be. She'd done some reading, covertly held a lesson with Gwendoline in her chambers, and then drifted off to bed while most of the house was still up and about.

Then, she was suddenly awoken an indeterminable amount of time later by someone parting the heavy curtains around her bed. Della was unsure of how to react. She was shocked still for a moment, until she recognized the wild hair springing free from the pins on her head. Della was almost certain there was almost no privacy between a lady and her maid, but Clara had surely never crossed this particular boundary before.

"Della," Clara almost hissed. "I fear I've done something horrible."

Without her permission, Clara climbed up onto the bed and let the curtains fall closed. There was absolutely no light around them now, and they were ensconced in a dark quiet. It was possible Della should feel more concern, but what Clara considered to be a horrible action on her part was usually something laughable, like going out dancing in the rain or letting her feet rest on the furniture.

"What is going on?" Della finally asked. She rubbed the sleep out of her eyes and tried to tame her unruly hair. She could feel little strands standing up at all ends on the crown of her head. Clara couldn't see her, but that mattered little.

"I fear I've done something horrible," Clara repeated. Della heard her move, tucking her legs underneath her body even though she still wore her proper dress.

"You've mentioned that, and yet I am still having trouble understanding."

Clara huffed. Della tried to sit up, but her hips were not agreeable to the action, so she slumped back onto her multitude of pillows.

"I was downstairs a moment ago, on my way to bid Harry a good night." As Clara spoke, Della's mind wandered. She thought of all the horrible things that could happen to Clara and Harry with her parents here. Her stomach turned violently. "He was still awake because your father was still in his library, and he refuses to go to bed until the viscount does, the bloody stubborn man."

Clara took a deep breath, and Della thought her own lungs hadn't breathed in years.

"I had planned to walk past, but it wasn't just your father. Your mother was with him, and they were speaking about you."

Della gasped, indignation rising in her heart. Not at her parents—she could hardly rouse feelings for them at all—but for Clara. For what Clara may have done in the name of defending her honor.

"Oh, Clara, please tell me you didn't confront my parents over some perceived slight. You should not have risked yourself, your entire livelihood, over something so inconsequential as their opinion of me. There are few things I care for less."

"I did nothing of the sort, I assure you." Clara reached out into the dark, and her fingers found Della's forearm. "I know I can be quite reckless, but I would never do anything so foolish. You are my dearest friend, but I'm afraid I could never stand up to the viscount and viscountess."

Della finally breathed a sigh of relief. That was the worst thing she could possibly imagine, Clara standing up to Della's parents at her own expense. Such was the problem, though. Clara couldn't confront them, and neither could anyone else.

"Well, then." Della relaxed some, certain this whole endeavor was just a fit of Clara's dramatics. "What did you do that was so horrible?"

"I listened." Clara stood up abruptly, like she could no longer tolerate her own stillness. She threw open the curtains that shrouded them, and some light flickered in from the dimming fire. "I stayed, and I listened. I cannot credit why, Della, but there was something that made me hang on their every word."

Clara had begun to pace, and Della was more confused than concerned. Her words weren't matching her actions. She walked swift laps about Della's chambers, but Della was still not understanding what awful misdeed she'd done. Overhearing was far from a crime, and this act of mild espionage was committed by all sorts of household servants all over England. Some considered the gossip a benefit of their position.

"I'm afraid I don't know how to tell you this, Della. Although perhaps you know already, and I am making a fuss for nothing. I do not think so, however. I'm almost certain you would have told me had you known such a thing." Clara's voice was uncharacteristically serious, and her face was downtrodden. She wouldn't meet her eyes, and Della began to panic in earnest. She moved to the edge of the bed, facing Clara. She'd hoped to interrupt one of her laps back and forth across the room. Horror scenes flashed through Della's mind. She thought of illness and death and grave danger.

"What is it, Clara?" Della whispered.

"They were discussing your inheritance. From your mother. Your true mother, not the viscountess." Clara stopped walking. She met Della's eyes.

"You must've misheard. I have no inheritance." Of that, she was sure. That the current viscountess was actually her stepmother was less of a secret and more of a rarely discussed truth. Esther was the only mother Della had ever known, her own having passed away in Della's first year. That left Della with no memory of her, and certainly no material possessions to inherit. That was true of her father, too. Everything that belonged to the viscount would go to her brother, who would be the new viscount upon their father's death, and she'd be dependent on his charity to live comfortably. Della paid little thought to that period of time an undetermined length into the future, in an effort to protect her heart.

"No, I'm certain that is what I heard." Clara sat down again next to Della on the bed. "What do you know of your grandmother?"

"Very little," Della admitted. Her parents were not especially fond of discussing their upbringings and their extended families. "I know nothing of her, truly. Father was her only child, and he only speaks of his own father, the first Viscount Morley. He received the viscountcy from His Majesty for his work in Parliament."

"I believe they were discussing your mother's mother," Clara said.

"Oh," Della muttered. "I know even less about her. You know we never speak about my mother. It makes Esther uncomfortable." Even referring to her by her given name felt odd to Della. She was not the person who had given birth to her, but she'd always been her mother. Speaking about her in such a way felt like disrespect even she wasn't owed.

It had never saddened Della before how little she knew about the feminine side of her own lineage. She could trace her father's line back several generations of wealthy businessmen and landowners, but she couldn't say the same for her grandmothers on either side.

"She was a baroness," Clara said. Her eyes were wide and frightened, and Della had never seen her so alert. "In her own right, they said."

"In her own right?" Della gasped. "I didn't know such a thing was possible."

Land and money and a title passed down to a woman instead of a man. The idea felt ludicrous to Della, and she was ashamed of her own reaction.

"I had never heard of a woman's inheritance either, unless it came from a generous father," Clara whispered. A generous father was a luxury provided to neither of them, but no one spoke of it.

"So, my grandmother was a baroness. What has that got to do with me?" Della could hardly believe the idea, it all sounded so far-fetched.

"The barony is yours, Miss Harris." Clara confessed. Della winced at the formality, at the distance it put between her and her friend, even though they remained seated right next to each other.

"That cannot be." Della was mystified.

"It must be," Clara insisted. "They were worried you'd discover your property. Your father said something about the letters patent, and the estate being placed in a trust until your marriage or your twenty-fifth year."

"Why, that's now." Della's hands shook.

Clara simply nodded.

A multitude of questions filled Della's mind. She wondered how a woman could own her own land. A baroness in her own right. Della didn't know where the barony was, or if it could really be hers, or why her parents would ever have hidden this from her.

It was nauseating and overwhelming, and this unexpected intrusion into her comfortable life tore at the very fabric of her being. The air started to feel too thin and her breathing too ragged.

"Clara," Della whispered, reaching around to grab her hands. "I need you to not speak of this. To anyone. I must . . . I must think, and I must find some answers."

Clara nodded again. Della knew it was as good as a promise. She had her discretion and her support, and up until this very moment, she hadn't realized how deeply she'd held her loyalty.

"Thank you, Clara." She squeezed her hands. "I'm quite certain I've no idea what's going on, but I think you've just changed my life."

Clara squeezed back. It was so strange to see her so quiet. She would almost appear reserved if her hair weren't a veritable mess. Wordlessly, Della climbed back into bed. She tried to get comfortable amongst her abundance of pillows, but her heart felt so restless she thought she may never settle down into sleep again. She heard the door close as Clara left, and her mind raced.

Della thought of trust, and of loyalty. She could never simply ask her parents about what Clara had heard. It would put Clara at risk, and that was one thing she'd never do. Even if she were to ask, they clearly couldn't be trusted to tell the truth.

She hated to admit it, but Della needed help. She needed someone who might be on her side. Who might favor her over her parents. Someone their power wouldn't intimidate. There was only one person in her life who fit that description.

Thinking of him and only him, Della fell asleep.

CHAPTER FIVE

WHEN ANDREW RECEIVED the letter, he breathed a sigh of relief. Even if it turned out to be a stunning rebuke, she'd written him back. He'd been so nervous he hadn't been able to sleep. Not without dreaming of her—this faceless, shapeless silhouette of someone he hadn't seen in years. It was less about what he saw in those dreams, and more what he heard: her laugh.

As he spotted the letter on the corner of the sideboard, he was so overwhelmed with relief that he forgot to temper his reaction in front of his mother.

"A letter came for you, my dear," she said, a smugness in her voice that Andrew was sure meant bad things for him. "Must be an interesting topic of conversation. Your Miss Harris has written back rather expediently."

Della had written back quicker than she normally would. Andrew knew precisely how long it took her to write back, and that average was much more than the few days since he'd sent his letter. That his mother also seemed to keep track of their correspondence should've bothered him. It didn't, particularly.

It was the price he paid for living with her, and he didn't mind. Most men had found their own bachelor's lodgings well before his age, but after so long abroad, Andrew was quite fond of getting to see his mother each day.

"Miss Harris belongs to no one, as far as I'm aware." He reminded her and himself. He took off his coat and loosened the cloth at his neck.

"Pity, that," said his mother. She sat in the middle of her sitting room, ensconced in fabrics. Mending clothes, or making them. Her skills as a dressmaker were highly sought after, and she seemed to always be carrying around some bit of her sewing, even though she had a studio for that purpose.

"What do you mean?" he asked, sitting down on the sofa opposite her. His mother was a remarkably progressive woman, and he knew she detested the notion of women belonging to anyone but themselves, as common a notion as it was.

"It's a pity what they've done to that girl." She put down her sewing, her hands falling to her lap that was still covered in loose pieces of muslin. "Stowing her away in the country like she's something to be ashamed of. As if once she fell ill, she didn't belong to them any longer."

So that's what she meant. A different kind of belonging. One Andrew definitely couldn't claim, no matter how much he might want to. No matter how often he did mistakenly think of Della as his.

His mother picked up her needle and began sewing stitches with a sense of indignation.

"She's always seemed well," Andrew said, and she had. During all of their correspondence, she seemed bright and positive and like the Della he'd always known. He'd hardly known her to say a negative word.

"I hope that she is, but she must be lonely out there all by herself." His mother made sure to meet his eye as she said this, raising an eyebrow for emphasis.

Surely she was not implying what he thought she was implying. As fundamentally progressive as she was, he could never imagine her suggesting such impropriety.

He hadn't told her he'd already suggested the very same, and he might have Della's answer in the palm of his hand. Despite their close relationship, there were some things his mother didn't need to know.

"Well, go on then." His mother flicked her wrist in his direction. "I suppose I've distracted you enough." She sent him another smug smile, and he really should have refused. He shouldn't have confirmed her suspicions. He should've sat there for another hour chatting about the weather and what they might have for dinner, just to prove to her that he didn't care so deeply about the contents of the letter in his hand.

Instead, he rose to his feet and bid her a good afternoon.

"Give your young lady my regards," she shouted after him.

He chose not to justify that remark with a response. On his way to his study, Andrew shifted the letter from his left hand to his right. Back and forth, over and over again. It felt weighty. Somehow more meaningful than all of her other letters, even though he'd treasured each one. He'd taken an immense risk when last he wrote her, letting the underlying disquiet plaguing his life show through his pen. It was more vulnerable than he'd been with anyone in years. Thinking about the last time he'd shown that vulnerability sent an ache through the middle of his chest. It was eight years ago, and for the very same woman whose letter rested in his palms.

Andrew sat behind the heavy wooden desk that had been his father's. He had many memories of the man they'd lost when Andrew had been just a young man, but he always felt most connected to him in this room. They shared a profession, and being surrounded by his law books and old notes filled Andrew with strength. Just enough to tear open the letter.

He was never so aggressive with her words. Even the paper she wrote on was important to him, but he'd spent enough time in the purgatory of waiting for her response.

Dearest Andrew, he read. Even her greeting had him smiling. He took a moment to enjoy that, being dear to her.

I miss you.

His smile swiftly faded. It was something she'd never said. Their distance, both the physical distance between them and the difference in their places within society, had always been unspoken.

He'd never considered the idea that she might miss him. Not after the way they'd left things eight years ago. After the way she'd left things. He was simply happy to have their friendship. Happy to have the ability to write her and receive a response. The idea that she'd want anything more than that was almost too much for his mind to process. It was too bright a light for his eyes to behold.

I fear I've found myself in a state. My parents are in residence. I'm certain I don't have to explain further, as you well know how their presence here dampens my spirits and those of the people I care so deeply for. Truly, an unexpected visit from them, and the accompanying silence and the berating of everything in sight would be bad enough. But there is unfortunately something more.

It appears my parents have been lying to me, Andrew. For all of my life, it seems. I don't know why, or how. Clara overheard something she almost certainly shouldn't have. I suppose Clara could have been the one telling the untruths, but if given the choice between trusting Clara or my parents, we both know I would choose Clara every time. I have been given that choice, and it only just occurred to me in this moment that Clara could've been lying, but I could never believe it of her.

I have an inheritance. A difficult concept to believe, to be sure, but I can only assume it to be true. I am not certain if you remember, or if you ever knew in the first place, but the woman I call my mother is, in fact, my stepmother. I was so young when my own mother passed that I have no recollection of her, and Esther and I look so strangely alike that most have forgotten my mother entirely and have always assumed Esther's place in my life. I had, of course, never considered there might be an inheritance on my mother's side.

My parents have withheld this from me, and they continue to do so. Perhaps they will forever, and take this secret to both of their graves. I'm of two minds about this. I cannot understand why they could keep this from me, but I also know exactly why. I have felt that exact type of cruelty from them before. Despite this being a fresh hurt, it's also horribly familiar.

I miss you, because the last time I saw you, things were simple. When you would stand outside the schoolroom window and make faces at me behind my governess's back. When you'd climb trees just to show me how high you could go. I was always so scared you'd get stuck up there. I think it's me who's stuck now. I'm stuck with this information I was never supposed to know, and for the first time, I actually feel stuck here in this house.

I like to believe I live a very charmed life here, with people who care for me and anything I could ever ask for. But to think that the very two people who brought me up, the people who were to protect and love me, have been holding me here like this. It's as if I've never known my own life at all, never known myself.

Except with you, I think. When I was a girl, looking up into the sky to spot you in the limbs of the tallest tree, I was myself. I wasn't thinking of illness or inheritance or how to apologize for someone else's horrid behavior. I was thinking of what I'd do if you got stuck. I'd have climbed up there after you.

I think I need someone to climb up into the sky after me, Andrew. And I think I'd like it to be you.

Somewhere in the middle of the letter, her tone had shifted. He felt it more than he read it. Her words took on a rapid pace in his mind, as if she were frantic. Almost panicked. And then, just as quickly as the frenetic outrage appeared, it faded.

And she was talking about him. About how they'd been as children. Together. He had climbed all those trees just to impress her. He had pulled the silliest of faces just to make her laugh. He couldn't believe she remembered all those things. Lazy afternoons and runs through the garden, those leisurely aspects of their childhood that faded as they'd gotten older. Turned into sneaking out to the stables and hiding from her parents just so they could speak to each other alone.

Would she really have climbed up those trees after him?

He hated to doubt her, but his mind flashed to the worst moment of his life. When she'd run and he'd tried to follow, only to be told she didn't want him to.

He finished the letter. He read it once more. His gaze was stuck on the last line. For once, he didn't know what she meant.

I think I need someone to climb up into the sky after me, Andrew. And I think I'd like it to be you.

He didn't have to ask himself if he'd still climb up into the sky after Della. Of course, he would. He knew he'd climb down into the very pits of hell for her.

He also knew she'd never mentioned his invitation to visit her at Westfield Manor.

CHAPTER SIX

I T WAS A splendid morning. Her parents departed in their three carriages at dawn, and Clara was dressed like herself again, in another men's shirt and loose-flowing tan trousers that Gwendoline had made for her. Those trousers were a wonderful thing. A passing onlooker might assume they were a skirt instead, but they held all the functionality of a pair of trousers. Della had asked Gwendoline to make some for her as well.

Clara ran a hand through the hair she wore unbound in long waves that draped over her shoulders and down her back. Her other hand held a letter, though she seemed unwilling to hand it over.

"Is something . . . amiss between the two of you?" Clara asked, folding her hands behind her back and beginning to walk around the large dining table in the center of the room. "You've been exchanging letters rather quickly."

"You are shouting," Della muttered. She rose to her feet, stretching her legs after spending too long sitting at the breakfast table. One hip cracked, louder than the stomping of Clara's feet on the carpet. The opposite knee threatened to buckle under her weight.

"So it seems I am," Clara shouted.

With an indignant huff, Della gave in. She resolved to the fact that she'd have to explain all of this, whether she wanted to or not. After she'd stretched her limbs out as best she could in a static position, she began to walk. Her pace was much slower than Clara's. Della was unhurried, taking a turn about the room as if she were at a party. Clara was on a warpath, as if she were heading off to battle.

"It seems Andrew may want to come here. To Westfield Manor."

"What?" Clara shrieked. "And you've neglected to tell me this? That your true love wants to reunite after eight years?"

"He *is not* my true love," Della started. She didn't know how to talk about this, but she knew that much was true. She couldn't love Andrew, and Andrew certainly couldn't love her. "We were not betrothed. We were not even courting. He is a dear friend to me, and he has been since we were children."

She stopped near the door and turned around, following her same path toward the window. Clara had slowed down a bit, enough that they were walking together.

"Why has he never visited you before?" Clara asked, in an unusually soft voice.

"I do not know," Della answered. "It could be because of my illness, or because he's been abroad for many years. Perhaps he's never had any interest in visiting the countryside, or me."

Clara threaded her arm through Della's. They reached the window and stayed there a moment, looking out at the verdant gardens below.

"What does it mean that he's interested in visiting now?" Clara spoke into the windowpane.

"I'm afraid I do not know that either."

Below them, they watched a bird fly from tree to tree. Della began to count the roses blooming on the farthest bush.

"Do you?" Clara asked. "Want to see him, I mean?"

It was a question Della had never asked herself, for she already knew the answer. Even though it felt impossible, like a fantasy she'd write about in her journal, she wanted to see him. Besides the people she lived with, Andrew was the only person in the world she wanted to see, in fact.

"Yes," she admitted. "I would love to see him."

Clara smiled, spinning herself around and letting her arms flutter the heavy curtains. Della turned around and approached the dining table again, albeit slowly. She was still not moving well this morning, despite all of the stretching.

"Oh," Clara suddenly righted herself, landing directly in front of Della. "I've an important question." She grabbed Della's arms again as Della lowered herself into the chair at the head of the table. "When your Mr. Lockhart comes, I don't have to wear gowns and pin up my hair, do I?"

Della could only laugh in response. Clara handed her the letter, finally, and then she left the room. Della needed privacy for moments like these. It wasn't that she didn't want anyone to see the unbridled joy Andrew brought her, it was just that she wanted to keep it for herself, to keep what little she had of him to be all her own.

Della held the letter in her hands. She ran her fingers over the paper as she always did. It smelled like him, that worn leather and fresh ink scent she wanted to inhale forever. Under normal circumstances, she'd carry the letter with her to her chambers, sit down at her writing desk and read the letter several times, then secure it in her drawer and put the next-most-recent letter in her trunk with the others. There was a routine, a course of action to this that she cherished. It was practically tradition. Today, she decided tradition could go to the devil.

She tore the letter open, then cursed herself for that bit of recklessness when a bit of the paper ripped. There went her nearly eight-year-long streak of perfectly preserved letters.

As she unfolded the missive, her heart sank. It was dreadfully short, only a scant few lines in that crooked script she'd come to adore. That couldn't be good, she thought. She expected a polite denial. Perhaps a gentle reproach for her casting up her emotional accounts on him. She feared even a neutral statement dissolving their friendship.

Dearest Della, she read, after she could take the suspense no longer. If she let her mind race any further, she would cast up her actual accounts all over the carpet at her feet. That would be an incredible waste of a good day gown. She continued on, heartened at least for the moment by still being something dear to him.

I must admit I was concerned after reading your last letter.

Della's breath caught in her throat, a painful tightening that felt like someone had tried to tighten a set of stays around her neck. She closed her eyes for a moment, bracing herself. It would be all right, she thought. She had to convince her own heart it would be so before she could read on. This was not the end of them, even if she so deeply feared it would be. For once, she chose to believe in her mother's philosophy of illness—even though it had no basis in anything scientific. As she lost herself in caring for Della, Esther began to believe that her remaining ill was Della's own fault. Her mother thought if Della believed she'd feel better, she would. In this instance, Della decided that if she believed that Andrew wasn't abandoning her as everyone else had, he wouldn't be.

She knew such a thing was impossible, that no matter how strongly she believed in anything, nothing could change the words on the paper she held in her tightening hands. She had to put her faith in that misguided philosophy just this once, because she could do nothing but hope. She took a deep breath. Opened her eyes.

I don't believe I've ever read a letter in such a tone, to be candid with you. I can't imagine what it must be like to find out about an inheritance in such a manner. I don't blame you for your alarm.

Oh. Della exhaled. The thick cloud of terror over her person seemed to dissipate. He was concerned for her. She hadn't thought that was a possibility.

Quite frankly, I blame your parents for many things. I hope you'll forgive me for insulting your family, but I blame them when my breakfast is cold. I blame them when I step in a puddle. I blame them when I lose the spectacles that I eventually find on my face. I can forgive these minor transgressions, but you can be sure that if they have in fact been hiding your own property from you, that will never be forgiven.

Della laughed, then she gasped. At first, the idea of stern, steady Andrew blaming her parents for his every inconvenience was comical. She could imagine him with wet socks cursing the viscount's name. She couldn't imagine the level of anger those last words held, though. Andrew had never been angry. She'd never seen him fly into a rage over anything. She simply didn't know if he was capable of such a thing. The idea that he'd be so aggrieved on her behalf was preposterous. The idea that her parents' slight was something unforgivable to him was remarkable.

If she'd bared her soul to him in her last letter, he was doing the very same thing now. There was a brutal honesty to his words that she'd never felt before. An almost aggressive tone that she didn't recognize, and it was for her.

There was one short paragraph left, and Della pressed a hand to the middle of her chest in an effort to calm her racing heart. It wouldn't do if she swooned right in the middle of the breakfast room. The doctor would have to be summoned, and she despised that wretched man. Besides, if she dropped dead right now, she'd never know what else Andrew had to say.

> ~~My ill-will toward your parents aside~~
> ~~Your parents' horrid actions aside~~

Della giggled at the words he'd hastily marked out. It was unlike him to send a letter that was less than pristine, but she guessed they were both feeling a particular sense of urgency lately.

Besides, if you are ever in need of help, you have it. You are the only reason I ever made it back down from those tall trees, after all. I'd hoped you knew by now that I am always at your service.

It might be terribly forward of me, but I plan to leave London for Westfield Manor tomorrow morning. You may turn me away at the door, of course, but it's my hope that you won't. I do not know if I am capable of climbing into the sky after you, but I can certainly travel to the countryside for that purpose. I've missed you, too.

Yours,
Andrew

Della's racing heart attempted some maneuver in her chest for which she was not prepared. It flipped or dropped or skipped a beat. Something terribly uncomfortable. The letter slipped from her fingers, drifting over her skirts to the floor.

"Clara!" she called, with as much vigor as her fragile body and even more delicate heart could muster.

She heard the sound of someone clambering down the hallway, each footstep a pounding on the wood. She made such noise for such a small person, especially one who did not even wear shoes. Della had no idea how she'd heard her from all the way up there.

"What is the matter?" Clara asked, strolling into the room she'd just left with a casual air about her, as if she had not been practically sprinting.

Della pointed to the letter laying at her feet. Her mouth was suddenly dry. It was difficult to form words.

"Andrew is coming here," she croaked. "To Westfield Manor. Now."

She looked up at Clara, who had yet to shed that casual air. Della wondered how she could possibly not be roused by this, the best kind of emergency.

"Oh. Well." Clara picked up the letter from the carpet. "You did not answer me before. Must I go change?"

CHAPTER SEVEN

THIS WAS QUITE possibly the most impulsive thing Andrew had ever done. He was a calm, rational person. He considered the consequences of his actions before he did things. Especially significant things. Except for fleeing the country eight years ago and spending most of a decade abroad, but that had been about Della, too. Something about her made him impulsive, and something about his own impulsivity felt dangerous.

His journey to the countryside had been rather pleasant, as he was used to traveling and had seen much worse accommodations than traveling inns and the mail coach. It was only as he made his final approach to Westfield Manor that he began to doubt himself.

He took the stone stairs two at a time, and he waited at the door. Stared at the tops of his boots. Suddenly they didn't feel shiny enough, even though they were brand new. Even in his own mind, he chastised himself. No one would give a passing thought to his boots. Nor should they expect him to be in perfect order after such a journey, but he wanted to be. He fiddled with his coat. Made sure his waistcoat was properly buttoned. He'd skipped a button exactly once in his life, but the embarrassment stayed with him, and the idea that he could look like such a fool in front of Della was unimaginable.

The door flew open. It was all very sudden, both the motion itself and the chaos that seemed to erupt out of the house in its wake.

"Bloody hell, Clara," Andrew heard. It was a masculine voice. Certainly not that of the slight lady who appeared in the doorway.

Though she was small in stature, her smile was quite frankly terrifying.

"We have discussed this. You are not to open the door. *I* open the door," the man's voice continued. "There could be all manner of danger out there, and you'd run headlong into it—"

The man finally appeared, standing behind the woman. She was little and frightening. He was enormous and somehow still not as formidable.

"Terribly sorry, sir," the man said, stepping back and pulling the woman with him by a gloved hand on each of her upper arms. He must be the butler, then. He didn't know why anyone else would be so attached to the simple act of opening the door.

"You must be Andrew Lockhart," the woman said, as she let herself be pulled away. Her eyes were wide with excitement, and it was only then that Andrew noticed how strangely she was dressed. He was almost certain that was a man's shirt, and she wore a divided skirt, as if she were going riding. Her hair was unbound as well, and a bit of a mess.

"I am," he agreed, because he was, but he had no idea what he'd just walked into.

"Wonderful!" She took his arm, as if they were taking a turn about the room at a London ball. The butler actually growled, which was objectively terrifying. It was enough to make Andrew take a half step in the other direction.

He did not want to be rude, but he would appreciate some context, or some idea of what was going on here.

"And you are?" he asked the both of them.

"Oh," she laughed, patting his elbow where her arm was threaded through his. "I'm so sorry, we do not receive many guests. I suppose we are out of practice."

She started to steer him toward the grand staircase, and the butler followed. It was entirely possible Andrew was being lured to his doom. Even so, he went willingly. There didn't seem to be another choice.

"I am Clara, Della's maid." She took to the stairs, climbing each step so fast that Andrew struggled to keep up. It was deeply impressive for someone with such short legs. At some point, Andrew realized she wasn't even wearing shoes or stockings. He was sure he'd never met such a lightning bolt of a person. "Oh, wait. You don't call her something awful like *Miss Harris*, do you?" she said, her tone shifting into something mocking as she said Della's proper name.

"I assure you I do not call her something awful." He laughed, just at the absurdity of it all. "She has always been Della to me."

Clara nodded, as if in approval. They'd reached the top of the stairs, and Andrew hadn't even a moment to look around. She dropped his arm, then turned around to face a closed door.

"And the large man towering behind me is Harry." She gestured toward him, where he stood near the top of the staircase. He also nodded, this time as if in recognition. "Though you may call him Mr. Stanton if you wish. He values things like formality and politeness that I do not."

Mr. Stanton nodded again. He stood there at the banister with his gloved hands folded in front of him. The picture of propriety. Andrew did not have significant experience with butlers, but he thought it was often their policy to make themselves scarce in situations like these. Instead, there he remained, watching Clara—Andrew really wished he knew her last name so he could address her properly—with a casual but intense interest.

"Now, I do fear Della might kill me for what I am about to do, but I have already decided to do it." Clara was one for dramatics, apparently. He couldn't imagine that—Della harming anyone—but he hadn't seen her in eight years. Perhaps she'd become ill-tempered. Andrew turned his head toward Mr. Stanton. The look they shared assured him that Mr. Stanton was remaining in the general area should any attempted murder occur. Andrew had a feeling that the butler would not allow even the slightest harm to befall Clara. Andrew was oddly jealous of that—knowing without a doubt you would always be there for someone you cared about. Even if they were about to do something ill-advised. He'd never had that ability. He'd never known he wanted it.

"And what are you about to do?" Andrew asked, hoping for some kind of warning, or any indication that this entire situation was not something his mind had concocted in the throes of a fever.

"Never mind that." She waved a hand in his direction. Her other hand held the doorknob, as if she were poised to throw the door wide open. "Before we go in, Della is feeling poorly today, and I must ask that you not be difficult about it."

"Of course not," Andrew scoffed. "I assumed Della feels poorly nearly every day, and I hope I have never been difficult about it."

Clara nodded in approval again. Andrew felt like he was in the middle of some impromptu examination, and he needed to pass in order to see what was behind that door. Who was behind that door, he should say.

"Forgive my boldness," Clara said. "I only try to protect her. When I can. You know her family?" Her tone indicated that was a question, rather than a statement of fact.

"I know her family," Andrew nodded. "I do not like them." He'd never said that before. Not to Della or anyone else. He had liked them, when they were children. He'd thought they lived a charmed life he'd never be able to attain. As he grew older, as he heard all they'd done to Della, he grew less and less fond of them. It felt freeing to actually admit it.

"We are in agreement on that." Clara nodded once more, then she turned the doorknob.

Andrew took a step forward, into the open doorway. Everything happened very suddenly, then. He was one half step inside when Clara whirled around him, trapping him in the fabric of those flowing trousers she wore. He was so disoriented he didn't realize what was happening until he heard the door close.

And there was Della. With him. Alone.

He was fairly sure he was in the midst of a grand sitting room with plush furniture and burnished golden wallpaper. Everything shone in a bright, metallic haze, but all he saw was her.

He remembered her eyes. They were deep, dark blue. Like a midnight sky, and her hair was dark, almost raven black with only a hint of brown showing through when the light hit it, flowing over her shoulders in waves. Her round face. Those freckles. Hell, he even remembered how her left eyebrow somehow arched higher than the right. She sat in an armchair in the opposite corner of the room. She couldn't be farther from him unless she jumped out the window, but he relished being this close. Her posture was stiff, and he noticed her wince as she adjusted herself.

Della was so incandescently beautiful and so close and so precious to him that it made him completely mindless, which is why he said something so foolish.

"Your maid unsettles me."

He considered himself a reasonably intelligent person. He spoke several languages and had conducted business as a solicitor on three continents, but somehow, for the first words he'd had the opportunity to say to Della's face in eight years, that was the best he could come up with.

CHAPTER EIGHT

DELLA WAS IMMENSELY grateful she'd been sitting down. Though she wanted to do Clara bodily harm for this incredible surprise, she may have actually swooned had this happened while upright on her feet.

Andrew was here. In her sitting room. Standing near the door, staring at her. He seemed overdressed, but perhaps that was because she never saw men in the latest fashion anymore. Everything about him felt polished and new and somehow still so achingly familiar. So safe. His hair was still the color of warm chocolate, with more of a curl than she remembered. His big, brown eyes made him seem so serious. So earnest.

His mouth quirked, not in a smile, but in what Della thought was an expression of abject discomfort. That dimple appeared in his cheek, and she was lost. Utterly, irrevocably lost.

"Your maid unsettles me," he'd said.

How long ago had he said that? Had she been simply staring at him wordlessly, as if trying to communicate by blinking? Della moved as her hip started to scream. She shuffled her feet back and forth against the floor. She crossed one ankle behind the other and hoped the pain she felt didn't show on her face.

"Clara has that effect on people," she responded, finally. Della had no way of knowing if she'd done so in an appropriate matter of time. She had no idea what she'd done with her face. Had she even managed to smile at him? She couldn't recall.

Andrew shifted, too, bearing his weight on one foot then the other. Almost fidgeting. Della remembered herself as she absorbed his awkwardness.

"Please do sit down." she gestured to an armchair opposite her. Much, much closer than he'd been before. She hadn't realized the impact those ten or twelve steps would have on her. First, she heard them. Soft footfalls on the plush carpet. Then, she felt him. A sudden hum of awareness down her spine as he entered her space. Della knew how improper this was, this man in her private sitting room. She couldn't care less.

Della had been lost ever since he came through the door, but she looked up at him now, and she was found.

Her rooms were not particularly sunlit, but the rays streaming through the window illuminated his face and Della had to stifle a gasp. He looked softer, somehow, in this light. The sharp edges of his cheekbones seemed to melt, and his lips relaxed into something that resembled a smile. Della realized all at once that this was someone she'd never met. The Andrew she'd last seen in London was a boy of barely twenty. This was a man who felt familiar but looked entirely changed.

Andrew sat. He observed his surroundings in silence, and his face scrunched up as he looked toward Della's writing desk. The dimple popped out on his cheek, and Della nearly sighed. Perhaps he was more familiar than not.

"How was your trip?" she asked him, just to break the quiet. He didn't look particularly travel weary, but she feared he never would. He was simply too handsome for something as trivial as travel to dampen his appearance.

He didn't answer for the longest time, continuing his perusal of the room. Although the lack of conversation felt less than comfortable to Della, oddly enough, so did the thought of talking. Perhaps he felt the same. They'd shared so much in writing for so long, that she found she didn't know how to speak to him anymore. She couldn't put on the mask she wore with the few strangers with whom she interacted, one of politeness and entirely artificial charm. Sitting in front of her at this moment was a true rarity in her life. He was someone who knew her, and she found she didn't know how to deal with that.

"Andrew?" she prodded, finally. He'd been looking so intently at the wallpaper she wondered if he were counting each bloom within the floral pattern.

"I am sorry." He shook his head and laughed, seemingly at himself. It wasn't the laugh she remembered. That had been open and free. This one felt sardonic and somehow guarded. "What is it you said?"

"I asked about your trip." She repositioned herself again, but she realized she was running out of comfortable shapes to contort her body into. Soon, she'd simply have to move, whether she liked it or not.

"Oh. Yes. It was quite an easy journey, all things considered." He stated simply. He was looking at her now, finally, and Della almost wished he'd go back to his study of the room. The deep, complex brown of his eyes was entirely too intense. There was a necklace her mother used to wear, made of large, heavy brown zircon stones. Della remembered that color so vividly, how it sparkled and shifted from gold to bronze to brown depending on the light. It was as if his eyes were made of such gemstones, and his gaze was much more than a woman so delicate should have to handle.

"You seem rather . . . focused on the room," she said. There had to be a topic of conversation, she supposed. So, she pointed out the obvious.

"I am," he confirmed with a polite nod that made a curl fall over his forehead. "It's not what I'd pictured. I suppose it was silly of me to have imagined you in some decrepit hovel all of these years, when you seem to be getting on rather well in your golden rooms."

Della wasn't sure what was more of an assault on her sensibilities—that one rogue curl or the idea that he'd been imagining her at all.

"I'm very fortunate," she said, simply stating a fact that she'd only recently realized.

Andrew raised one eyebrow, as if in suspicion. He crossed one leg over the other, resting his left ankle over his right knee. He rearranged his jacket. It drew her attention to his hands, and she looked away so sharply her neck creaked.

"You consider yourself fortunate, then? Living here?" His tone had smoothed some. Before today, if she'd closed her eyes and tried to imagine what his voice might sound like, it would have been this. Gentle. Slow. That feeling of safety washed over her again, and some part of her wanted to rebel against it.

He was a man she was alone with in her private chambers. She was not supposed to feel safe right now.

"I do," Della said. She stood up, taking slow, deliberate steps in an effort to regain control of her aching limbs. "I have many wonderful people here with me, and I am content. I have far more than many others, especially those in my condition without any support."

Della couldn't see his face from this angle, still walking slowly on her path to nowhere. He was silent again for long moments, and as she ran a hand over her still aching hip, she wondered if they'd truly lost the ability to talk to each other. Maybe she'd write him a letter and hand it to him instead of sending it through the post. That seemed easier.

There was a knock on the door. She was close enough to open it herself, so she did.

"Time for dinner," Clara said, her fist still raised to the now-open door. Her smile was that of an excited child. Della half thought Clara was more thrilled about Andrew's visit than she was herself. "Mrs. Goldsmith sent me to see about you and Mr. Lockhart. Will you want a tray in your room, or will you be joining us in the dining room?"

Della turned around to ask the same question of Andrew, but he was suddenly much closer than he'd been before. He stepped up right next to her, in fact. Their bodies took up the entirety of the doorway. She looked up at him. He looked down at her. They were stuck in silence again, but this quiet wasn't heavy with awkwardness. This was alight with possibility.

"I should like to go to dinner, but I might require some assistance," Della told Clara. Her pain today was becoming such that movement hurt less than stillness, but the staircase was an entirely different beast. She'd never make it down and back up without help.

"Please," Andrew said, extending his arm in her direction. "Allow me."

Della froze. Clara let out a pleased little giggle that made her seem girlish.

"I'll tell Mrs. Goldsmith to prepare for two more," Clara said, promptly leaving them alone once again.

Della tried to communicate by blinking again. Once, twice, three times. His eyes weren't responding to hers. They were such deep pools of amber. She forgot what she was trying to say in the first place.

Slowly, so slowly, Della wrapped her fevered fingers around Andrew's elbow. At the first touch of her ungloved hand against his greatcoat, she sucked in a heaving breath. Or maybe that was him. Perhaps it was them both. She dared to squeeze his arm, even though the action made her knuckles twinge.

"Shall we go?" he asked in that same quiet voice she'd already become so fond of. She nodded and grabbed her trusty walking stick from its ever-present place by the door.

They took tentative steps toward the grand staircase, lost again in an absence of conversation that was starting to feel comfortable. Della could smell him, musk and leather and rain. She could feel the fabric of his coat against her fingers, the warmth of his skin beneath. Della realized she'd never been on a man's arm before. She wondered if what she enjoyed so much was being on someone's arm or being on Andrew's.

They took the first step gently, but even so, a low hiss slipped out from between Della's teeth. Andrew did not respond. Not verbally, anyway. Instead, he shifted their stances until her nagging hip was resting against his. They took the next step in tandem, him bearing some of her weight.

"Is that better?" he asked, that low voice becoming a near whisper.

"Yes," she told him honestly. Even if he hadn't helped her pain, she would always assume things were automatically better being this close to him.

The remainder of the stairs were easier, but they took them at a snail's pace. She wasn't in any rush to be parted from him, and he didn't seem to be in a hurry, either. They made it to the ground floor, and the grand hall was suspiciously empty, but Della could hear that the revelry had already begun in the dining room.

"Thank you," she whispered, squeezing Andrew's arm once more for good measure, and just because she felt as if she could.

She'd been trained in the art of the marriage mart. Had dances with all manner of tutors. She'd worn gowns straight from the best designers in Paris. Despite all that, Della couldn't recall experiencing anything as lovely as this simple trip down the stairs.

"My pleasure," Andrew said.

He smiled, a genuine, charming grin wide enough to make those fathomless eyes crinkle and both of his dimples appear.

It was almost boyish, and in it, Della saw the only man she'd ever loved.

CHAPTER NINE

ANDREW THOUGHT HE might've stepped into another world. A beautiful realm in which he had the privilege of walking about with Della on his arm. Where he couldn't so much as breathe without the hair around her shoulders ruffling in waves. Where they stepped into a room and everyone smiled.

If he'd left his home and everything he knew for this unknown place, he just might be grateful.

He hadn't expected so many people, though. Not at the dinner table. He'd never been permitted to join them in the dining room at the Harrises' London townhouse. At first, he was too young, as they all were. He and Della and David. Then it was a matter of their noble birth and his working-class upbringing. When he'd so abruptly decided to come to Westfield Manor, he hadn't thought about this bit. The little things. This small raucous crowd that greeted them—greeted her—was appropriate, though. This was the kind of joy he wanted for her, and the kind of joy he ached to be a part of.

"Come in, come in," Clara said, standing behind the chair at the head of the table. She slid the chair out and tapped against the ornate cushion at the back. Della broke away from him, and Andrew mourned.

He was directed to the seat at Della's right, and Clara sat to her left. Andrew took a moment to appreciate the fine china and the artful display of flowers at the center of the table. When he looked up, he noticed every pair of eyes was on him. Della. Clara. Mr. Stanton. Another man about his age who appeared to be slightly dusted in dirt. A younger girl who was quite possibly the blondest person he'd ever seen. An older woman who was fussing with the dishes.

"Where are your manners?" said the older woman at the opposite end of the table. "You are making the poor lad uncomfortable." She turned to look at Andrew. "I hope you still like jellied eels. Miss Della told me they were your favorite."

She remembered. Della wasn't looking at him anymore. She was shifting her silverware across a still-empty plate.

"I love them," he told the lady he assumed to be the cook.

"Thank you, Mrs. Goldsmith," Della said, finally.

Everyone seemed to take that as permission to begin eating, and platters and bowls were passed around. There were his jellied eels, as well as white soup and potatoes and mince pies.

"You know," Clara said, leaning her elbows on the table and avoiding the food she'd placed on her plate entirely in favor of conversation, "Della has never told me how this . . . friendship of yours came to be."

Della looked at him then, a chunk of boiled potato on the fork she held frozen halfway to her face. She nodded once. He interpreted that as a nonverbal passing of the torch to him.

"I grew up visiting Morley House. My father was the viscount's man of business, and their home was a more fun place for a child than my mother's studio."

He stopped speaking for a moment, and he realized that the silence he left behind was rather tense.

"Good lord, Clara," Della sighed. "Go ahead, say it. I know you want to." She ran a hand over the wrinkles in her forehead.

"Their home was . . . fun?" Clara asked. "For a child?" She looked around the table, as if to confirm that everyone else was as confused as she was. They appeared to be.

"It was," Andrew confirmed. Even if he wasn't on particularly good terms with the Harrises now, he still looked back on his time there with fondness. "David is several years younger than me, and while we had . . . different upbringings, we had many good times together in our youth. He was rowdy. Always bored by his nurse and tutors. It seemed the only thing that could entertain him was a boy with the same boundless energy and a few more years' worth of sense."

Clara leaned back in her chair. She crossed her arms. "And what about Della?" she asked.

Della dropped her fork. "Please do not speak of me as if I am not sitting right here."

Andrew did just as she said. He looked directly at her, even though the sight of her ethereal face made his chest constrict. As he'd made the journey all the way here, his wild imagination couldn't conjure up how this would feel, being this close to her again. Her eyes on him. Her voice in his ears, his mind. His heart. Every time he blinked, the image behind his eyelids was her.

"Do you remember the day we met?" he asked. He didn't expect her to. They were so young then, it was an entire lifetime ago. There'd been so many days and miles and memories between them, he could never assume she'd kept a hold of this one moment in her mind.

"Of course," she said. So simply, as if all those years of keeping that memory was as easy as breathing. "Though the story does not paint me in a flattering light." Della laughed, and Andrew nearly fell off of his chair.

There it was, that one sound that had haunted his dreams for the better part of a decade. Under the table, he pinched the skin above his knee, then he regretted it immediately. Even if this were an aberration, he didn't want to wake up.

"Oh, this I must hear," Clara said. She leaned forward on her elbows again. Andrew supposed he'd been forgiven for whatever had made Clara so defensive before. Not defensive, exactly. Protective. He could understand that, being protective of Della. They were alike in that way.

Clara's plate still appeared untouched, and Mr. Stanton wordlessly tugged on her left elbow, removing it from the table and placing her fork back in her hand. She rolled her eyes, but she ate.

"It's David who was the menace," Andrew said. He shook his head. He could hardly reconcile the boy he'd run amok with as a child with the man full grown who he saw parading around London as if he had been elevated by His Majesty himself.

Della hummed in agreement, and he could tell she was thinking the same thing.

"He liked to sneak away from his tutor," Andrew laughed, thinking of all they'd done that they shouldn't have. "Not for any important purpose or with any destination in mind. It was a challenge, and he loved winning. As my father worked with the viscount, I roamed about the grounds. David and I made a game of it. I'd try to find him before anyone else could."

It was silly and juvenile, but they were boys. Andrew only wished that David had matured a bit since then.

"It always struck me as odd, how often David was able to escape," Della said. She'd stopped eating, sitting with her hands folded in her lap. Just watching him. He felt the warmth of her gaze like a thick blanket on a cold morning. "His tutor only had the one pupil. I don't know how he kept losing him."

Andrew had never known, either. "One day, I was looking for him," he continued speaking, though, because he was just getting to the good part. "I was looking in the stable stalls, which was ridiculous, because David's never been much of a horseman."

"Oh, no," Della laughed, that brilliant burst of air ringing out like a church bell, "he's not fond of strong smells."

Everyone around the table burst into laughter, but Andrew was suddenly deadly serious.

"I was searching for him," he smiled, "but I found you."

Della softened right in front of his eyes, her eyes heavy lidded and her lashes resting on her barely flushed cheeks. Her smiling mouth fell into something more demure, almost shy.

"In the stables?" Mrs. Goldsmith blurted. Andrew had briefly forgotten there were other people in the room.

"Yes," Della admitted. "David would tell me of all of the adventures he went on, so I had snuck out as he always did. I'm not sure I even remember how I ended up there, but we had the kindest stable boy back then, and he let me brush the horse's mane."

"That's what she was doing when I found her," Andrew told the rest of the table. "Brushing the mane of a horse twice her size. She had to stand on a wooden box to even reach the horse's neck."

"That's what I remember." Della laughed again, this one a soft, nostalgic chuckle. "You were but a year older than me, but so much taller. And you were so worried I'd fall."

He was. That moment began his mission of keeping Della from harm. David had never thought to include Della in their games. Andrew had, though.

She was as good at seeking as she was hiding, but he always, always found her.

CHAPTER TEN

I T WAS TOWARD the end of breakfast the next morning when Andrew asked the question that Della had been dreading.

"So, what are we to do about this inheritance of yours?" He wiped invisible crumbs from the corners of his mouth with a napkin, and Della wondered, not for the first time, how anyone could look so dapper this early in the morning.

He'd dressed more casually today, forgoing his coat in favor of only his ivory shirtsleeves and a light-blue waistcoat. He'd spilled porridge on the tails of his cravat, so he'd simply unwound it from around his neck. There was truly no end to the improprieties he brought to this house.

Della loved it.

"Let's . . . discuss that another time," she managed to say once she looked away from the slice of bare skin at the base of his neck where his shirt draped open. She tried to convey her meaning with her facial expressions, widening her eyes and shifting in the direction of the dining room's open door, but she could feel his confusion.

It was just the two of them at the moment, but anyone could walk in or walk by, and Della didn't know how to explain this to anyone else. She didn't know yet what there was to explain. The subterfuge made her intensely uncomfortable, and she was no good at keeping secrets. The only secret she'd ever kept was the illness that had eventually become public knowledge, and the resulting alienation was enough to make Della avoid hiding anything from anyone ever again.

"Meet me in the library," she whispered across the table. "You leave the table first, then I'll follow."

She thought this was an excellent plan, but then she remembered he had no idea where the library was. He seemed to be poised to say just that, but she continued on.

"Right down this corridor, third door on the left."

He nodded. She waved her hands in a motion that indicated he should commence phase one of their plan and leave the room. A moment too late, she realized that was an incredibly rude thing to do. Della blamed him for that, though. He was forever making her too comfortable. Too safe for her own good. Her manners went the way of her good sense, vanishing at the first sight of him.

Andrew smiled, his lips just barely curling up enough to make his dimples appear. Wordlessly, he stepped back from the table and departed. He was rather stealthy, actually. Must have been all that hiding and seeking they'd done as children. It had made him sneaky and made her adept at hiding herself.

Della stood, trying to make as little noise as possible. The chair had other ideas, scratching against the dining room floor as if its only purpose was to produce a horrible sound. She stayed still for a moment, both to stretch her tightened limbs and to determine if anyone heard her moving about. Everyone in the house was always so attentive, and it felt like betrayal to be avoiding them all like this. There simply wasn't another choice. She couldn't throw their very livelihoods into upheaval, not until she knew the facts. Right then, it was all just speculation. The whole ordeal was made of overheard whispers in the night.

Walking on the tips of her toes, Della left the dining room. She looked both ways at the door and hauled her shawl higher up on her shoulders. The hallway was always drafty, and she found that her elbows just could not bear the touch of the air.

Della kept her head down the entire way, but she acknowledged that was beyond foolish. It was not as if they were in a crowded ballroom, and she could pass by a stray partygoer without being recognized. If anyone saw her, she'd say she needed a novel from the study. Or that she'd decided to take a walk about the house instead of outside in the gardens. She'd lie and say that something about the absolutely perfect weather outside was unamenable to her.

Even as she praised her own quick thinking, she didn't need it. She made it to the library without seeing a soul, and she heaved a sigh of relief as she opened the heavy door and gently closed it behind her.

"I am sorry for speaking so openly," Andrew said. "I should have known you wouldn't want everyone to know." He was roaming the wall, looking at the spines of books she'd collected over the years. It was quite a selection, if Della did say so herself.

"It is not that I don't want them to know," she sighed, lowering herself into the chair in front of the enormous oak desk in the center of the room. "I simply don't want to cause a stir until we . . ."

Her voice trailed off as she realized what she'd said. We. Implying present company was included in whatever this was. He hadn't agreed to anything, and she hadn't truly asked, so it felt like a rather bold assumption.

"Until we know more?" Andrew finished for her. He still walked slowly, his hands folded behind his back. It was a slow march across the room, and it was making Della nervous.

"I suppose," she agreed. "Please, sit down." She gestured to the admittedly overly plush chair behind the desk, and Andrew's eyebrows raised in a way that was almost comical.

Still, he sat.

He looked out of place there, almost disheveled with no cravat and no coat. It made Della imagine things she shouldn't. Walking into a room like this, seeing Andrew in the midst of his work. Perhaps with his curls all rucked up and ink all over his fingers. She'd step closer and he'd smile and—

"I would never presume to sit behind a viscount's desk," Andrew remarked. He'd interrupted her barely blooming fantasy with thoughts of a harsh reality, and she didn't appreciate it. He seemed to be observing, too. He ran his hands over the ornate carved wood of the chair's arms, and Della had never in her life been so envious of furniture.

"Does it make you feel duplicitous?" she asked. She tried to keep the scorn out of her voice, but it was no use.

"No." Andrew's face fell. Those dimples hid themselves away in the shadows of his discontent. "I wish it did. Then we could blame it on the desk."

Della sat with that for a moment. Andrew had always been this way, blunt and honest and always forthright with his thoughts and feelings. He simply didn't know any other way to be. She'd expected a laugh at her suggestion that the viscount's recent behavior was underhanded and deceitful. She hadn't expected him to agree, and so readily. She remembered his letter, though, in which he'd said he liked to blame her parents for inane, trivial things like puddles and lost spectacles.

This was so much more significant than any of that, and it really was a pity they couldn't just blame the desk.

"I am sorry, Della," he began again. His soft face went suddenly sharp. That face was so dear to her, and it caused her physical pain to watch that immediate transformation. "I know they're your family and I shouldn't disparage them in front of you, but they're so . . ."

His voice trailed off on a frustrated sigh. Della watched as he tried to smooth wrinkles out of his suddenly creased forehead. She was momentarily mesmerized by those slow, rhythmic circles. Her breathing slowed, the beat of her heart relaxing into something lazy and soothed. It was almost hypnotic enough to make her forget everything, like where they were and who she was. That she had any problems at all in the world. That there even was a world outside of this room.

"You needn't apologize, Andrew," she emphasized. "You apologize too much."

He stopped the mesmerism, his hand falling away from his face. Now, she could see him in earnest, and that was much more exhilarating than relaxing.

"Is that a habit of yours with everyone?" she asked, because she suddenly had to know. "Or is it just . . . a reaction to me?"

Andrew looked at her then. Their eyes met, and it was as if there was nothing and everything between them. Things like physical space and time ceased to matter, evaporating like morning dew in the midday sun, but their history remained. In those eyes, she saw the boy with the curls and the wide smile. She saw the only person who'd ever come looking for her.

"I am sorry if I apologize too much," he sighed. She laughed at the irony, but his eyebrows pinched in response. "But I cannot be like them. I cannot be another person who hurts you."

Her laugh fell into abrupt silence, like a drop of rain suspended in midair.

Della's instinct was to refute and deny and dismiss. That passed, though. The raindrop of hurt resumed its fall until it crashed against the ground and shattered. She was hurt, and there was something about Andrew being so incensed on her behalf that brought warmth to the frigid emptiness in her chest.

Her parents were not well-liked people. Everyone she knew had something disparaging to say about them. They were rude. They were arrogant. They represented all the thoughtlessness and vapidity that defined high society.

No one had ever been upset with them because of her, though, and as much as she hated the sight of that normally genteel face tensing up in indignation, knowing all of that was on her behalf tugged at some previously unexplored chamber of Della's heart.

"So what do we do?" she asked him, leaning forward in her chair and wrapping her shawl tighter around her chest. "How do we . . . resolve this?"

It felt like an impossible question, as if none of this were ever going to be settled. Her world had been upended, and the only thing she knew was that Andrew Lockhart sat in front of her, ready and willing to help. Even that was difficult to fathom.

"Do your parents keep any important documents here?" He began to look around, peering into desk drawers and eyeing the shelves on the wall behind her. "We could find the letters patent or look up the barony in *Debrett's*. But there might be something here. I've no idea how many estates they have, or where they'd keep their records. I don't believe my father ever dealt with things of this nature on the viscount's behalf—"

He stopped speaking so abruptly, and Della could almost see the path of his thoughts.

"I am sure your father knew nothing about this," she assured him. "And if he did, I could not blame him for choosing not to risk his position by sharing that information."

Della remembered Andrew's father. He was always kind to her, with that same warm smile she was so glad to see Andrew had inherited. There was nothing in her heart that could find ill will for him, even if he had been a part of keeping this secret.

"I am—" Andrew started again.

"No, please don't apologize." Della smiled. She took over the conversation from there, rubbing her palms on the skirt of her gown to keep the joints in her hands warm. Her mind raced with thoughts of where her parents might hide any tangible proof that the property in question was indeed hers.

Her mind came up empty, her thoughts trapped in a dense fog that accompanied her worst pain. It was not the time for this, she decided. She was holding too much hurt already. She simply couldn't add any more.

"Would you excuse me?" Della stood up too fast, and her entire body wobbled as her knees debated whether or not they'd support her weight.

She fled the room without looking back, and without another word from Andrew.

CHAPTER ELEVEN

TODAY WAS THE worst of all days. It was time for the doctor to come attend to her, as he did yearly. Sometimes more often, if she fell particularly ill. More so than usual. That happened occasionally, and those visits were thankfully usually brief. He'd prescribe rest and constitutional walks and occasionally laudanum for her pain. These yearly examinations, though, were thorough and thoroughly vexing.

"Dr. Seagle." Harry presented him to the parlor that was empty except for Della. She sat in an armchair in her best day dress. It mattered little that the style was out of fashion, and it featured no lace or embroidery. Her mother always sent gowns in dark colors, as if Della were in mourning for her own life. Today's was a light blue, the brightest option available to her. She wore it as if she would a ballgown on the day of her debut into society, had such an event ever occurred.

"Good morning, Miss Harris." The doctor bowed, placing his leather bag down on the sideboard and approaching her. "I must admit I'm surprised to see you out of bed, let alone sitting downstairs as if to receive callers."

Della sighed. This was why she'd dressed up. Why her posture was ramrod straight. Why she'd let Clara form her hair into some aggressively tight coiffure. The doctor always assumed she'd be abed, even though she'd been downstairs in this very chair for his last four examinations. For him to be surprised that she was well enough to receive callers, that comment carried a particularly sharp sting. She was often well enough to receive callers. They never came, except for Andrew, who had been politely asked to stay in his chambers until the doctor left, but that was not the point of the matter. She had to appear competent. Stable. Or else the power to make her own decisions, the last power she held in this world, would be taken away from her.

Dr. Seagle stepped into her personal space without asking for permission. He pressed his fingers into her shoulders, running them down her arms. His fingers wrapped around her elbows, tight enough that Della felt pain.

"So interesting," he murmured. Della knew he was not speaking to her. He'd have to consider her human to do so, and Della knew he did not. "It's almost as if you've a fever in only your joints."

Della knew this to be a symptom of her disease. Something she dealt with every day. That it was such a novelty to her long-time physician bothered her. Everything about him bothered her, so she tried to let it go.

Dr. Seagle never asked her questions while he was conducting his examination. He'd run his cold hands all over her body without a word in her direction, then he'd sit back and interrogate her while he wrote scribbled notes in his files.

"Hm," he noted. He picked up her hands in each of his, fingertips glancing over her swollen knuckles. "Your hands are becoming deformed."

Della had noticed the changes in her hands, the way the bones in her fingers seemed to rub together. How the swelling in her knuckles seemed to have become permanent. Her fingers weren't straight anymore, and if she placed her first fingers side by side, she noticed they pointed in different directions. She wouldn't call herself *deformed*, though. That word ate at her as he continued on. Her mind drifted far away, and she pretended she couldn't feel the press of hands against her knees, her ankles.

She was simply not here. Not in the parlor at Westfield Manor, not in the house at all. She was taking a walk by the lake. The air was crisp, an early autumn breeze that fluttered against her unbound hair. The chill made her hip ache, or maybe that was the walk itself. Either way, she didn't mind. It was peaceful out here. Tranquil.

"And how have you been feeling?" he asked, sinking into a chair opposite her and pulling out his leatherbound journal. His voice quite ruined her tranquility.

"I've been well," Della told him. She always found it difficult to discuss her pain with anyone, to summarize the past year of her life in a matter of few words. It was impossible. Besides, she could tell him that she spent most days bleeding from her eyes, and he'd have no other treatments to give her.

There was nothing for it. They'd tried acupuncture and bloodletting and the consumption of a variety of different metals. Each was more tortuous than the last, and Della had decided years ago that the only treatment she would accept was the use of heat, and the occasional pain medication when things got dire.

The doctor, however, saw this as a failure on her part. He saw it as a weakness, saw her as a woman not willing to fight hard enough. In her mind, though, battles were something that could be won or lost. Her illness was something that must be lived with, like a strange elderly aunt. She'd chosen to accept her elderly aunt, even with all of her quirks.

Dr. Seagle would never understand that choice, and Della was well past the point of caring.

"Your mother mentioned that you'd be willing to try some new treatment." Dr. Seagle seemed so pleased at the notion, that he'd be able to load her up with metal and steal her blood and make her eternally fucking miserable, all in the name of health she'd never get back.

"Absolutely not," Della wanted to scream, but her voice came out even-keeled. She couldn't be aggressive, lest she give all the power back to her mother. "She must be mistaken. I am doing quite well as I am, taking my daily walks in the garden and traveling up and down the stairs several times a day."

Several times a day might be an exaggeration, but she didn't care. All she cared about was getting this man out of her house without boxing his ears or convincing him she was incompetent.

"My apologies," the doctor spoke as he wrote. "I must have . . . misunderstood."

It was not a misunderstanding, of that, Della was certain, but she wouldn't address her mother's duplicity. Not about this, anyway. Della hated the fact that her mother knew everything about her visits with the doctor. She felt there should be some notion of privacy, and she'd always considered Dr. Seagle a spy who would report any impropriety back to her mother. That was why she'd told both Andrew and Clara to hide away upstairs.

"It's quite all right," Della assured him, her fakest smile in place. She swept her hands over her skirts, dusting off imaginary debris and trying to regain her dignity. She didn't think she ever could, not with him. Still, she tried.

"I'm so pleased to see you up and about," he said, standing and packing up his belongings. She wanted to pick up that leather satchel and hit him with it. "But I do wish you'd heed your mother's request for more treatment. It must be so difficult for her, having a daughter so ill. It would mean so much to her if you'd just try."

Della's blood boiled, but her face smiled. She simply nodded at the doctor as he took his leave. She hoped she wouldn't see him again until next year. She hoped that someone else would take over his practice by then.

Frustrated tears sprang up, and she actually groaned. The action was deeply unladylike, but it felt good. She was so incredibly angry. He'd dared make this about her mother, as if having a sick daughter was worse than being sick yourself. Della knew full well that her illness had ruined her mother's life. She needed no reminder. He'd accused her of not trying, as if she hadn't put forth an incredible effort just to sit upright in front of him this very morning. When he'd expected her to be in bed, fragile and alone. The way everyone seemed so determined to keep her forever.

Most of all, Della was frustrated because there was no way to win. Either she was trying too hard or not enough. Either she was too active or too lazy. Either she was too sick or not sick enough.

There was no way to win, but like she'd always thought, this wasn't a battle.

"Miss Della?" There was a knock on the parlor door, left open since the doctor's departure. The voice was Gwendoline's, as was the name she called her. Miss Della. It was unique to Gwen and Mrs. Goldsmith, and it was completely unnecessary. "I heard the doctor leave. I hadn't realized he was coming today. We can postpone our lesson if you'd like. If you aren't well."

Postpone. What an excellent word. Della was so proud.

"No, no," Della waved in her direction, gesturing for her to come in instead of lingering in the doorway. "I'm quite well, thank you."

Gwendoline sat in the chair the doctor had just vacated, her posture timid and her clothing more fashionable than Della's. She had incredible skill with a needle, and Della was always impressed with her. Gwendoline was naturally impressive. She was beautiful, the kind of classic, round-faced, soft-eyed beauty that would have suitors in every London ballroom fighting to dance with her. With her demure speech and her soft-spoken nature, she'd be the diamond of any social season. Instead, she was here with Della and Mrs. Goldsmith, making strange clothing and hiding whenever they had guests.

"How are you this morning?" Della asked her, partially re-laxed by the horrors of the day being over, and still partially angry at what had transpired. What had been said. Her muscles should be loosening, and instead, they were still held tight in frustration.

"I'm well," Gwendoline nodded, the blonde hair framing her face jostling with the movement.

Della was about to send her to the library to retrieve the

books they used in their lessons, when she had a better idea.

"Would you mind terribly if we skipped our lesson today? And we simply had a chat, instead?" she asked her. Della found that she'd never really spoken all that much to Gwen, not about anything that mattered, besides the lessons she taught her.

Gwen nodded again, this time hesitantly.

"I did not see the doctor today because I am unwell," Della tried to explain. "Not acutely, anyway. I am ill, as I'm sure you know. I have pain all through my body that has lasted for years, and it will linger for all of my days."

"I understand that," Gwen said, wringing her hands together where they sat in her lap. She appeared uncomfortable, and Della hated to be the cause of it. She hated that even talking about these things made everyone so uneasy.

"So I see the doctor once a year. He attends me, makes his notes, and reports to my mother."

"Your mother?" Gwen's face twisted in suspicion. Della noticed she was rather pale, as she often was. She worried about her.

"Yes," Della laughed, something bitter and forlorn. "I'm afraid we don't all have excellent mothers like yours."

She didn't want to talk about the viscountess. She wasn't even sure why she'd brought it up. Perhaps because an indignant rage still simmered in her blood, lingering where the flutter of her pulse beat against the skin of her neck. Even the high collar of her dress felt hot with that particular rancor.

"She is an excellent mother." Gwen averted her eyes. She picked at a stray thread in the embroidery on her dress. They were simple, gorgeous flowers made out of the delicate thread she'd sewn into the muslin. "I am lucky to be here with her. With you."

"We are lucky to have you." Della smiled. "I don't know anyone else who would make trousers short enough to fit Clara."

Gwen giggled, met her eyes once again.

"It is always so interesting, what Miss Clara asks of me. I

believe now she's wanting a pair of loose trousers made out of the fabric we'd use for a nightgown. It seems so odd to want to wear trousers to bed. *Men* don't even wear trousers to bed."

Della laughed, but she did wonder how Gwen knew what men were wearing to bed these days. She wouldn't ask, but she wondered.

"I think that's a delightful idea. Seems wonderfully comfortable, perhaps even for lounging about the house. I should like a pair myself."

"Of course." Gwen nodded seriously. So serious, their Gwen. She was too young to be so . . . burdened.

"Is that what you'd like to do?" Della asked. "In the future. Work as a dressmaker?"

Gwendoline froze, her fingers stilling against the middle of one embroidered flower. She'd been running her hands over each one, tracing the pattern she'd sewn. Della cursed herself for opening her mouth. This was what happened when she didn't think her words to death before she spoke them.

"I . . ." Gwen looked at her, and those soft eyes were rather afraid. "I am not certain."

Della thought to speak again, to tell her it wasn't important, they didn't have to talk about this now, it was all right if she didn't have a plan for the rest of her life. Remarkably, Gwen kept speaking.

"I mean, yes. That is what I'd like to do." She balled her fingers into fists and that pale face turned an almost frightening shade of red. "I just do not know if I can. I don't know if I am . . . able."

Her voice broke on the last word, and immediately, Della understood. She'd long suspected what Gwen had just seemed to confirm. That was something about being ill, it allowed her to sense illness in other people. To notice the signs, even when they tried to hide them. That pale countenance couldn't be hidden.

"Have you fallen ill?" Della asked simply. She was not one to speak in riddles and metaphors. She wanted direct confirmation of the topic they were discussing, however delicate it may be.

"I am not sure, Miss Della." Gwen sighed. Her rigid posture fell all at once, and she sank into the oversized armchair as if it were a warm bath. "So often, I think it must be a problem of my own creation. That it must just exist in my own mind."

Della nodded, for she knew that exact feeling all too well.

"I thought the same thing, dear." Della shifted her own posture, as her various bones and joints were beginning to stiffen. She attempted to cross one leg over the other, as she'd seen Clara do so easily. That took the pressure off of one hip but put it all on the other. Even more deeply uncomfortable than her last position. Della righted herself again, crossing her legs at the ankles instead.

Gwen's eyes met hers, and she saw the face of true solidarity. An understanding borne of shared experience.

"I thought that everyone had weak ankles. That all hips were structurally unsound. That all knees burned as if with fever." The more Della recounted the days of her youth, the more pain she remembered. It was all so easy to brush off when she'd been swimming and running and sneaking out her bedroom window to look at the stars. "It was not until I couldn't get out of bed for days at a time that I ever considered something was amiss."

"And what did you do?" Gwen asked. She'd abandoned fiddling with her dress in favor of leaning forward to follow Della's every word. It felt like a responsibility, to be the person Gwen talked to about this. It was a welcome weight on her shoulders, the thought of being listened to so intently.

"I hid it as best I could." Della was loath to admit this to anyone, as she'd become more than ashamed of her own behavior over the years. "It was foolish of me, but I was young. My mother was training me for my debut. Pianoforte lessons and gown fittings and rehearsing all manner of dances. I'm quite sure it's exhausting for all future debutantes, let alone for a young girl of seventeen trying to hide an illness."

Gwendoline seemed to be stunned into silence. Della hadn't

spoken about this with anyone in so long, it felt oddly refreshing to confess to someone how she'd treated herself so badly.

"How did you hide it from everyone?" Gwen asked, her voice almost an awed whisper. As if they were young girls telling secrets in the schoolroom.

"I pushed myself until I broke." Della spoke the words through gritted teeth, still angry at herself for all of that unnecessary pain. "I played until my fingers locked into place and I danced until my knees wouldn't hold me up any longer."

Her mind and her words painted a brutal picture of that time, but the pain her body remembered was so much worse.

"Why would you do that to yourself?" Gwen asked, then she seemed to catch herself. "I . . . I understand why you would, I'm sure. So you didn't lose all of your prospects just before your debut?"

Gwen was partially right. Della had been worried about her prospects. She'd worried about what would happen to her if her debut into society didn't go exactly as planned. She'd never dreamed that it wouldn't happen at all. That was a nightmare not even her overdrawn mind could've predicted.

"I had a friend. Her name was Mercy. There can be competition among young ladies on the marriage mart, and there is almost an expectation that we consider each other a threat. I was supposed to assume that Mercy could steal my future husband, but she was amazingly kind to me. There could be no competition between us, as she was a diamond of her first season. She would surely have married before I made my debut the next year. My mother wanted me to model my own future after her."

Gwendoline watched with wide eyes, hanging onto Della's every word. She briefly wondered if she should tell Gwendoline about this, the harsh truth of what so often happened to young women like them.

"She received several offers, and she accepted a proposal from an earl. I was thrilled for her, and she seemed so proud to be elevating her family."

As if Gwendoline sensed the impending tragedy, she leaned back, resting against the chair like she could protect herself from the blow.

"But she was hiding an illness. I've no notion of what it was. There were many rumors, of course, but I do not know if any were true. Her earl rescinded his offer, claiming her illness made their agreement fraud. And Mercy just . . . disappeared. Knowing what I know now, I'm sure she was sent away to the countryside, or Scotland, but I never heard from her again. No one knew what happened to her or how she fared."

Della felt her own voice thicken with the threat of tears, though she choked them back for Gwendoline's sake.

"I suppose society would say the same about me," she remarked. "Though I am doing quite well here. I can only hope the same is true for her. I did end up modeling my life after Mercy's, it seems. Just in the last way my mother would ever have wanted."

Silence reigned between them, and with a sigh, Della took the opportunity to tell Gwendoline a few more vulnerable truths.

"I never particularly cared about my prospects, if I am honest." Della sighed wistfully. This was the bright spot in this story. The waxing moon in a cloudless sky. "My mother had hopes of me marrying a duke. She thought I had the potential to elevate the family much further than my father's recently established viscountcy. When she discovered I was ill, she threw herself into trying to cure me. She was obsessed with it, to the point that she became someone else. She was never so . . . ill-tempered before she had to care for me. When she finally accepted that I'd be sick for the rest of my life, it was as if I'd done it to personally insult her. They sent me here, saying it would be for a season. Perhaps a year. I'd delay my debut, and everything would be fine. I'd find my duke eventually. I don't know if she truly believed that, but it was what she told me."

Della rolled her eyes. The idea was preposterous. Even as a bright, healthy debutante, she didn't belong as anyone's duchess.

"Wait," Gwen said, her delicate face crinkling up. "What did you care so much about, then? If you didn't want to marry a duke . . .?"

Della smiled ruefully. Here was her bright spot. She could easily grow tired of speaking about this time in her life, but she'd never tire of speaking about him.

"I wanted Andrew. I cared about him." It felt freeing to admit that. That he was the only thing she'd ever really wanted. "Marrying a duke would've been miserable, because it wouldn't have been him. I hid my illness for so long because I was afraid, so deeply afraid, that Andrew wouldn't want me. That he'd turn me away like Mercy's earl."

Gwen simply nodded, as if she understood. Della sincerely hoped she didn't.

"But I was sent away. He traveled abroad. Suddenly I had all this time to consider what I wanted out of my life. I've come to realize that being here, ill and at peace, is a much better existence for me than that of a duchess in hiding."

Della breathed a sigh of relief. Something in her chest felt lighter. More free. There was a note of acceptance ringing through her heart that she'd never truly felt before.

"And Andrew?" Gwen asked. She seemed so enraptured just by Della's simple words, by her explanation of how she'd ended up here.

That was the question, though. What about Andrew? Della hardly knew. She hoped, radically so. Even if hope was a faint notion that seemed almost foolish.

"I am not sure," Della said, using Gwen's own words. "He is here. I know nothing more than that."

Gwen opened her mouth to speak, but they were interrupted. Harry was a shockingly quiet man, despite being both overly tall and broad. Della had always thought he'd make an excellent soldier, defending the Crown with his deceptive silence and alarming stature.

"Pardon me, but Clara would like to know if she can come

out of hiding now." The knowing look in his eye, and the softening of his usual overt formality could only mean one thing. "I believe Mr. Lockhart would also like to know."

Della felt herself smile. He was here. That may be the only thing she knew for sure about Andrew, but it was a truly incredible thing.

CHAPTER TWELVE

ANDREW WAS QUICKLY growing restless. He'd tried not to pace the floor of the overly spacious room he'd been placed in, as he thought it was uncivilized, but he'd given up on that mission nearly an hour ago, because he'd run out of other things to do. Something about this didn't feel right. He didn't begrudge Della her privacy, of course, but the notion that she was so afraid of repercussions from a simple doctor's visit concerned him. The situation nagged at a specific corner of his mind. It was one he considered a part of his instinct. He didn't know why yet, but he trusted that piece of himself. If it told him something was wrong, then it was.

There were three quick, consecutive raps on his closed door. He briefly considered whether he was authorized to open it, but he assumed anyone knocking meant the doctor had left. He turned the knob, and Clara stood there, poised to knock again. Andrew thought he'd answered the door in a reasonable amount of time. Perhaps she was just impatient.

"Good news," she said, dropping her fist and settling her hands in a clasp in front of her. "We've been freed."

Clara took two steps back into the hallway and turned toward the grand staircase. Andrew guessed he was expected to follow, so he did.

"Does this always happen when the doctor comes?" he asked

her. "The hiding, I mean." She descended the stairs at a rapid pace. He was getting used to her whirlwind speed, but she did still unsettle him just a bit.

"Oh, yes." She reached the first floor ahead of him and kept walking toward the sitting room. "Besides the fact that Della does not like him, we cannot trust the doctor. He reports back whatever he discovers here to the viscountess, whether it is related to Della's health or not."

He stopped in his tracks, but Clara continued on. That instinct that told him something was wrong sparkled again. It was just a tiny twinge in the back of his mind. It pinched something just enough to make him uncomfortable. He had to sit with that discomfort for a second. Eventually, he followed, deciding against speaking to the back of her head.

They entered the sitting room, and there was Della. He was still not accustomed to this, walking into rooms and just . . . seeing her there. He was truly taken aback each and every time.

She looked downtrodden. Somehow defeated and angry and sad all at once. He wasn't even sure he could identify all of the emotions he saw in her eyes, but he was certain he hated all of them.

"How bad was it?" Clara asked. She sat next to Gwendoline on a long cream-colored sofa. She tucked her bare feet underneath her. Andrew felt a little ashamed he hadn't even noticed Gwendoline was in the room.

"It was . . . what it was." Della sighed. "The same as every year, I suppose."

Andrew thought he should say something, instead of simply standing alone in the corner, but he was silent in the face of all of those feelings of hers. Anything he had to say felt woefully incomplete.

She noticed him then. It was just a raise of her eyes, a shift from where she'd been discussing something so intently with Clara. She smiled, and there was nothing he could say that was better than that.

"Thank you for making yourself scarce," she told him with that smile still in place. "I am sorry to ask that of you."

"Of course." He returned her grin with one of his own, though he knew his could not compete. "You know I do enjoy a bit of hiding."

Her gaze broke away from his, but he caught the pleased twitch of her lips.

"I thought I might go out for a walk, since I've yet to see much of the estate. Would anyone care to join me?" This was not an invitation to Della specifically, he assured himself. He looked at each of them as he spoke. His eyes did not linger on her. Not even for a moment.

Clara jumped up off of the sofa, and she pulled Gwendoline with her. Gwendoline bobbled the slightest bit, as if she were dizzy, and Clara took hold of her more firmly, supporting her with an arm around her shoulders.

"Oh, we would love to, but Gwennie and I are so very busy. Another time, I'm sure." Clara began to move, still dragging Gwendoline bodily with her.

"Busy with what?" Gwendoline asked. She seemed so utterly confused by this turn of events. So was Andrew.

"Making trousers!" Clara huffed. They left the room abruptly, and Andrew and Della both stared after them.

"I suppose it will be just us, then." Della stood, getting her balance with the help of her walking stick. Her face, which was still displaying that myriad of emotions, was now tensed in pain.

"Are you well enough to take a walk?" Andrew couldn't help but ask.

"Yes, of course." She waved a hand at him, as if in dismissal. When she reached his side, he extended an arm, and she rested her free hand in the crook of his elbow. "I have been sitting for far too long. I need to walk, anyway."

They headed out the front door, and they took the few stone steps slowly to the ground. He turned right, heading out toward the overgrown gardens he'd only seen from afar. He hadn't had a destination in mind, and with Della clinging to his arm, he didn't care if it took them forever to get there.

"Walking helps your pain?" he asked her. There was a stone path through the middle of the courtyard, but it too had been overtaken with weeds. It was hardly visible anymore. As he asked the question, he found he didn't know all that much about Della's illness, and he wanted to learn.

"Very much." She nodded. Her footsteps had started out unsure, as if her gait was restricted. Now, she seemed to have loosened up some. "Much of my pain comes from stiffness. If I sit or stand for too long, all of my joints start to freeze. My hips, especially."

"And the doctor, is he able to help you?" Andrew side-stepped a missing stone along the path. They reached the end of what used to be a nicely manicured courtyard at the side of the manor house, and Della tugged on his arm as she started down a large hill toward the lake he saw glistening in the distance.

Where she led, he followed. She seemed to be considering her answer as she took small, gentle steps down the hill. His other hand came to hold hers, where it rested at the crook of his arm. He was afraid she'd fall, he told himself. It was not a baseless excuse to touch her. It was a matter of her ultimate safety.

"When I first arrived here, I dove into reading. I must've kept the town bookseller in business with all I bought. So many of those purchases were medical books, because my illness still seemed like such a mystery to me. I thought I would make peace with it if I could just understand." Della looked out at the water, her face a murky mixture of expressions.

Andrew had no idea how this was an answer to his question, but he was still unwilling to interrupt. They reached the lake's edge, and she stood there for a moment. Her gaze focused on the toes of her boots, just inches away from the gently lapping waves.

"I learned so much, but I never really came to understand. It's an illness with no cure, and that is difficult to fathom. But I learned something important about medicine, about doctors."

Della shifted, letting her walking stick fall to the ground beside her. She raised one foot and fiddled with the laces on her half-boots while she still held onto Andrew with the other hand. He had no idea how she balanced like that. She wiggled out of one shoe, and Andrew nearly choked when he caught sight of her stocking slipping down her leg. Once again, he had no understanding of what was going on, but no desire at all to stop it.

"They all take an oath. It is supposed to be sacred, this promise they make. To do no harm." She wrestled her other boot off and tossed her stockings aside, presumably so they wouldn't get wet. "Of course, I can only speak to my own experience with this one doctor, but he has no respect for that oath. At least when it comes to me, anyway."

"What do you mean?" Andrew finally asked. He held onto her as she dipped her toes in the water.

Della hissed, as if in pain, and Andrew's arm reflexively tightened. He expected her to take a step back, free her feet from what had to be bone-chillingly cold water. She didn't. She stayed right where she was.

"He has done me harm, whether he intended to or not. He continues to do so, every time that I see him. Just because he has this strange . . . loyalty to my mother. They think they can fix me at all costs, no matter what I want."

He watched as she wiggled her toes in the mud, turning the clear water a dirty brown.

"And what is it you want?" he asked, finally.

The wind blew the hair around her face into frizz, and he suddenly worried that she'd come out here without a cloak on. She stepped back out of the water, twiddling her toes again in the grass in an attempt to dry them off.

"I wanted to dip my feet in the water. So, I did. Even though it hurt."

"All right, then." It was a simple enough wish, and he was glad to have been here to support it.

"You asked about my parents yesterday. If they kept any

important documents here. I didn't think so, but it occurred to me that my mother always prefers rooms in the west wing of the house. I'd always thought that she wanted to be as far away from the rest of us as possible, and that very well may be, but do you think she could be hiding something there?"

Andrew gathered up her boots and stockings, then handed her the fallen walking stick. He turned around and headed back toward the house with her still on his arm.

"I suppose we could find out."

$$\underrightarrow{\;\;\;\;\;\;\;\;\;\;}$$

CHAPTER THIRTEEN

H ELL, NOW SHE had to deal with the blasted stairs. Della was immensely proud of herself for making it back to the house in one piece after her little stunt at the lake, but she'd somehow forgotten that just beyond the front door were those damned steps. It was not always such an exhausting trip. If it were, she'd have moved to a chamber on the lower floor long ago. It was just on days like today, days where she felt as if her limbs were weighty and unyielding, that it became such a Herculean effort to move.

"Do you need a moment to rest?" Andrew asked, still holding her hand against his arm. He must've seen some anguish on her face at the thought of climbing back upstairs. Or perhaps he was just perceptive.

"Just a moment," she admitted. "If you would hand me my shoes." Della broke away from him and sat on the ivory velvet bench near the sideboard, the only pieces of furniture in their entry hall. Andrew passed over her boots, and she sighed in relief as she slipped her stockings over her aching toes. She did not even bother pulling them up or tying the ribbons. Nor did she notice Andrew's eyes widen at the sight of her bare ankles. Della tied her boots as tight as the laces would go, just to prevent any swelling.

It was reckless, what she'd done, but she refused to regret it. She'd needed that dip in the water to wash away someone else's sins.

"Shall we go digging for secrets?" she asked him. Della stood up on her own, without the help of her walking stick, just to test the stability of her legs. They seemed sturdy enough, even though her toes still throbbed.

"It seems this house is full of them, metaphorically speaking. Stands to reason there's some physical proof somewhere." Andrew once again offered his arm, and she took it in one hand and her walking stick in the other.

"Speaking of secrets . . ." Della started. Something had been nagging at her since her conversation with Gwendoline earlier in the day. She briefly wondered if she had the courage to ask him about it, but then she thought of the shock of cold water on her toes, and she decided just to dive right in. "I was speaking to Gwendoline this morning, telling her about an old friend of mine. She disappeared, in the eyes of society. I realized that everyone in London must think the same of me."

Andrew nodded. They took the stairs slowly and carefully, and the conversation helped pass the time.

"How did you find me?" she finally asked. "I thought I'd never see or hear from anyone again, but then your first letter arrived."

He laughed, just a bright chuckle that was entirely too brief. Della thought she could see his cheeks blushing out of the corner of her eye.

"My mother. She often . . . overhears things, working in her position. You know how some pretend the servants aren't there, capable of listening. It took her a while, but she discovered where they'd sent you. When I went abroad, she made me promise to write weekly, no matter where I was. And she made sure your letters got to me, and mine to you." He was fully blushing now, and so was she. Della tried to assure herself it was from the exertion of the stairs, but that was difficult to believe.

"I am grateful to her, then." They'd reached the landing, and she led him toward the essentially abandoned half of the house.

The hallway had been dusted recently, because of her parents' trip. Otherwise, this wing existed in darkened silence. Midafternoon light streamed through the windows, and all of the furniture and carpets were faded because the curtains were always left open.

At the end of the long hallway, Della opened a creaking door. The bedchamber within was shadowed, but sparklingly clean. She sat on a beautiful carved wooden chair near the door, exhausted from the walk. Andrew threw open the curtains her mother had clearly left closed. While she rested, Andrew searched. He opened the wardrobe, sifted through the trunk in the corner, and examined the drawers in the bedside table. He was meticulously careful, and Della appreciated it. No matter what they found, if her mother came back into this room and saw even a hair out of place, there would be consequences.

Della looked around, observing the dressing table with beautiful, old perfume bottles and expensive cosmetics—more than anyone could ever use. There was a champagne silk dressing gown thrown over the privacy screen near where she sat, and a pair of pink slippers left abandoned beside the bed. It was a startling combination of wealth and carelessness, just like her mother. She tried to remember the mother she'd grown up with. The one who'd truly loved her, cherished her like a parent should. There was no evidence of that person left. It was all gone, lost forever to the depths of caring for Della.

"I don't believe we'll find anything of use here," Andrew muttered. He shut the last drawer and rose to his full height. He came to stand in front of her, then sat down on the plush and overly ornate bed.

There was something heady in this, sitting in a bedchamber with him. Alone. That overwhelming feeling wasn't the goal of this adventure, but Della let it wash over her anyway. It amazed her, how he was all at once so calming a presence and so exciting an idea.

"In fact, I have another thought." His voice was low and

comforting and a tingle ran down Della's spine that had nothing to do with the lingering cold from their walk. "I'll go back to London, speak to a few people. See what I can find out."

Della's heart skipped an agonizing beat at the thought of him leaving, but she'd always known he'd leave. He'd left her once before, and she knew he'd do it again. His life was in London, hers was here. Men like him didn't want women like her, anyway. Not in the long term. Not to marry, and not to love. She had his friendship, and his loyalty, and she told herself to be grateful for that.

"I couldn't ask you to do that," she said. Her eyes wouldn't meet his, no matter how hard she tried to appear unaffected.

"You did not ask, and I am more than happy to do it. There are many people I need to get reacquainted with in town, anyway."

Della was silent for long moments. It seemed there was nothing more to say.

"Thank you, Andrew," she finally murmured. She forced herself to look up at him again, to memorize that face she held so dear. Messy curls. Sharp jaw. Tensely held mouth bracketed by frown lines. Those fathomless eyes she'd never be able to forget if she tried. The ache in her toes spread throughout her whole body, and that cold took root in her chest.

Della didn't know what she was thanking him for. His willingness to help? Or for being the one to leave?

❦

CHAPTER FOURTEEN

THERE WAS SOMETHING about the dark that made Della foolhardy. In the dead of night, she was thoughtless and hasty, unheeding of her own rationality. She knew this, and yet, she continued on.

Down the hallway, walking in the pitch black. Sensing where she was only through muscle memory and the feel of her fingertips against the walls she hugged. She'd been counting doorways since she'd left her own. This was the right room, she knew it. The pads of her fingers drifted over the wood. They wrapped around the doorknob.

This was hide and seek all over again, but they weren't children anymore, and never before had she needed to find him so desperately. That desperation was as senseless as this entire endeavor. She'd climbed out of bed on a whim, tossing a warm robe over her night rail to protect her fragile joints from the pain of cool air. Only then, when she stopped in front of his door, did she realize what she was doing.

The silence around her was brittle, broken by the echoes of her soft footfalls. Trying to fight against a sudden wave of her own good sense, she closed her eyes. She stood so close to the door she thought she felt her eyelashes brush the wood.

Della blinked exactly three times to gather up the courage she'd somehow lost in the space between her own bedroom and his. As she twisted the doorknob, she heard a creak, and she couldn't be sure whether it was the door or her own wrist. At the sound of a click, she realized he'd left his chambers unlocked. She hadn't considered what she might do if he hadn't. There was a rush of air as the door opened. Her room was cooler than his. Della attributed the new warmth she felt to Andrew himself. Surely any place where he lay would naturally be as warm as the therapeutic baths Della loved to sink into every night.

For a moment, she stood frozen. Two steps inside the room, the door still wide open. She took a couple of breaths. She watched the rise and fall of his chest, just a hazy outline. He was a shadowed silhouette, but the briefest glimpse was enough to stop her in her tracks.

She must have moved eventually, shifted her weight to ease the terrible ache in her left hip. He stirred, made some noise that was halfway between a gasp and a groan, and then, "Della?" he said, and his voice was a dim whisper, as silhouetted as his form itself.

There was some clutching sensation behind Della's ribs. A gnawing that left her almost bereft. She wondered if he recognized the shape of her in the fading firelight or if she was simply the first person he'd thought of as he startled awake.

"Della?" he repeated, because she'd been too busy trying to move her heart back into its rightful place in her chest to answer him. She rolled her eyes at her own behavior.

He was so, so close, and still entirely too far away.

"Yes," she said, finally. "It's me." She didn't know what to do. This mission was entirely improvised, and she hadn't thought much past getting out of bed. She'd never even considered what she might do if she ever got this far.

Abruptly, she realized she still hadn't closed the door. Anyone could be roaming about the house, even at this hour. Stranger things had happened. She peered out into the hallway, looking left and right to make sure no one had seen her. As gently as her clumsy hands could, she eased the door closed.

"Come here," Andrew murmured. She was still turned away from him, and she pressed her forehead to the door's scratchy wood. She needed a reminder that she was here, in reality. That she remained grounded on this planet, and not truly in a world where Andrew spoke to her like this, so softly and so close in the dark. She had to maintain her awareness of the circumstances. She'd done something ill-advised and inappropriate. Absolutely irresponsible. She should be deeply afraid of the consequences. The aching sense of anticipation she felt at those two words were completely misguided. This was not a moment she was going to remember as long as she lived. This was not the single best night of her entire twenty-five years. It simply wasn't.

Della turned, and she couldn't make herself look at him as she took slow steps across the room. She had to focus on her gait. She stared at her bare feet, willing them and the rest of her traitorous body to behave. She reached the edge of the bed, and she had to look at him then. There was nowhere else for her gaze to fall.

All the air in her lungs—all the air in the room, the world, maybe—was suspended in motion. That indistinct silhouette was gone, replaced with Andrew's true profile highlighted in sharp relief. Moonlight danced through the gauzy curtains and hit the high points of his cheek bones. It emphasized the way his bottom lip was just the slightest bit fuller than the top.

"Della?" He wouldn't stop saying her name, and she didn't want him to. "What's the matter?" He'd sat up, his torso leaning against the pillows and his shoulders resting against the head-board. Once again, she became devastatingly distracted by the skin at the top of his chest his nightshirt didn't hide. She wanted to run her fingertips over the dip between his collarbones.

"Nothing," she said, reflexively. Then she cursed her own strange behavior again. There was no reasonable explanation for sneaking into his room in the middle of the night if nothing was amiss. Unfortunately for Della, there was no reasonable explanation at all.

She hadn't liked how they'd left things after their discussion in her mother's rooms. Hated it, in fact, and instead of speaking to Andrew at some point during the day as most people would, she'd allowed herself to sit and stew and overthink every word and every gesture, until she'd ended up here. In his bedchamber. Hovering uncomfortably at the edge of the bed and staring so intently at the fine hairs on his chest that she thought she might be able to count them. Perhaps it was time to admit that indeed everything was not all right.

"I . . ." She twiddled her fingers, but that made her realize how much they were starting to curve in different directions, and she was no longer soothed by the motion. "I couldn't sleep."

In the fading light, she thought she saw concerned crinkles form at the edges of Andrew's eyes. He turned down the counterpane next to him and fluffed an extra pillow.

"Come here," he said again. Della closed her eyes against the force of longing that threatened to overwhelm her. It was no use, she was swept away. She hadn't allowed herself to be caught in the undertow, but her heart hadn't asked for permission. She inhaled one quick breath, and it smelled like him. Like leather and pine and ink, more potent than any sensation she'd ever felt.

This wasn't her intention, not really. She'd never imagined herself ending up here. She'd only wanted to talk. She'd only wanted some assurance that when he left Westfield Manor, it wouldn't be forever.

Della slid into the bed as gracefully as she could with a body that was actively in decay. Suddenly, she could feel him. That warmth all around her was Andrew. He pulled the coverlet over her legs, his arm brushing over the fabric of her robe, and she shivered.

They didn't speak for long moments, and already, Della felt better. The racing beat of her heart slowed, and the constant panic in her mind quieted. It was peaceful. Just being with him in a way she'd never been with anyone else. Her soul was much more tranquil than her body, which was struggling to find comfort in this half sitting, half reclined position. She scooted down the bed, resting her weight on her right shoulder, which began to throb. So, she lay on her back. That was murder on her hips, and the inflamed joints between her ribs made her feel as if she were suffocating. Della tossed and turned, shifting each limb in an attempt to calm the stabbing pains shooting through her bones.

With a huff, she gave up. She rolled onto her stomach, her head facing him. That damned hip was agonizing, but she rearranged herself in a way that helped some, with her left knee bent. She rested one hand in between her pillow and her face and let the other tangle in the sheets between them. Andrew wordlessly mirrored her position, lying on his back and turning to face her. Della stifled a gasp at the closeness. He was so warm and steady, and she was overcome with emotions she couldn't define. She felt his hand drift to the back of her calf, draping her leg over his. That gasp slipped out into the air between them without her permission.

"Is that better?" he asked, his thumb rubbing slow circles over the back of her knee.

"Yes," she whispered. It was such an indulgence, being with him like this. She couldn't help but ask for more. She couldn't help but reach for everything she'd ever wanted while she could.

So slowly, Della let her hand move up to his chest. She pressed into his skin, her fingertips dancing under his shirt. Giving in to that devastating longing, she felt the dip between his collarbones and the smooth line of his throat. Despite the warmth he radiated, his skin was cool to her fevered fingertips, and Della thought her mangled hands were never more useful for anything than touching him. Her thumb brushed the edge of his jaw, and he sighed. His chest rose and fell, and she felt him move, turning his face to melt into her touch. She sank her fingers into those curls, and she didn't even know if the sharp intake of breath she heard was her own. His eyes had become drowsy, what was usually the brown of tree bark had turned an almost as inky black as the night itself.

"Why couldn't you sleep?" he asked, low and slow and gentle. Della thought she might have actually felt the imprint of his words on the delicate skin of her cheek. She wanted to keep them there, as a talisman of this moment. She wouldn't need anything to remember this by, though. As much as the seconds ticking by felt ephemeral, she knew the memory was beyond eternal.

"You'll come back, won't you?" Della finally asked. She spoke her fear out between them, and for a second, it felt heavy and dense, like she'd exhaled the black smoke of an overburning fire.

Under her hand, those lines appeared in his face again. On his forehead, around his eyes. She smoothed them out with her febrile fingertips.

"Of course," he whispered, his lips drifting over her forehead so briefly she thought she might have imagined it. "That's the best part of traveling. Coming home."

CHAPTER FIFTEEN

ANDREW HADN'T KNOWN what it was to hate until that very morning. Everything even remotely hateful he'd ever felt paled in comparison to how he loathed to get out of bed. For long minutes, he just lay there and stared. The curtain of Della's unbound hair had fallen over her face, and he swept it back behind her ear. His eyes started to draw lines between her freckles, forming abstract shapes across her cheeks and up over her nose.

Waking up next to Della was the most precious gift of Andrew's life, and getting up and leaving her behind felt like handing it back. As if it were somehow unwanted, and not something he cherished.

He stood up with perhaps more furor than was necessary. He just knew he had to stay in motion, because if he stopped moving, his body would naturally gravitate back to hers. Breaking that pull took all of the strength he had and more.

Andrew surveyed the room and realized he'd made a bit of a mess in only the few days he'd been here. He couldn't let Della see this in the light of day and think him slovenly. He packed as he tidied up, wrinkled shirts and lonely socks going into his satchel with little fanfare. He dipped behind the privacy screen to change, and the fabric of his last clean shirt felt stiff and starchy. Tying a cravat around his neck was intensely uncomfortable now that he knew the sensation of Della's fingers running up and down his throat.

She was still asleep when he returned to stand in front of the bed, fully packed and fully dressed. It was almost impressive that she'd managed to sleep through the flurry of him pacing about the room. Andrew sat down on the edge of the bed at her side, his hip resting against the crook of her bent knees. Della was facing away from him, and he spent entirely too long watching her, counting her breaths. He thought he might be able to see the beat of her pulse against her neck if he tried hard enough. He would. Try hard enough, that is. As he watched her exhale on a dreamy sigh, he promised himself this wouldn't be the last time he got to see Della like this. It was the end of the beginning, not the beginning of the end. He'd get so many more cold mornings and warm nights and he'd collect each of her smiles like the treasures they were.

"Della," he whispered, even though he suspected she wouldn't wake so easily. Maybe he was just prolonging this, wanting to spend each last moment he could in this bed with her. That was shortsighted, though, he told himself. The sooner he left, the sooner he could come back.

"Della," he tried again, a bit louder this time. He found her elbow, resting at her waist, and it was radiating heat even over the blankets. His hand drifted to the curve of her shoulder, and it was burning, too.

She woke up then, as he gently shook her. Her eyes were bleary at first, almost startled, and then they seemed to melt as they focused on him. Andrew tucked that miniscule moment away for later. On a particularly bad day, it would hearten him to know Della's first instinct was to trust him.

"Andrew," she said, her voice nothing but a confused breath. "What's the matter?"

She must have sensed it, then. His disquiet. The way it would pain him to leave this room. He was sure it was written on his face.

"I have to go," he said as plainly as he could. He didn't want to worry her, but he also didn't want to give her false hope. If he told her all he'd be willing to do on her behalf, she wouldn't ever let him leave her sight.

"Oh . . . I—" she started to say, but she cut herself off mid-sentence. "All right." She seemed suddenly resolved. Gone was the innate trust and natural warmth in her eyes. It had been replaced by a guardedness he hated to see. Something chilled and resigned.

He tucked a strand of that rogue hair behind her ear again. He ran his thumb over the apple of her cheek, trying to memorize the feel of those freckles.

"Goodbye for now, Della," he whispered, as if she were still asleep and he didn't want to wake her. In reality, he just didn't want to hear the words from his own lips.

"Goodbye," she whispered back. Her warm fingers wrapped around his wrist where he still held her face. For the briefest moment, her lips pressed against the skin just above the sleeve of his coat. His breath caught in his chest as he fought against an onslaught of unwelcome emotions.

He couldn't do this right now. He had to go.

He stood from the bed just as he had earlier that morning, abruptly and vehemently, though his hands lingered. They drifted slowly over her, not feeling the sensation of the counterpane but the heat of her skin beneath. He reached the door entirely too soon, and he paused for a single moment in the doorway. He'd lost all the warmth of her body, and he shivered as a bereaved chill swept over him.

"Andrew?" he heard her say, still in that faint whisper.

This was another moment he'd keep. Not saying goodbye, not leaving. But the sound of his name in her early morning voice. Against his better judgment, he turned back to face her. She was stunning. All he could see was her pale face and her dark hair and the faint lines of displeasure around her lips.

"Don't forget to write."

HE HADN'T RESPONDED. Della lay there for what felt like hours, absorbing what was left of his scent on the sheets and considering everything he'd said and everything he didn't say. She'd asked him last night if he'd come back, and she didn't like his answer. She'd asked him to write to her, and he hadn't answered at all.

It had been a long while since Della had felt this hopeless. All of the contentment she'd worked so hard to build was long gone. It was in a carriage headed back to London, perhaps never to return. She tried to go back to sleep, but she was haunted by the sight of him walking out the door. It repeated over and over in her mind, and the relative silence around her served as soul-stirring background music.

"Mr. Lockhart?" Della heard, along with a particularly aggressive knock at the door. "Have you seen Della? I cannot find her anywhere, and its long past time for breakfast. I've never once walked into her room to find her missing."

Della rolled her eyes. She'd failed to account for Clara when she'd decided to lie here forever, and that was a critical mistake.

"I should be concerned, but I'm hoping that you have"—Clara's voice abruptly halted when she opened the door—"an explanation," she finished.

"It's terribly rude to enter someone's chambers without knocking," Della chastised.

"I knocked," Clara responded. She entered the room in earnest, taking slow steps until she reached Della's side of the bed. "And there was no answer. I tend to take silence as permission."

In spite of herself, Della laughed. Clara leaned against the bedpost and crossed her arms. Della's laughter fell away at the sight of that posture. She felt as if she were being reprimanded by her mother. This interaction held all of that protective energy, but none of the existential terror.

"Dare I even ask why you are here?" Clara began to tap her

foot against the carpet impatiently. Della rolled her eyes again like a misbehaving child. "And where is Mr. Lockhart?" Clara looked around as if she'd just realized the man to which this room belonged was in fact nowhere in sight. Well, this room used to belong to him, anyway. Della feared once she left, she might never be able to set foot in this chamber again.

"He's gone," Della forced herself to say. She crossed her own arms, assuming a defensive posture now that she'd been awake long enough for her arms and legs to move at least somewhat.

"Gone?" Clara fell into the armchair next to the bed, succumbing to yet another fit of dramatics. "What do you mean?"

Della sighed. She loved Clara. She loved everyone here at Westfield Manor, but she found the thought of explaining this to any of them exhausting beyond belief. Already, it weighed on her. It made her eyelids heavy and her bones ache. That her bones always ached was not the point of the matter.

"He's gone," she repeated, her voice broken by another heavy sigh. "He left. He went back to London in search of answers. I don't know that he'll ever find any."

She closed her eyes, letting the heaviness take over. She was emotionally treading water, and she was getting tired. It felt like the time to let go and lose herself in the watery depths.

"So you are telling me that he's left, what, in the middle of the night?" Clara's voice bordered on hysterical, and Della couldn't tell if that was anger or vexation or a deep sadness she heard there. Perhaps a devastating mix of all three.

"Early this morning," Della clarified. "Right at dawn, I believe." Her head was beginning to ache, too, and she wasn't sure if it was because she'd been holding back tears, or if it was the screech of Clara's voice, or if it was simply a result of missing breakfast. She never missed breakfast. Clara had been well within her rights to worry.

"Without saying goodbye?" Clara asked. Della's eyes were still closed, but she could almost imagine the look on her face. Wide eyes. Probably leaning so far forward in her chair that she'd have fallen by now if not for her death grip on the arms.

"No, he said goodbye." Della rubbed at a sore spot in the center of her chest. "To me, I mean. I suppose he didn't speak to anyone else before he left."

"I'm sure Harry would've told me if he'd seen him leave," Clara muttered.

That sore spot bloomed into a deeper ache. Clara was so certain of Harry. Of her relationship with him, whatever that may be. Della had briefly thought she had that security, too. That certainty. Now, he was gone, and she wasn't sure of anything at all.

"Did he have business back home?" Clara asked. Della actually winced at the use of the word. *Home.* The best part of traveling, he'd said.

"I don't know," Della admitted.

"Well . . ." Clara replied. She was silent for a moment, and Della could feel her carefully collecting her words. That was a terrifying notion, Clara being careful. "I'm sure he'll find whatever he's looking for."

"I don't know," Della repeated. "I don't know what we do now."

She heard a rustling and an indignant huff. When Della finally opened her eyes, Clara was much closer. Standing over the bed in a way that was almost menacing.

"We eat breakfast." Clara extended a hand, pulling Della to a sitting position. "That's what we do now."

Chapter Sixteen

B Y THE TIME Andrew got back to his home in London, he'd begun to feel a familiar sort of restlessness. He'd had ample time on the journey to confront those admittedly confusing feelings and to identify them, but they still circled around him like vultures. The restlessness had been his constant companion for years. It had followed him as he'd traversed the globe, and it had made all of his accomplishments feel hollow.

He'd long ago identified the source of that particular feeling. He needed a purpose. He needed something to do, some way to make an impact on the world around him. He'd thought studying the law was the way to do that, and he'd done some good in his legal career so far, but none of it felt grounding. None of it felt like the reason he was brought into the world.

When he saw Della again after eight years apart, he knew he'd found his purpose. As soon as he'd left her behind, the restlessness crept back up. It felt like a snake slithering across his body, a scaly sensation climbing up his spine and down his arms. Even now as he stood hovering at the entrance to his own home, the itching unease remained.

He couldn't place just how long he might've been standing there at the door, suspended in motion but not in time. Eventually, he shook his head, as if to dispel the lingering confusing feelings. Or maybe to shake the snake of disquiet off of his back.

Luckily for him, his mother was waiting. He'd scarcely taken two steps inside the house before she was approaching. Her hair was just starting to gray around her ears, and she wore a light-blue day gown and an ivory shawl. She was always cold, his mother. She wrapped her arms around him, and even though he was taller and broader and a man full grown, he still felt like the boy who hugged his mother every chance he got. In many ways, he was still that boy.

"Welcome back!" she said, with all of her usual enthusiasm. She patted his cheeks then looked him up and down, as if to assess him for injuries or determine if he'd somehow gotten taller. "How was your trip?" she asked.

They gravitated to the sitting room, and he pondered how to answer. His trip was incredible. It was life changing. It hadn't felt like a trip, like all the rest. It felt like coming home. He simply didn't know what to do with that, or what to say. As much as he wanted to confide in his mother, and she was perhaps the only person in London he trusted, it didn't quite feel like his story to tell.

"How did you know that you wanted to be a dressmaker?" he asked her, answering her question with one of his own and completely changing the subject of their conversation.

His mother didn't bat an eye. This kind of non sequitur was common practice in their relationship, and she'd always done her best to follow the path of his winding thoughts.

"I was very young," she started, sinking further into the old divan she sat on. It was becoming threadbare, and it needed reupholstering. His mother hadn't changed the furniture since the death of his father, and that was almost a decade ago. She insisted she loved the old-fashioned furnishings, but it suddenly seemed rather dated to Andrew. "My mother taught me how to sew and how to make clothes. I made my own church dresses as a girl, and I loved it."

She smiled, and Andrew knew that fondness. He'd heard all of this before, but he had a feeling he could do with a reminder.

"I suppose I had other choices, but it never really did feel like a choice." Her eyebrows pinched and her gaze turned contemplative. It was in the slight tilt of her head. Andrew saw himself in that. He'd always favored his father, and it was almost a comfort to find pieces of himself as he looked at his mother.

"You know my work was always rather . . . unusual." She seemed to emphasize the word with the raise of one of those previously pinched brows. She threaded her fingers together in her lap and brushed dust off of her skirt with her littlest finger.

"Unusual?" Andrew asked. "How do you mean?" He was surprised at this turn in conversation. That sort of pivot was usually his to make, and he wasn't sure he was still following.

"My mother made dresses for everyone around her until her fingers gave out." She sighed, and Andrew didn't know if it was wistful or an expression of long-held grief. "And she did so by the book. Maids were in drab muslin and cooks were in stiff aprons. She did a wonderful job, but there was such little fun in that."

Something in her gaze shifted, and Andrew decided she was truly wistful.

"I had fun." Her mouth tipped up in a rueful smile, and she was almost mischievous. "I made wedding gowns out of old curtains and communion dresses for girls out of tablecloths. The rich are so bloody wasteful."

She rolled her eyes, and Andrew did too. He wasn't surprised at her unsavory language—she was often quick to swear when she truly got started speaking.

"But I took what they didn't want, and I let it shine."

Andrew was beginning to follow the strangely winding path of her speech. Perhaps he was more like her than he'd originally thought.

"What I mean to say," she leaned forward, spearing him with her intense focus, "is that being a dressmaker wasn't the choice I made. The choice I made was the *kind* of dressmaker I wanted to be."

He sat with that for a moment. He generally considered his

mother to be correct in all matters, and the reality of what she said began to resonate with him.

Maybe this sense of restlessness came not from the fact that he was a solicitor, but that he wasn't yet the kind of solicitor he wanted to be. Her words repeated in his mind. *I took what they didn't want, and I let it shine.*

The rest of society, even her parents, didn't want Della, but he did. He desperately, fervently did, and he could let her shine.

❦

CHAPTER SEVENTEEN

DELLA WAS LISTLESS. It had been mere days since Andrew had left, and she'd already begun to question how she'd ever gone entire years without seeing his face, hearing his voice, feeling the warmth that he uniquely brought her.

Andrew's absence, like the worst of her pain, made her deeply emotional and almost destructively reflective. Whereas the flaring of her pain often made her quietly introspective, this puddle of overwhelming feeling in which she'd suddenly immersed herself prompted her to speak. Clara was, as always, her chosen confidant. They sat in her chambers, and Della tried to get comfortable in the one chair in this house she actually liked, her feet propped up on a matching stool.

"This is all very formal," Clara remarked. "I feel as if I've been summoned because I am in trouble."

"That is ridiculous. You are never in trouble. Not with me, anyway," Della scoffed. "I simply wanted to talk."

"We talk every day, do we not?" Clara asked.

"Yes, but this is important." She spoke as sincerely as she possibly could, and as soon as her hip unlocked from the painful position in which it had been stuck, she readjusted herself to set her feet on the ground and face Clara where she sat on the floor with her back resting against the bedpost and her fingers tangled in the thick carpet. It was not unusual for Clara to prefer the floor to the furniture. Many who knew her thought it one of her many charms. Della thought it a luxury to have a body durable enough to regularly rise from such a position.

Clara nodded, and she looked oddly serious.

"I'm sure you know," Della started, "I've been feeling . . . rather alone, lately. It seems that feeling worsens every time I see my parents. And to know that they've been keeping something like an inheritance from me . . ." Her voice trailed off. She didn't have words to describe how that felt. She didn't think there were any.

"And then Andrew came, and that first meal we all had together was so wonderful. It was so incredibly nice to just sit down and look at all of the people I'm surrounded by. It's such a privilege to have all of you."

Clara simply smiled, surely knowing that Della had more to say. Where Clara always spoke with immediacy and conviction, Della was typically more thoughtful about each of her words. Overly so, such that she often regretted uttering them in the first place.

"I have been thinking," she sighed, waiting for her words to settle into order in her own mind, "about my parents, and the way that we as a society treat those who fall ill."

"They," Clara gently interrupted, wrapping her hands around her knees and pulling them to her chest. "Not we. The way *they* treat those who fall ill."

"Right, yes," Della nodded. At least in this instance, she appreciated the reminder that she was no longer a part of polite society. "When my parents sent me here, I don't think I ever stopped to consider what that meant. I'm certain I always knew their reasoning was not as they say it was. It did not take me long to discover it was never for my benefit.

"I am alone." Della continued. Clara opened her mouth to speak, to refute that claim, almost certainly, but Della continued. "I am alone, but not alone. Because I have you, and everyone else. But that is . . . purely luck. I've no ability to go out into the world and make my own friends or develop my own interests beyond the walls of this house."

Her hip began to ache again, the kind of pain she knew meant she needed to move. Della stood, wobbling only a bit as she took the first steps around her room. The ache subsided some as she slowly paced, avoiding where Clara sat, so as not to trip over her. She heard that familiar, loud crack that she really didn't think bones ought to make.

"I was angry for a bit, as I'm sure you remember. There were tears and hateful writings for no one's eyes but my own." Della sighed, remembering that period of her life. At twenty-five, eighteen seemed so unbelievably long ago. As if all of that had happened to a different person entirely. She wondered how she'd managed to change so much when nothing else had. The scenery, the house, the people.

"I do remember," Clara laughed. "I was terrified myself, starting my first job. There were rumors of your mother, of why this house had been closed for so long before you arrived here. No one wanted to work for her—that's the only reason I was given the position as a girl of eighteen with no experience or reference to speak of. I thought you'd be everything people thought your mother to be. But you were just a girl, like I was."

Della continued to pace, her footsteps slowing until she leisurely ambled across the room. She couldn't recall ever speaking about this with Clara, of those first days they'd all been at Westfield Manor.

"I'm certain the rumors were awful, but some of them might have been true."

"I certainly hope not," Clara laughed. "The one about your mother hating the country so much that she'd ordered the house closed, sure. And how she sent your first maid away. But not the one about her pushing a servant down the stairs in a fit of rage."

"She would never," Della gasped. Her mother was many things, but she was the furthest thing from violent. Physically, anyway.

"I know," Clara nodded. She released her legs and extended them out in front of her, pointing and flexing her toes in her oversized boots that were made for a man. Della was surprised to see her still wearing them. Usually, they'd be abandoned somewhere by this point in the day. "It all got very out of hand. You know how people talk."

"Exactly," Della said, returning to the comfort of her armchair in the middle of the room. "People talk, and things get out of hand, and that's the reason people like me end up in horrible situations. The idea of their sick daughter remaining at home for all of polite society to see was too much to bear, so they sent me here. And I meant what I said, Clara, it is truly a privilege to have you all here. Not all are so fortunate."

"What do you mean?" Clara asked, her entire face scrunching up like a confused child.

"As I sat in front of all of you that night, I thought of what it might be like if I were truly alone. If I'd been abandoned by my parents and everyone else. Not all families can afford a household for one person. Not all even care enough to employ them. Think of what could happen to me once my parents are gone and my livelihood depends on David."

Clara shook her head immediately, like she couldn't give the idea any space within her brain. Della couldn't blame her for that, for she often felt the same. She naturally avoided thoughts of that upcoming portion of her life. It was a terrifying prospect, the idea of having no control and depending on someone who seemed to care so little for her. Della suppressed a shudder. As difficult as it was to prod at the sore spot in her own future, she felt she had to. They had to. There was good to be done.

"Think of the others. Those who don't have a country house to be banished to. Those who are made to feel as if they are burdening their families with their very existence. Those who end up alone, for one reason or another."

Della stopped to catch her breath, as her mind had been racing faster than her mouth could speak. She thought of Mercy, wherever she may be. She hoped she wasn't alone. She pressed a warm, aching hand to the center of her chest just to feel the racing beat there. Suddenly, that rhythm felt like one of purpose.

"But what are we able to do for those people, beyond thinking of them?" Clara asked. Her face still appeared confused, and the furrow of her brow made Della realize that she wasn't entirely making sense. That happened sometimes, when she forgot herself in the furor of her own thoughts.

"I've an idea," Della said simply. She smiled, and something about that twitch of her lips was freeing. She felt some of the rebelliousness her eighteen-year-old self had been known for coming back. It crept into her psyche slowly and quietly, like a child sneaking back home after dark.

It was there, in the shadow of her teenage petulance, that Della found herself again.

"Should I be concerned?" Clara asked, crossing her arms and shifting that expression of confusion to one of amusement. "The last time you had an idea, we ended up walking back from the lake after a swim in the pouring rain. It was frigid, and you nearly caught your death."

That had been a horrible idea, one of those moments of teenage immaturity. Della had known it would rain. She always knew. She'd thought if she caught her death out here in the country, it would be a kind of poetic justice. How wrong she'd been. Dying in misery was not justice. Living in utter contentment was.

"I think that we could help these people. Some of them, anyway. If my parents speak the truth, I am owed an inheritance. Property that could be used as a haven for young, ill girls like myself. Girls who have nowhere to go."

"We?" Clara asked. "You'd take me with you?" Her voice was fragile and quiet, so unlike her that Della did something equally out of character. She stood from her chair and lowered herself to the floor next to where Clara sat. The motion was ungraceful and inelegant, but she made it.

"Clara," she grasped her hands, "that day at the lake, I told you to run ahead back to the house and I'd make it there eventually. You wouldn't leave me, not for anything. We both nearly caught our deaths out there, together. No one is left behind—I'm fairly sure that is the entire point of the idea."

Clara smiled. She was so rarely emotional like this with anyone. Radiant happiness was at the core of her personality, but there was also a deep vulnerability to her that not many ever got to see.

"I've no idea how we are ever to act on such an idea," Della sobered. Reality was swift in setting in, as soon as she'd formed this grand idea, she'd realized the magnitude of what she was actually trying to execute. "My parents will never allow me my rightful property."

"Well," Clara smiled again. This one was cunning and almost smug. "Thankfully you've retained the services of an excellent solicitor."

CHAPTER EIGHTEEN

Andrew hadn't been to Morley House in years. It was in an overly regal neighborhood, somewhere he'd never had a reason to be outside of his father's work, and he'd been too young to realize it the last time his boots fell onto the stone steps. A chill of terror ran through his body as he thought of that last time. He'd been such a fool. It was a moment of desperation, and it had broken his heart. Upended his entire life. His memories of this place were fond outside of that one ruining moment, but something about the grandeur of it all made him ill at ease.

He was sure it was beautiful, but all he could see was a place where Della wasn't welcome, and that was nowhere he wanted to be.

The butler opened the tall, heavy door, and he and a footman bowed as Andrew approached. He wanted to tell them such an action was wholly unnecessary, but he didn't want to let on just how out of place he was here. Though he was sure as experienced domestics in a home like this one, they could smell the commonness on him. They could probably tell by his lack of finery and general disposition that he belonged with them more than he did with the viscount. Truly, it was an act of boldness in and of itself to be standing in their front hall. He had no right to, and he certainly hadn't been invited.

He'd come here to give them the benefit of the doubt. He

remembered the Harrises as kind people. They'd treated his father well, and they'd let Andrew spend most of his childhood roaming about the grounds of their estate. It wasn't that he didn't believe Della, it was just that he had trouble reconciling the owners of the home he'd practically grown up in with the people who would do such a thing to their own daughter.

He was about to ask to see if the viscount was seeing visitors, but the man himself walked through the hall just then, seemingly headed for the grand staircase. He stopped in his tracks at the sight of Andrew, and it seemed that neither man had any idea what to say. Andrew braced himself to be swiftly thrown out by the aggrieved looking footman who stood in the corner. The man seemed to be prepared for some kind of violence. Instead, Viscount Morley's face broke out into a wide smile. Andrew barely recognized that face. It was staggering for a moment, how much older Morley looked. Andrew realized he'd been robbed of the opportunity to see his own father age in the same way.

"My God, Andrew Lockhart, that must be you." Morley stood in front of Andrew, vigorously shaking his hand. "If I didn't know any better, I'd think you were your father. I haven't seen you in an age, my boy."

At that very moment, Andrew regretted even coming here. He was still shaking his hand, and Andrew was growing more and more uncomfortable by the second. It wasn't just that he didn't belong there, though the gilded wallpaper and marble flooring were clues that led him to that conclusion, it was the overly familiar greeting. Despite his words, Morley acted as if they'd just spoken last week. As if they often played whist together at a club somewhere in the city.

How could the man in front of him greet the son of an old business associate with such demonstrative familiarity when he didn't even care to see his own daughter more than once a year?

Andrew withdrew his hand as swiftly as he could. Something about being so close to the man made bile rise up in his throat.

"Yes, well . . ." Andrew started to respond, once he realized that was what was expected of him. Of course, if you called upon someone at their home, you would be presumed to speak. "I've been abroad for many years."

Practically since the last time he'd walked these halls. Much had changed since then, Andrew noticed as he looked around. He wasn't surprised. Della had always lamented her mother's constantly changing the furniture and the paint and the carpets. Della had always preferred to be outside because the landscape didn't change nearly as much as the interior of the home, only once a season. Andrew was amazed he could still recall memories like that, happy ones, as he stood in the place where his world had been shattered. That was the power of Della, and that was something he should never doubt.

"Come and sit, we'll catch up." Morley smiled, and Andrew felt himself grin in response. He hoped the discomfort he felt wasn't showing through his face. It was a relief to be invited in, and he hadn't even needed to ask.

As he walked further into the home, relief turned to dread. Andrew's stomach turned as they headed for Morley's study. He still knew where it was, because it was where he'd always been able to find his father if he needed him. Andrew felt as if he needed him now, and there was a pinch of grief in the hollows of his chest at the thought that he wouldn't be there this time.

"I had heard you left for the Continent some years ago, just after your father went to his rewards, but I hadn't realized you were back." The viscount sat behind his large oak desk and fixed Andrew with a gaze that made him squirm.

For a moment, Andrew just looked around. He was taken back in time. Nothing in this room had changed, it seemed it had been spared from the viscountess's garish taste. In fact, the room reminded him of the study at Westfield Manor. Sitting here with Morley was nothing like sitting across the desk from Della, though. It was night and day. Harsh cold and searing warmth.

"I am," Andrew answered, because he was. He found he didn't have much else to say.

"And how is your mother?" Morley asked. He picked up his spectacles off the desk and began to sort through a slurry of papers strewn about the surface.

"She's well," Andrew answered. He wasn't making eye contact. He was focused on those papers. He might be a bit of a mess in other aspects of his life, but he was ruthless in the organization of his work. The sloppy bookkeeping he saw before him was maddening.

They fell into silence, and something about it made Andrew bold. Everything had been so easy so far, he decided to test the waters. See how far Morley could be pushed before he fell.

"And how is your daughter?" Andrew asked. He was almost proud of the way he feigned nonchalance. As if his daughter was an old acquaintance, or she was just the subject of a natural progression of polite conversation. As if she weren't the fulcrum Andrew wanted to balance his entire life on.

The last time he'd been in this house, the last time he asked anyone about Della, it wasn't her father. Andrew hadn't even made it that far. Now, he didn't know how much Morley knew about what had happened between them. About what Andrew had wanted to happen, anyway. It was a risk to even mention her name.

The viscount put down his papers, somehow leaving them in more of a tangle than when he'd started. He must be trying to bait Andrew into anger at this point, the disorder was so deliberate. He took off his spectacles, leaned his elbows on the desk and intertwined his fingers as if in prayer.

"She is ill," he said, on a long-suffering sigh.

Andrew knew that, of course. Everyone knew that. Della was ill. She'd been ill for years. Andrew wondered if that's all they'd been telling anyone who asked about her welfare. He wondered if that was truly all Morley knew about her.

"It's quite a loss," Morley continued. "She had such promise. Such prospects." He shook his head, and then he was back to sifting through his work.

Andrew was astounded. So much so that he didn't dare speak, lest he ruin this entire visit by letting the vitriol he felt fly from his mouth. He shouldn't have come here. He shouldn't have doubted the level of callousness these people were capable of. Even now, it felt as if the very air he breathed was contaminated with it. Like he might be influenced by their evil just by sitting here.

He realized that an unusual amount of time had passed since anyone had last spoken, and he supposed he ought to fill the gap of silence with something. A comment on the weather, or a compliment on the exquisite grounds they kept. Something. Anything. He couldn't, though. There was no way for Andrew to continue conversing with someone who spoke of Della as if she were dead.

Describing vibrant, brilliant, perfect Della as a loss. He couldn't even imagine it.

After a few more moments of interminable silence, Andrew had decided the only thing to do was excuse himself. Before he could move, the study door flew open in a rather forceful manner. He thought there must be some emergency. There'd be no other reason to interrupt the man of the house from his work. He didn't see Morley taking too kindly to an intrusion like that.

To Andrew's utter surprise, he watched as the viscount's face softened. His expression went from enraged to mildly irritated in an instant. He couldn't imagine what could cause such a spectrum of emotions so quickly. Andrew turned his head. Oh. Well. That explained it, then. Standing in the doorway was someone Andrew hadn't even considered as he attempted this ill-fated trip to Morley House.

The future Viscount Morley. He'd be the third, if Andrew remembered correctly. David. Andrew's first friend, and someone he'd not spoken to in over eight years. He appeared to have already overindulged in spirits, even though it was only the early afternoon. His coat was hanging off one shoulder, and his cravat was askew, some of the buttons on his shirt were even undone.

There was no telling where he'd gotten that light-blond hair, when Della's was so dark. Much like their father's.

"Father," David slurred. Andrew wondered if the other man had even noticed his presence in the room.

"David," Morley acknowledged. The thinly veiled irritation was beginning to come to the surface. His face had turned a mottled red, and Andrew could see veins in his temples starting to bulge.

It seemed it wasn't good for a man's health to have an heir like David. What a pity.

"David," Morley repeated, his tone as docile as if he were talking to a child or a lost dog. "You remember your friend Andrew, don't you?"

Andrew wouldn't have called them friends. Not anymore at least. Friends rarely went eight years without speaking, and that, regrettably, was why Andrew didn't have many. Besides, in his adulthood, there was no reason for Andrew to befriend a future viscount. They might have played around the same estate as young boys, but their paths couldn't have diverged further.

David seemed to look him over, squinting his eyes in what Andrew assumed to be an attempt to ward off double vision. David approached, Andrew stood. David extended a hand, and Andrew met him halfway because his bleary eyes seemed to be severely lacking in depth perception at the moment.

"Been a while," David said.

"So it has." Andrew nodded. He let his hand go.

"I'll be taking the carriage again this evening. After dinner." David turned to speak to his father as if Andrew had simply vanished.

"And I suppose you'll be needing more money," Morley sighed.

Andrew wasn't sure what he was watching, but it felt like he was trapped somewhere he shouldn't be. Intruding on a private moment of a rich father spoiling his equally rich son. David simply nodded.

"You should join me at the club tonight, Lockhart. Enjoy yourself for once in your life." David smacked Andrew on the shoulder. The invitation felt sincere, even if the words themselves were less than kind.

"I'd love to," Andrew said, despite the fact that he'd most likely hate nothing more. He didn't belong in that club any more than he belonged in this palatial house, but it was an opportunity, he realized. He'd come here today to find some proof that Della's family wouldn't do this to her. This outing might just be his opportunity to find some proof that they actually had.

David left the room as abruptly as he'd entered, and Andrew was once again in a battle of silence with Morley.

"My apologies for his behavior," the viscount said. It was so reflexive, Andrew got the hint that he made this particular speech often. "You know how young men are these days."

Now that, Andrew didn't understand. He and David were only a few years apart, and he was long past considering himself a young man. He'd been a young man when he'd left England, thinking he'd never return. Since then, he'd studied and worked and done enough around the world that he'd grown bored. David was still clearly acting the part of a young man, though. In a way Andrew had never been permitted to.

"You could join us for dinner, if you'd like." Morley smiled in a way that set Andrew on edge. He was so polite. It was almost certainly artificial. It was a thin veneer that Andrew knew he had to break through. He feared there was something malignant lingering beneath.

"Thank you for the kind offer, but I have business to attend to this afternoon." Andrew smiled at his own words. The power of Della, shining through once more.

"Very well then." Morley stood up, shook his hand again. "It was good to see you, Andrew."

He left the room without another word, striding down the halls with his head held high. He nodded at the butler and the footman on his way out, waving off their still unnecessary bows.

Andrew would come back later. He'd go on this galivant through the night with David. *Enjoy himself for once*, he'd said. The arrogant prig. He wouldn't enjoy himself, but maybe he'd find something useful.

Andrew headed toward home. He didn't have business to attend to this afternoon. Not really.

He had a letter to write.

✦

CHAPTER NINETEEN

Andrew watched as David dozed off in the carriage, leaning for a moment against the squabs until they hit a bump in the road and he was jostled awake. It was the first moment he'd been able to relate to the man since they'd been reacquainted that afternoon. Andrew was exhausted himself, as this trip to the club was already extending well beyond his usual bedtime. He knew he wasn't a young man anymore, but this was all the more proof.

David's head bounced off the back wall of the carriage, and Andrew struggled not to laugh. It wouldn't be appropriate, even if he did seem to deserve a good smack about the back of the head.

"So," Andrew tried to make conversation, just to avoid more bodily injury. "What have you gotten up to all of these years?"

David laughed, something that was both light and bitter at the same time. He gestured all around them and provided no other answer, which Andrew took to mean this was all he'd been doing for the better part of a decade. That was rather sad. David had all the money and the privilege and the support in England, and he'd done exactly nothing with it. Meanwhile, Della had none of that, and she'd still built a lively, beautiful home for herself.

Despite all he'd said in his letter to Della this afternoon, and most of that was rather impolite where her family was concerned, Andrew thought it was astounding how swiftly he'd come to feel pity for the man in front of him.

Their carriage rolled to a stop, and David seemed to come alive. Where he'd been drowsy and sad, he now appeared energetic and thrilled to be where he was. It was as if Andrew watched as a mask of exuberance settled over his face. He departed the carriage without the use of the steps, and Andrew followed behind. He politely thanked the footman and the coachman, ensuring he actually spoke to the people that had thus far seemed invisible to David.

As they entered the loud, dark space of the club, Andrew felt himself tense up. This was not the place for him. He was made for quiet and calm. This was raucous and chaotic. David, though, was having no such problem. He'd assumed some kind of absolutely feral character, accepting drinks and speaking to people in loud, passing shouts. David hadn't introduced him to anyone, and Andrew would never be able to recognize a soul if he saw them again.

By the time they settled at a table in the corner, David had a whisky in each hand. He'd already finished at least one and replaced it with another. It had been only minutes, but Andrew had already lost count of how much the other man had consumed. Andrew had been almost deathly seasick on a trip to America once, and he imagined that's how David might feel in the morning. Though if this kind of intoxication was commonplace for him, perhaps he'd just roll out of bed and start the process right over.

"I don't see you enjoying yourself yet," David yelled, taking a sip from the glass in his right hand, then his left.

"I suppose this is not my kind of . . . enjoyment," Andrew answered. He knew his face was wrinkled up in disdain. It was the visual representation of the way his body rebelled at being in this place. He didn't like the way he had to raise his voice to be heard. This was how he imagined Hell, if fire were music and the devil were a barman with a particularly heavy pour.

"What, do you think yourself above the rest of us common degenerates?" David smirked as he spoke. He was making eyes at a scantily clad woman across the room, and everything about it made Andrew uncomfortable.

"Certainly not," he responded. He didn't think himself above anyone, especially not the men of high society by which he was currently surrounded. "And you—a future viscount—consider yourself a common degenerate?"

"Perhaps not common, but a degenerate nonetheless." David extended a glass in his direction, as if they were in on the same joke. Like they were actually friends.

Andrew remained silent. He found he didn't have anything to say. There wasn't much they could talk about, a worldly solicitor and pompous jackass heir to a viscountcy. Eventually, though, the silence began to prove worthwhile.

"I'm merely biding my time, you see." David placed his glass back on the table, and he ran the tip of his thumb clumsily over the rim. He attempted to wink, or at least that was Andrew's best guess at what that erratic facial motion was. "Until I can do something worthwhile."

Andrew leaned in, resting his forearms on the table and sliding his drink across the surface from one hand to the other. He saw this for the opportunity it was, but he took a moment to consider how best to use it. David had accelerated to quite a level of drunkenness, those whiskies stacking upon each other exponentially in his blood. Andrew almost wanted to know what that felt like. It must be freeing, that kind of intoxication. To be free from your thoughts and expectations. Hell, David even seemed rid of the burden of operating his own limbs. That was why Andrew could never be that loose. He valued his sense of control.

"And what might that be?" Andrew asked him. He was treading carefully. Although he was almost certain David wouldn't remember this conversation in the morning, he knew a volatile man when he saw one. Andrew couldn't get this wrong. Not when it was Della's future on the line.

"My father is far too lenient," David said. He rolled his eyes, and they seemed to get stuck at the back of his head. As if his body had forgotten how to process that particular action. "He's not had a man of business in years. There were a few after your father, but they came and went. Now he does it all himself, what he does not force upon me."

Those eyes rolled again, and Andrew just sat, absorbing the information he was so readily handed. The more David loosened up, the more Andrew stood to gain from their time spent in this hellish bar.

"*You must learn,* he says," David began in a truly abysmal impression of someone. Andrew guessed it was his father given the context, but there was otherwise truly no way to know. "*This will all be your responsibility one day.*"

Andrew realized this display was quite insensitive. Not only to Viscount Morley, who was so horribly butchered by David's less than flattering impersonation, but insensitive of himself, too. To mock your own father in front of a man who had none—that was the kind of thoughtlessness he was beginning to recognize as a cornerstone of David's ethos.

As he looked at the sloppy, slurring man across from him, Andrew thought he'd completely lost all respect for him. Then, he kept talking.

"And then there is Adelaide." The way he said her name set Andrew's teeth on edge. It was almost a hiss. His hands formed into fists and pressed against the wooden seat of his chair. "They tell me all the time, *You'll have to take care of her when we're gone.*" He resumed that grating impression, and it took all of the control Andrew had to stay seated.

He'd never been prone to violence, not even as a boy. But something about this moment, David's smug face, the whisky he dripped everywhere, or the vengeful tone of his words, pressed at an angry spot on Andrew's soul. He should've known if he could ever be tempted into brutality, it would only be for Della.

"That is rich, coming from the people who are mismanaging her estate as we speak." David spat all over himself as he spoke, and Andrew didn't think he'd even noticed. Andrew's own ears perked up immediately, though, at the idea of them stealing from Della. "They doted on her when we were young. She was always perfect. Smarter than me and better mannered. Everyone she met loved her, and I was just the bloody heir."

Yes, Andrew wanted to say. Della's the physical embodiment of sunshine, and David's the physical embodiment of a stubbed toe.

"When she fell ill, there was a sense of justice in that. She was sent away, and I've lived the life of an only child." David raised a glass, as if to salute to something. To what? His sister's illness? Or his own power? Andrew knew the life of an only child. It was all he'd ever known. He knew it could be lonely.

"I don't like the way they've coddled her. She's no need for a full household at that country house . . ." David rattled on, listing grievances his parents had committed against him on Della's behalf. Andrew's ears were beginning to ring. He thought that was the sound of his own self-preservation, trying to keep him from strangling a future viscount with his bare hands.

"At least they've not seen fit to let her have the barony." At that, Andrew's senses heightened once more. The roar in his ears subsided, and he froze. He even tried to slow the beating of his heart, as if the blood flowing through his body too fast would upset the delicate balance of this conversation. A discussion that had suddenly become much more important.

"I wasn't aware your family held a barony," Andrew remarked. He thought he was handling this rather well. Before tonight, he could've counted on one hand how many times he'd ever lied. Now, the untruths seemed to flow out of him freely. He wasn't sure yet if that was something to be proud of.

"*We* do not," David made sure to emphasize. "I've no claim to it, as the title belonged to Adelaide's mother. You do know she is my half sister, don't you? We don't discuss it much, especially in public. It bothers my mother, that she brought no title to the marriage like my father's first wife. Makes her feel somehow inferior."

David rambled on, raising a glass to nothing in particular as he stopped to consider his words.

"They never told Adelaide. The estate was placed in a trust in my father's care, and they'd planned to tell her after she married, so that her husband could run the place."

David seemed to be getting rather flushed. Andrew couldn't tell if that was from the alcohol or the rage he seemed to be simmering in. Perhaps a dangerous combination of both.

"It was a fine plan, but then she fell ill." He rolled his eyes again. "She became a burden no one will carry, and now that she is of age, we have quite the problem. The Crown will come calling eventually. They'll manage to find her, even secluded in the countryside."

"And that is what you are afraid of? That she'll learn the truth?" That overloud ringing was back in Andrew's ears, and he thought it might actually be the hiss of steam from his blood boiling.

He'd had a similar thought about how His Majesty would eventually have a vested interest in the property and finding the title's rightful owner.

"Oh, I am not afraid of anything." David's face shriveled up into a horrid grin. "We were going to find her a husband we could trust to run the estate as we have been, but her being sent away worked just as well. It's true that it becomes more complicated now she's of age, but Adelaide is just as easy to control as any husband of hers would have been. Likely even more so."

"Control?" Andrew nearly growled. Under the table, his hands balled into tight fists.

"Mmhm," David raised his glass again with a shaking hand, his words beginning to slur. "My mother has been sending a physician—a friend of hers—to attend her every so often. He reports back what he's seen, and he can be persuaded to linger around a bit longer than he should."

"What exactly does that mean?" Andrew asked, suddenly stilled by fear that the doctor had seen him at Westfield Manor.

"It took time," David sighed. "But we've learned what is important to Della. She loves the domestics my mother hired, and she likes her peace and quiet in the country. My mother didn't believe it, so they recently went to see for themselves, and she was finally convinced. Said she'd never seen Della happier. So we're going to tell her that as long as she complies, and we get control of the barony—and its money—with her having the title in name only, she'll get to keep the comforts of home. If she doesn't, well, things will get even more complicated."

It was astounding, the audacity of the man in front of him. Of his mother, his father. Their entire family. Taking advantage of Della's illness. Banishing her to live a life of solitude in the country, instead of running an estate where she belonged.

"All she has to do is inform whoever comes knocking to inquire about Kinloss that she is in ill health, and therefore leaving the running of the estate in the care of her father, as it has been for decades. It's quite simple, really. It won't disturb her a bit."

A wave of nausea threatened to overwhelm Andrew. His head spun. Andrew wasn't sure if the amalgam of emotions in his chest were rage or devastation or hurt. All he knew was that they were all for Della. He stood up abruptly because he couldn't take one more second in this disgusting place with this despicable man. And to think, Andrew had once considered him a friend.

"What's the matter?" David asked as Andrew began to step away. He was sure he looked frantic and irate. He could feel the aggrieved line of his brow tightening up.

"Nothing." He tried to play it off. "I've got an early meeting tomorrow. Better be off."

David shrugged. Andrew considered it a good excuse. If he so much as mentioned something related to an actual job, David wouldn't know the difference. Briefly, Andrew considered staying. Making sure the stumbling drunk got home safely. It only took a moment of recollection on their conversation for Andrew to dismiss the thought as quickly as it came.

Without so much as another word, he left the noise and the rancor of the club for the quiet darkness of the street. The cobblestones were damp with rain, and every breath of cold air felt like renewal in his lungs. Even if it was heavily scented with the unsavory aromas of the city.

He stopped at the corner, unsure of where he was or where he was going. Andrew had always known when he needed to take a moment to himself, so he did. He leaned against the wet bricks of a nearby building and let his head fall into his hands. His mind raced through every cutting word, the motion behind every sip. The ferocity of his own rage shocked him.

Once he calmed down, he knew what he needed. A plan.

⁕

CHAPTER TWENTY

ELLA DIDN'T LIKE this. She didn't like it at all. She'd had a premonition about Andrew's letter before it arrived, and not the kind she welcomed. It wasn't the rush of warm feeling and the tightening of anticipation in her chest. It was vivid anxiety. It was impending terror.

> *This has been an enlightening trip. I would love to tell you that your father sends his warmest regards, but I can't. I'm not certain what regards he has, to be honest with you. Though I'm certain they're not warm. And to say nothing of your brother, whose words I dare not repeat. A true waste of humanity, that one. I've not seen your mother, and that does feel like a stroke of good luck on my part.*

He'd crossed that one bit out, but she could still read it. She could still feel the uncharacteristic anger exploding off the page. Even the slant he wrote with seemed more aggressive. Like he'd used enough pressure to break his quill right in half. It was all so unfamiliar to her—this Andrew who wrote such things. Who felt such things. Della knew something must have happened. Something significant and potentially horrible, and it must have been about her.

That was what she didn't like. Thinking that Andrew was out there somewhere in London, roaming around with his head full of vengeful thoughts and his heart full of completely unnecessary anger. She couldn't stand the thoughts of him doing all of this alone, whatever it was he was doing. Never had she more hated her distance from what used to be the center of her life. Him. Her family. All of London and society. This feeling of impotence, the way it seemed as if everyone were dancing through the ballroom of her life and she was standing alone watching along the wall, was more than she could handle.

She poured over his letter once more, both absorbing the words and trying to find their hidden meanings. There was a message here she couldn't see, an invisible layer to his correspondence that held the key to figuring all of this out.

> *Forgive me for speaking ill of your family again, but I cannot tolerate them, Della. I won't discuss what I've heard unless I can do so in person, but just know that I wish they'd never even known you. It's a privilege they've so thoroughly abused.*

"Again?" Clara remarked. Her eyebrow quirked up in that way she did when Della was being stubborn, and Della rolled her eyes in response. She was allowed to be stubborn, as far as she was concerned. She was a lady of her own free will, and if that will happened to be particularly strong, then so be it.

> *Once again, I find there's unfortunately no point to this letter. I simply needed an outlet for what has gone on the past few days, and you've always been my favorite person to write to. I feel better already, actually.*
>
> *Don't worry about a thing, Della. I'm going to fix this.*
> *More soon.*
>
> *Yours,*
> *Andrew*

"I just don't like it, Clara." Della sighed. She was certain this wasn't the first time she was saying those same words. It had been her constant refrain since she received the letter. Even before. Since the moment that preemptive panic had set in. She ran her thumb over his signature. Even though his penmanship had become scrawling and chaotic throughout the letter, that signature was as sharp as ever. She could hold the paper up to a torch and line it up with any of the signatures from any of the other letters he'd ever sent her. It was always so pinpoint perfect. So sharp and reliable and consistent. Just like him.

"I know, Della." Clara lowered herself down on the edge of Della's bed, facing where she sat at her writing desk. "But it's been days. All you've done is read the letter over and over again. Have you considered that it might be time to do something else?"

Clara's eyebrow raised again. Not to indicate stubbornness, Della didn't think. This was different. She did this sometimes when she was trying to lead Della down a certain path. She was trying to get her to follow the progression of her thoughts. As if that were not a winding path to certain trouble.

"And what would you have me do?" Della asked. It was better to just come right out and say it, she believed. The less speaking in metaphors and riddles the better. That was for someone with a much stronger constitution than herself. She had such little energy for mental luxuries like those. Della shifted her legs again. One of these days she was going to hurl this damn desk chair out the second-story window. There was no possible way in which she could contort herself to achieve even a modicum of comfort in it. Someone in such pain should really have more plush furniture available at their disposal.

"Have you written back?" Clara asked. She tucked her feet underneath her, getting her dirty boots on Della's clean bedding. Della didn't mind. That wasn't the side of the bed she slept on, anyway. In fact, she'd come to think of it as Andrew's, even though he'd never slept there. She knew that was the side he preferred, and that was enough.

"No," Della admitted, and it felt like an expression of guilt. She often took several days to write Andrew back. She enjoyed taking that time as part of her process. It was an effort to extend the life of the blissful feeling his letters always brought her, but she wasn't trying to extend anything now. She wasn't feeling that particular delight at the moment. She was still swamped in dread, and she didn't know how to paddle her way out. She didn't know which way was up.

"I've tried," Della nodded to several pieces of paper she'd desecrated in her attempts to write a single bloody letter. It was a terrible waste. Another sigh hissed out between her teeth, and Della realized she was completely at a loss. "Words feel . . . inadequate, somehow. I've always been able to write to him, even if no one else. But I need to know what happened, and he won't tell me—"

"Then go see him," Clara interrupted, the words blurting out of her mouth like the strength of Hercules couldn't have held them back. "I am sorry," she muttered after the outburst. "But I have wanted to say that for days. I thought you'd come to that conclusion yourself, but that process is taking entirely too long."

"What do you mean?" Della asked, certain she'd misheard. Or misunderstood. She knew Clara couldn't be suggesting what she thought she was. It was preposterous, but then again, so was Clara.

"Go to him," she explained simply, as if he were at the manor next door and she could go by and call on him first thing in the morning. "Go to London. You said it yourself, you need to know what happened and he won't tell you. Not in writing, anyway."

"Yes, but . . ." Della stammered, all of the reasons she couldn't just make a trek into the city flowing through her mind. None of them would form into words, though, and Clara continued to look at her expectantly. "I cannot go to London."

That was all she'd been able to say, and it had to be enough. She believed that *no* was a complete sentence.

"You can't," Clara hiked that eyebrow up again, this time in challenge, "or you won't?"

Della rolled her eyes. In her mind, there wasn't a difference. It was semantics. Either way, she was staying right here. She had to. There was no other choice.

"With all of that money you've been saving, I think you could make it to London rather comfortably. Perhaps even quickly." Clara's entire face turned into a smirk, and Della fought off a gasp.

"How do you know about that?" she asked, feeling surprisingly more impressed than betrayed or violated.

"There are no secrets between a lady and her maid." Clara winked. She was leaning so far forward that the elbows resting on her knees threatened to slip out from under her.

Della straightened up her posture. Another sigh escaped her lips without her permission. She hadn't wanted to have this conversation. She didn't want to list all of the reasons that this plan could be nothing more than another one of Clara's grand ideas. Nothing more than an appeal to her sense of adventure.

"That money is for the future. I had hoped no one knew I've been skimming off the top of the monthly allowances my parents send. But it's to protect all of us. Their generosity is going to run out one day, and I needed some way for all of you to keep your livelihoods."

There were a multitude of reasons they didn't discuss this— the period in the future that seemed so uncertain. Not the least of which was their lack of power, their inability to control the way that story would unfold.

"Don't you see?" Clara's eyes had softened. They might even be tearing up, and Della couldn't remember ever seeing Clara cry. Not in all these years. "This is a risk we have to take. You can keep socking away coins here and there to try to save us from destitution, or we can go to London and take what's rightfully yours." She'd stood up, knocking dusty dirt off her shoes and making her rousing speech all the more convincing.

"We?" Della asked. She'd been fixated on that.

"Della, of course. We. Harry and I would go with you, at least. No one left behind, remember?" Clara had begun to pace the floor. Della could practically see the thoughts steaming out of her ears and mingling with the open air.

It was a preposterous idea. As much as was the idea that she could actually have things like property and a future and a home of her own. And Andrew. If she went to London, maybe she could have Andrew. She could find him and keep him. If he'd let her.

"I cannot allow you to do that, Clara. Risk your positions on a fool's errand to the city? There is too much at stake. If my family even so much as sees you, if they knew you'd helped me leave the manor—"

"Della, listen to me," Clara leaned against the desk, resting one hand on Della's shoulder. Her presence, for once, was steadying. "I think you'd find that the moment you left Westfield Manor, for London or otherwise, we would follow you. There's no *allowing* anything. No one gets left behind." She emphasized the phrase again, as if she couldn't underscore its importance enough.

"You've discussed this with Mr. Stanton?" Della asked. She still didn't like this. There was so much to lose, for her and everyone else, but she was beginning to consider it, just because she didn't see any other way. Sitting around here waiting for news was not her place. Nor was it Clara's.

"Well, no." Clara turned to face Della. Her cheeks were flushed, and she didn't know if that was from the exertion of this conversation or from the mention of her Mr. Stanton. "But I believe he could be convinced." Her smile turned almost smug, and Della felt a flash of envy.

"It must be nice, having a man so willing to do anything for you," she muttered. It was a whisper, a sentence she felt guilty even uttering.

"Della," Clara looked at her with almost annoyance on her face. It was gentle, but it was annoyance nonetheless. "You have a man of common birth going all over London, confronting a viscount, not to mention your mother, who is a beast of her own, just to help you get what is yours. Please do not act as if you do not have such a man."

That guilt rose up again, and as the cloud of her own mixed feelings dissipated, Della finally saw the path forward. It was dark and shadowed, possibly far too difficult to pass, but she had to take it. There was no other choice. Andrew was on the other side.

More soon, he'd said. From the bottom of her heart, Della fervently hoped so.

CHAPTER TWENTY-ONE

I N THE END, Mr. Stanton had been able to be convinced. Della knew no further details of how, and she didn't particularly want to. She watched them now, Clara and Harry, sitting on the other side of the carriage. Clara's head rested on Harry's shoulder, and his head had sort of drifted over to rest atop hers. They made an excellent pair. Della had never seen them quite that close together. At Westfield Manor, they seemed to revolve around each other. Hovering, moving in the same directions, but never exactly meeting in the middle. To see them now, pressed against each other with their faces relaxed in sleep, it would seem that they ended each day this very same way. In truth, Della felt as if she were intruding on some private moment.

She turned her gaze toward the window, her fingers peeling back the curtain just slightly. She couldn't see much, given the impending dark. They could be anywhere by now. She'd lost track of things like the day or the time. Della let the curtain go, flexing and fisting her hand over and over in an attempt to ease the throbbing, as even that miniscule action had sent an ache all the way up to her elbow. This journey was proving to be more physically taxing than she'd thought. Her own fragility had been a reason she'd immediately rebuked Clara's idea to go to London, but it was much less significant than the realities of how their lives would change should this all go wrong. She could lose

Andrew. She could lose Clara and Harry and Mrs. Goldsmith and Gwen. The family and the home she'd built at Westfield Manor. At the slightest mishap, this trip could cost her everything.

Just as she had that sobering thought, the carriage hit a bump. Her hips slid forward, and she had to grip the seat below her so as not to pitch forward into the floor. A hiss left her lips. Her hands were well beyond the point of comfortably clutching anything, and every point where bones connected between her knees and her chest felt as if it were aflame.

"Are you all right?" Clara whispered. It was a quiet huff for her, but it was a normal volume of speech for anyone else. Harry hadn't moved, his eyes still closed in the comfort of sleep.

"I'm well, thank you." Della tried to appear so. She straightened her posture, went through as much of her daily stretching routine as she could in the close confines of the carriage. She didn't know how well Clara could see her. The light was low, almost nonexistent, and most of it drifted in intermittently from the window when they passed something particularly well-lit along the road.

"Do you suppose this is dangerous?" Clara asked. She'd turned toward the window, and a sliver of light hit the contours of her face.

"Traveling into the night, you mean?" Della responded. They had perhaps pushed too far, choosing not to stop at the last coaching inn they'd passed before evening set in. They'd stop at the next one, but she worried that their quick pace would prove costly.

She did feel some better, though, having moved around a bit. Her body had made truly terrifying creaks and groans, but Della had long ago accepted those as a particular eccentricity of hers. She considered them the sound of the pain leaving her body. It hadn't left just then, not completely. It had subsided. Calmed. It had taken a few steps away from her, but it had not left her alone entirely. She supposed she wouldn't know what to do with herself if it did.

"That, too," Clara remarked. Her face had pulled into a smirk, an expression of her natural humor. That was something Della had always admired about her. She could tell a crowd the most heartbreaking story and still make them all laugh. The problem was that those heartbreaking stories were usually Clara's own. Della sensed an anxiety in her that she found unfamiliar. She couldn't see it on her face, not past that smirk, but she felt it thicken the air between them.

"We can turn back, Clara. I promise. I don't want you to risk yourself like this for me, and I don't want you to worry. This is dangerous, and we both know it." Della didn't know how to make her understand. That she didn't need to do this for her. That Clara had already done so much more than anyone else ever had. Than anyone else had ever considered doing.

"No," Clara shook her head. That smirk was nowhere to be seen, but Clara wasn't looking at her. She stared out the window, her expression inexplicably blank. "We have come too far."

"I don't even know where we are," Della argued.

"No," Clara repeated. She met her eyes now, a desperation there that begged Della to understand. "That's not what I meant. We have come too far."

They sat with that for long moments. Time was transient here, in this liminal space of the carriage. There was no way to know how many minutes passed before Della dared to speak again.

"If you are certain you don't want to turn back, then why are you so . . ." She struggled to articulate what she meant. What she saw in Clara's eyes. "Forlorn?"

Clara laughed, it was something sudden and inappropriate and almost surprised.

"I'm not certain I even know what that means." Her voice had become oddly wet. Della couldn't see her well enough at the moment to confirm that she was crying, but she would almost bet she was. She didn't know how to handle a crying Clara. It was an experience they'd never shared.

When she spoke again, her voice was more sure somehow. Perhaps there was something cleansing about this, crying in the dark. Suspended in time and space.

"I am not . . . forlorn." Clara sniffed. "I've just been thinking, along this journey, about what happens after this is all over. It feels as if nothing will be the same when we return home, no matter what."

Della nodded, and she realized that was an exercise in futility in such a darkened space. She'd just wanted to silently acknowledge that she understood. That she knew what she was asking of them.

"You are the only family I have, Della," she said in a low voice. Della could see the tears now, streaming unbidden down her face. She made no effort to swipe them away. It was as if she were pretending they didn't exist. That she was only really crying if she admitted she was.

"As are you to me," Della whispered back. "You may not be the only family I have by blood," she sighed. "But you are the only family I care about."

She reached around in the dark, feeling for Clara's hand. She took it, grasping it between her own. Clara still wouldn't look at her, and now the barely there light seemed to only be highlighting the rivulets of tears dampening her face.

"You are my sister in everything but name, and that will always be true." Della squeezed Clara's hand, willing her to understand. "I don't know what's going to change after all of this, but I know we will stay together no matter what. Always."

Clara finally met her eyes. "Even in Hell?" She smiled, even through the tears.

"Yes, I suppose so." Della laughed, too. They were delirious with exhaustion, riddled with anxiety, and laughing like schoolgirls. "Even in Hell."

Their laughter roused Harry from sleep, and he awoke abruptly.

"What's going on?" he asked, as if he needed no time to adjust to consciousness. He was asleep one minute and wide-eyed the next.

"Nothing," Clara assured him, patting his arm where her shoulder bumped his. "It's nothing. Go back to sleep."

He turned drowsy again in an instant. "You too," he mumbled. Clara attempted to get comfortable against him again. She wiped away the remnants of her tears.

"You too, Della," Clara whispered.

They'd drifted into a moment of pitch darkness, and Della could only hear the rustling of the carriage moving. She shifted around for a bit, trying to relax her pained limbs. She stretched out, she curled up. There was nothing for it.

They must be getting close to London, she realized. She could tell from the tense set of her burning joints and the hardening of her fragile heart.

CHAPTER TWENTY-TWO

I T CAME TO him in a dream. The idea that just might fix all of this for them. For her. He'd lain awake in bed that night, considering his options. He knew the barony was Della's. It was an irrefutable fact. He knew if he went digging through public records, he'd find all the proof in the world that Miss Adelaide Harris was a baroness. The proof wasn't the problem, though. It was her family. They had always been the problem.

The idea had come to him in a dream, but it was his mother who actually convinced him to put it into practice. It was that talk of hers, about being her own kind of dressmaker. It made Andrew realize that perhaps Della didn't need a solicitor to help her with this. Perhaps she needed a specific kind of solicitor. One who didn't care about things like rules, not when it came to her.

It was almost poetic, the way he'd been able to connect the pieces of this particularly convoluted puzzle just in time. The way he'd been able to resurrect an old, sneaking suspicion and use its confirmation for exactly what he needed. Well, it would be poetic if it worked.

As Andrew approached the doctor's surgery, he noticed the many people out and about under the midday sun. It was a rare break in the rain, and Andrew found himself sweating under his many layers. Perhaps that was just the nervousness seeping out of him. It didn't matter either way. Sweat stains on his shirtsleeves would definitely undermine the authority he needed to project in this moment, so he willed his body to stop.

He paused at the door, taking a much-needed moment and holding it open for a mother and her son to exit. The young boy smiled at him. He was missing both of his front teeth. The mother didn't smile at all, so Andrew had no way of knowing whether any or all of her teeth were present. It was unusual, seeing people walking in and out of the doctor's offices. He was known to make house calls all over London, even as far as Westfield Manor, when Lady Morley requested.

Andrew hoped he was right about those house calls. Hoped he was right about the doctor at all. He was hedging his bets on it, and there was so much at stake. One misstep could send the doctor running to Morley House, killing their entire plan before it had a chance to live.

If there was one thing Andrew had learned in his time abroad, it was to follow his instincts. Nothing was as valuable as his internal compass, and he hoped beyond hope it wouldn't steer him wrong this time.

He took a step into the office, and he spent a heartbeat thinking about what he meant to do. It was a despicable thing out of context. In reality, it was the only next step he could think to take. All he had to do was remind himself that this was for Della, and any reservations he felt faded away under the force of his adoration.

"Doctor Seagle?" he asked the man sitting alone behind the desk. It seemed fairly safe to assume that he was correct, but he needed to be sure.

"Yes." The man set down the papers he seemed to be sorting. Andrew wanted to roll his eyes. It seemed everyone in London had gone lax on their document organization just to spite him. "May I help you?"

As the doctor looked at him over the half-spectacles that were too small for his face, Andrew could see the resemblance. That familiarity, even though they'd never been formally introduced, was heartening. A visual representation of the cards Andrew held so close to his chest.

"I need to speak with you," Andrew said, his tone all business. "My name is Andrew Lockhart, and I'm a solicitor."

"Lockhart?" the man said, taking off those awful spectacles and twirling them between his fingers. "I knew an Elias Lockhart. Took care of him before he went to his rewards."

Andrew nodded. He'd expected that. He wouldn't let it deter him.

"He was my father, but I need to speak with you about one of your other patients." Andrew stood with his hands clasped behind his back. He refused to sit, but he couldn't even remember if he'd been invited to do so. This duplicity made him anxious. He knew he wasn't good at this kind of thing, but he also knew he had to be.

"And who might that be?" The doctor regarded him suspiciously, and Andrew could feel the tension in the room start to build. The suspicion was warranted. He was sure a strange man walking into his office enquiring about a patient wasn't an everyday occurrence for the doctor.

"Miss Adelaide Harris," Andrew said, even though her full name sounded wrong on his lips. She was Della to him. She always had been, and he hoped she always would be.

The doctor hummed. "She's a very ill young lady. An incredibly sad case."

"I suppose that's a matter of opinion." Andrew stepped forward. It had never occurred to him to attempt intimidation, especially not in a physical manner. Still, he tried, standing up straighter and looking down his sharp nose at the man sitting in front of him. "I don't consider her particularly sad, and she is owed both your respect and mine, as a baroness."

"A baroness?" Dr. Seagle scoffed. "What nonsense. Miss Harris is very ill, and besides, she is no baroness."

The doctor stood up, and now they were facing each other with only the desk between them. Andrew took a deep breath.

Seagle was already suspicious and on his guard, his cheeks puffed up and reddened in anger. Andrew knew he had to move quickly and efficiently. He could do this. This was a matter of stealth and finesse.

"I don't know how much Viscount and Viscountess Morley have told you," he leveled the doctor a blank stare, "about what they are doing with the information you give them. I shouldn't have to tell you that you're despicable, a doctor taking advantage of an ill young woman, but I don't believe you care about my opinion of your character. But I suppose you *do* care for your own best interests."

Seagle leaned back on his heels, affronted. Andrew felt his eyes tighten into a squint. His vision narrowed into a pinpoint. If this were a hunt, this was his one remaining shot.

"Is that so?" Seagle crossed his arms. "And how do I have any interest at all in this matter?"

Andrew watched as those spectacles hit the desk, bouncing off a stack of disheveled papers. He felt the resulting echo of silence in the middle of his chest. All he could hear was the beat of his own heart in his ears.

"Oh, I do believe you have quite an interest." Andrew didn't smile. He didn't gloat. He stated the facts simply and quickly. "You have been acting as a spy, sharing secrets, all the while keeping to yourself that the heir Viscount Morley dotes on is in fact yours."

There was a sharp intake of air. So much that the man sounded like he'd created his own gust of wind. The doctor fell backwards into his desk chair, as if his limbs wouldn't support his weight anymore. Andrew had his doubts about this, the entire plan, but they melted away at the sight of Seagle's pale face.

"I'm certain it doesn't matter to David, as his birth is legitimate in the eyes of the Church. It may not even matter to Lord Morley himself that the only child he cares about isn't even his. But it would be a terrible scandal. For the physician that the aristocracy so favors to be carrying on an affair with a lady—"

"Enough!" Seagle shouted. His voice was so strained, so broken. He stood back up in a fit of rage, his hands balling up into fists and slamming against the desk's wooden surface.

That was the moment Andrew knew he'd won.

"You've no proof," Seagle tried to say, but his reaction was proof enough.

"Of course not," Andrew admitted. "No such proof exists. But I cannot be the only one who suspects. Proof is not necessary when rumors and allegations are more than enough to ruin lives."

The doctor hung his head. Andrew took that as another sign of the man's defeat, and he thanked God for it, because he'd fired the only shot he had.

"I'm not sure if you are aware, but you are quite the pawn in their little game. I'm sure that you thought discussing your visits to Westfield Manor was a convenient cover for your dalliance with Lady Morley. In fact, they intend to use whatever information you've fed them to keep Miss Harris under their control. I don't know yet why they are so intent on keeping the barony theirs, when they've never publicly claimed the title. But I will find out, and when I do, you will be collateral damage."

Seagle swiped an angry hand over the surface of his desk. Papers were strewn everywhere, all over the floor at Andrew's feet. Out of the corner of his eye, he watched those spectacles shatter.

"How did you know?" Seagle asked in that voice that was as destroyed as his lenses.

"I hadn't seen David in years," Andrew answered. He finally sat down. There was no need for intimidation any longer. "I've been abroad. He walked into the viscount's office when I was visiting him the other day, and I thought he was you. I'm certain you don't remember, but you were the person who told me about my father's death. I've forgotten a lot of faces in this life, but yours won't be one of them."

There was malice in Seagle's gaze. So unlike the expression

Andrew hadn't been able to forget all those years ago. He'd been polite, then. Professional in the way he handled Andrew's father's passing. Now, he seemed to be seething. Andrew was sure he'd never forget this face, either.

This was why he didn't hunt, Andrew thought. The kill was so rarely worth the mess.

"It's because no one ever sees them together. Esther and Morley and the children. They don't eat together, they don't travel together. They don't even have portraits of the four of them. Some part of me thinks Morley knows. How could he not? He must look at David and see nothing of himself."

The other man had begun rambling, and Andrew did nothing but listen. That particular policy had served him well so far, so he might as well continue.

"Adelaide, she favors her father, but she looks oddly like Esther, too—" he began, but Andrew interrupted. Seagle had mentioned Della, so he must.

"She has her mother's bone structure and her father's coloring. I never met Della's mother, but Morley must've chosen his next wife by who looked the most like her." That, Andrew knew all too well. He thought of her now, her dark hair and fathomless eyes. That round face and those high cheekbones.

"And David . . ." Seagle tried again. "He has—"

"Your bone structure and your coloring," Andrew interrupted once more. Fair-haired David was a bit of an outcast visually in his family, but the doctor was right. No one could compare them if they were never together.

"What do you want from me?" Seagle finally asked. He'd seemed to compose himself some. A bit of that professionalism slipped back over his face like a mask.

"I have what I came for." Andrew nodded. "I couldn't bring this to the viscount and viscountess on my own suspicion, and I appreciate your confirmation."

"How did I get so wrapped up in this?" Seagle huffed, raking his fingers through his hair. "I am just the girl's physician."

"She is not a girl. She's a baroness, and you will address her as such." Andrew leaned forward, almost hovering over where the doctor sat. Seagle raised his hands, as if in surrender. "I don't think you doctors realize the power you hold in the lives of those who are ill."

Seagle looked up, the proud jut of his chin had softened to something guilty. Like he was a misbehaving child being told off.

"And you'll tell no one?" Seagle asked.

"Not a soul," Andrew confirmed. "Unless I have to."

Andrew had begun to feel bad for the man. The doctor had years' worth of tender feelings for a woman he could never have. Andrew understood him. He hated to exploit those feelings.

Though even if Andrew wound up the same way, loving someone he couldn't be with in the end, he'd make sure Della knew she was just that—loved.

CHAPTER TWENTY-THREE

DELLA THOUGHT SHE could sense a change in the air. It was subtle, but everything became stiffer and more congested the closer they got to London. She tried to assess her own feelings on the matter, but she came up short. They were too complicated to navigate. There was joy, for she thought she'd never return to the place she'd once called home. There was fear, for everything it meant that she was here. There was, more than anything, a longing. London represented so much for her, and returning after so long away was beyond strange. Some part of her longed to be the girl she was when she'd last left. So full of youth and promise, only to be swept away into a banishment she'd grown to love. The more dominant part of her, though, simply wanted what she always had.

Andrew. He brought about an even more overwhelming deluge of emotions, and the thought that she'd get to see him again was the only thing getting her through the last of this arduous journey.

Across the carriage, Clara practically vibrated with excitement. At their last stop, Della had begged Clara to change into clothing that the good people of society wouldn't find immediately reprehensible. She had, but she was wearing it all wrong. Her day gown hung loosely from her frame, and she was still wearing those men's boots she always had on. Her hair was escaping its pins, and she wouldn't sit still. Harry didn't seem to mind. He was gazing out the window and tapping a beat with his hand against his knee. They seemed rather at peace, actually. As if the tumultuous feelings raining over Della had escaped their notice entirely.

"I believe we are almost there," Harry muttered. He leaned in closer to the window, trying to see all he could like an eager child.

"What will we do first?" Clara asked. She climbed onto her knees and peered over Harry, resting her palms on his broad shoulders for balance. Della thought she should discourage that kind of disregard for her own safety, but that would be like trying to tame a wild horse. Recklessness was an integral part of Clara's character. It was quite possibly the reason they were all here in this carriage.

"I am not sure," Della sighed. Not for the first time, she realized how impulsive and ill-advised this trip was. "I've told the coachmen to take us to Andrew's house, but I do not know what we are to do if he is not home. Or not receiving visitors."

Della knew most weren't so formal, even in London. Those of the working class didn't require things like public drawing rooms for guests and specific hours of the day for calling. She couldn't help it, though. She could feel her genteel manners overtaking her once again. Something about the London air made her posture straighter and her accent sharper. She wasn't sure if she liked it.

Harry laughed. She'd been so caught up in her own musings that she almost hadn't heard it. She couldn't credit why he'd laughed, and he looked less than proud to have done it.

"I am sorry, Della." He shook his head. "But I cannot credit the idea that he might turn you away at the door."

She didn't know what was more surprising, his assessment of the situation or the fact that he used her name. That may very well have been the first time. It was almost as if they were becoming friends.

"You must admit it is possible," she tried to tell them—both of them—as they were smirking and giggling at each other in much too close proximity. It was usually very charming, watching them flit around each other like birds. She didn't particularly find it so now. "We haven't sent word that we're coming, and we haven't been invited. He left our home abruptly, and I've heard very little from him since."

"I know, Della, but—" Clara began to say, but then the carriage rolled to a stop. She abandoned her sentence and practically dove past Harry out the door as soon as it was opened. She didn't wait for the help of the coachman or Harry or anyone else, even the stairs.

"Good lord, Clara," Harry fussed as he followed her into the fading sunshine. "You could've injured yourself." He continued to grumble at her, and she argued back. That was something that wouldn't change, then. That was a slice of home she'd brought with her.

Della sat right where she was. She needed a moment to unfreeze her limbs. They were stuck, almost completely immobile. With no one on the other side of the carriage, she could extend her legs out in front of her. That was a start. She leaned forward and rocked back, stopping as it began to feel like the bones in her hip were ripping apart.

This happened sometimes, her entire body locking up. Each time, Della considered her surroundings. If she had to live forever in the bathtub or on the second stair or at her seat at the dinner table, then so be it. This place didn't seem so awful, a rented carriage. She could still be mobile, then. She cracked her knuckles. Rolled her shoulders. Tried to shift some weight onto her knees. She was in the middle of this exhaustive process when she heard a voice.

"Della?" he said, and suddenly he was there. In the open carriage door, backlit by the sun. Beautiful and golden and disheveled. All messy curls and a stern brow. His mouth hung open in what appeared to be shock or awe, and it was enough motion to remind her of that dimple in his cheek.

"Andrew." She smiled back, and she hoped. That's what this uncomfortable swelling inside of her chest was. Hope. It was intense and terrifying. She felt it like nausea in her stomach, like the tingling of pins and needles running down her spine.

He extended a hand into the carriage, and she suppressed a shudder of delight when his palm met hers. In another world, this would've been her life. Traversing the city with her friends and coming home to a man helping her down from the carriage. It seemed important, even in this fantasy she'd suddenly made up, that Andrew be that man.

Della took exactly one step toward the edge of the carriage platform, and the effort was considerably painful. All at once, she wasn't bearing her own weight anymore, and she was flying through the air with Andrew's hands pressed against her waist. It was an all too brief journey to the ground. Once her feet were under her again, she felt considerably lighter. With her own hands against his shoulders and his still resting just above her hips, Della truly realized what a torment this trip could turn out to be. She'd never again know contentment if she couldn't have this man.

"What are you doing here?" Andrew finally asked, after they'd spent entirely too long staring at one another. He looked around in confusion, as if he'd never seen his own home before. Clara and Harry had begun unloading the meager belongings they'd brought with them, little more than a traveling bag each, and talking to the hired coachmen.

"I came to see you," she told him. Her fingers flexed against the collar of his coat. "We . . . we came to see you. I kept thinking of you doing all of this—God knows what you've been doing— for me, alone, and I couldn't take it."

Della felt him squeeze her waist. Pull her closer just slightly. It was blatantly inappropriate conduct for the middle of the street, but Della didn't think anyone would pay them any attention over the commotion Harry and Clara were causing just by existing in their proximity.

"Della—" he started to say, but he was interrupted.

"What is going on out here?" It was Alice Lockhart, Andrew's mother, and Della was mortified. Here she was, with her ragtag family and all their belongings, standing in front of this woman's home with her hands all over her son. Della took an abrupt step back that hurt both her heart and her knees.

"Mother, you remember—" But Andrew was once again interrupted.

"Adelaide!" Alice nearly threw herself at Della, enveloping her in a hug so tight it brought tears to her eyes. It was actually uncomfortable, the combination of the almost-maternal affection and the devastation it brought her. Della had so missed this. Not just Alice herself, but having a mother to hug.

She was splendidly dressed, and that was no surprise. Her gown was emerald green with gold finishings. Her graying hair was upturned in a neat coiffure, and she smelled of some fragrant flower that Della couldn't place. It was all a bit much for Della's senses, this kindness and warmth. She simply wasn't used to it.

"I'm so sorry to intrude," Della said as soon as Alice let her go and she could resume breathing. "I . . ." She tried to explain, looking from Andrew to his mother, and she felt all of her capacity for speech drain away.

She had no idea what Andrew had been up to, or what he'd told his mother about all of this. There was no way for Della to speak to Alice about her presence here without revealing herself to be someone leading her son on a path to ruin. It seemed there was so much to apologize for that the words just wouldn't come.

"Let's all go inside, hm?" Alice said, grabbing Della by the arm and leading her toward the door. Everyone else followed, and they all shuffled into the charming home.

Della had never been here before. She'd never been allowed. Andrew's home was beautiful. Modest by the standards of society, but it was teeming with character. Alice was known to have a rather eclectic aesthetic as a dressmaker, and it showed in their furnishings. Nothing matched, there were jewel tones of all varieties everywhere. A green velvet divan in the entryway and deep-purple curtains covering the front windows. Beneath the veneer of Alice's oddly charming design, Della could see Andrew's natural sense of messiness. She'd never told him that, how she adored the sense of disorder he brought to the world around him.

"Oh," Della began, once she realized everyone was staring at her. "I'm so sorry, this is Miss Clara Fletcher, and this is Mr. Harry Stanton." She gestured to them both. Clara was swaying back and forth on her planted feet like she just couldn't help but move.

"Please, call me Harry. You've a lovely home," Harry remarked. He was always such a gentleman.

"Come in, come in," Alice gestured down the hall. "Please, put your things down."

Clara and Harry looked at Della simultaneously. It was eerie sometimes, watching their innate connection play out. Della didn't know what to say. She looked to Andrew.

"Please, go ahead." He smiled politely and stepped aside, letting Clara and Harry pass him. They walked toward his mother, and she and Clara began a lively conversation that they could hear even as they disappeared out of sight.

"I really am sorry," she started to say, as soon as they were alone. It had felt right, leaving Westfield Manor abruptly to see him. Now, though, it felt like she was being even more of a burden on his life.

"You apologize far too much," Andrew remarked. It wasn't what she'd expected him to say, and she was taken aback.

"So do you," she told him.

"Well, what are we to do about it? Apologize?" He smiled, that full, big, open grin and she got lost in those dimples again.

Della laughed. She was heartsick and in pain and worried beyond belief, but she laughed. With him, it seemed she could always find something to laugh about.

Alice reappeared then, without Clara or Harry.

"They are lovely people," she said. Andrew had her smile, and the laugh lines around Alice's face proved she used it well and often. "They're going to prepare the guest rooms for the night."

"Oh, Alice, we don't—" Della almost got her full sentence out this time. Almost.

"No, I'll hear of nothing else." Alice held up a hand. "It'll be nice to have guests. We haven't had a chance to use both rooms yet, and that's why I converted Elias's old study into another bedroom in the first place. For guests."

"Thank you," Della said sincerely. "I promise there is a reason we're here, and a good one. We didn't make the trek to London just to bother you." It was a joke, but it was a weak one. If she couldn't apologize, humor was the next arrow in her quiver.

Alice took two steps closer. Her face turned serious. Della recognized Andrew in that, too. It reminded her of the face he'd make when he first found her during all those hide and seek games. So serious at first, then his expression would melt into that dazzling smile.

"Is this about your family, dear?" Alice asked. She'd kept her voice low, but there was no need.

"How did you know, Mother?" Andrew asked. He'd leaned in, too, like the three of them were sharing a secret. Della supposed in some way they were. She looked between them, mother and son. She knew Andrew favored his father, but she could just feel Alice's spirit in him.

"I wish I'd just assumed," Alice sighed. "Because they're awful." She nodded. Della nodded back. "I'm sure I'd always assume if you were in any kind of trouble, it would be to do with your family. But you have been acting strangely since you returned." She pointed to Andrew. "And something happened today. You won't tell me what, but I know it was something."

Della flashed a look at him, and she'd never seen him appear so guilty. Unease churned in her stomach. Perhaps she'd been too late, and she really had let Andrew walk into ruin all alone. If she had, she'd never forgive herself.

"So it is about your family, then?" Alice asked, more gently this time. She was speaking to both of them, her gaze dancing back and forth. Della had never felt like this. Like she had someone literally at her back to help her solve a problem.

"Yes," she admitted.

"Then please follow me," Alice turned on her heel, her green-and-gold skirts swishing behind her. "I need to show you something."

❧

CHAPTER TWENTY-FOUR

ANDREW THOUGHT HE might be having some sort of episode. As he followed his mother and Della into the front room, he again blinked several times and attempted to set his world to rights. The scene before him was so strange it could not possibly be real, hence the episode. His mother and Della were not in the same room. Della was not in London. He hadn't extorted a doctor on her behalf today. None of that was happening.

"Perhaps I should have shown you earlier," his mother said, sitting down behind the small desk she used for writing and cutting fabrics for her dresses. "And perhaps I should not even be showing you now . . ." Her voice trailed off.

Andrew stepped forward, as he'd been lingering in the doorway, waiting for himself to wake up from this strange dream.

"What is it?" he heard himself ask. Della stood at his side, warm and welcome, and he was so intensely grateful that it felt as if every piece of him wanted to reach out and close the distance between them.

"It's your father," his mother said. Her tone was grim, and this wasn't the way she usually spoke of his father. She spoke of him fondly, usually with a touch of longing. She was rarely still visibly or audibly sad. Instead, she preferred to treasure his memory, as did Andrew.

From one of the desk drawers, she produced a stack of letters. They were held together by a piece of fraying twine.

"I told you I'd finally cleaned out his study. To make another guest room. I thought we might have guests once you got back out into the city, you know." His mother nodded, and he nodded back. "I found these. They are your father's, and I'd forgotten about them."

She sounded ashamed of that. A despair he rarely heard entered her voice, and it haunted him.

"He'd told me, when he fell ill, to give these to you, but only under certain circumstances. You went abroad, and I thought you'd never need them. Never need to know."

She looked up at him, at them both, with tears in her eyes. Now she appeared haunted herself. In her face, he saw the same guilt he'd felt after he left the doctor's office today. It was spreading like wildfire, somehow.

"What is it, Mother?" Andrew found himself repeating. He hated this, being the last to know something. He couldn't stand not having all of the information.

"Maybe I should . . ." Della mumbled, already twirling on her indelicate feet and making a move to flee.

He grabbed her arm. It was instinctive. He feared it would always be that way, him reaching out to stop her from leaving.

"No," he said, threading his fingers through hers and tugging her gently back to his side. "Stay."

She stayed. Thank God, she stayed.

"These," his mother picked up the hefty stack of letters, "are for you. Your father wanted you to have them."

Andrew felt the weight of the papers in his palm. Della squeezed his other hand. His heart skipped a beat, and he didn't know if it was from fear or elation.

"But you said," Andrew thought back to just a minute ago, "there were certain circumstances."

Alice hung her head. Andrew sensed that she'd hoped he wouldn't ask. She didn't know him very well if she thought he wouldn't.

"He told me to make sure you read them if you were to ever get involved with the Harrises."

Della let out a gasp, and her hand fell from his.

"No," he almost growled. He didn't know why. It was all he could think when he felt Della pull away from him. Just no.

"No," his mother repeated. She rounded the desk with her arms raised and picked up the very hands that had just slipped through Andrew's fingers. "No, I didn't mean you, dear." They were silent for a moment, and Andrew felt the weight of those letters as if they were made of stone. "I know my husband didn't, either."

Andrew wondered what Della must be thinking. She appeared horrified, her face ashen and her posture tense. She must assume anything his father had to say about her family was some stunning reproach. Something that would make him despise her by association. As if such a thing were possible. These letters could say Della herself was a man-eating succubus, and Andrew would still willingly walk to his own doom at her hand.

"I'll give the two of you some privacy." His mother looked between them both, patting Andrew's shoulder as she walked by him out of the room.

Then they were alone. In his mother's front room. He was still having trouble processing all of this, but those letters felt like they were burning his hands. Andrew sat. His mother's desk chair was short and small and not fit for a man full grown, but he felt as if he needed to be sitting for this.

"Are you sure I shouldn't go?" Della asked. Her head was turned, looking at the vacant space his mother had left behind. "Shouldn't I—"

"No." It was a complete sentence. He knew he shouldn't interrupt her. All anyone had done since they'd arrived was interrupt her, and it was terribly rude and a touch disrespectful, but damn it, she had to stop assuming everyone wanted her to leave.

Andrew tore open the stack of letters, spreading them out in front of him in the way he hated to see everyone else do. For a moment, he just ran his fingers over the old paper. What a gift, he thought. So many more of his father's words than he ever thought he'd have. No matter what they were—even if they had the potential to ruin his life—those words were precious. As they spilled across the table, he realized they weren't all letters. They were all sorts of papers. Ledgers and receipts and notes. Andrew had no idea what he was looking at.

He unfolded the letter that had been at the top of the stack. In front of him, Della paced the length of the room, one hand at her collarbone as if to calm her racing heart. She wasn't even roaming in straight lines, she walked in chaotic swirls and loops.

"Darling, could you sit down, please?" he asked her, flattening the first letter. "I cannot read and watch you in motion at the same time."

She looked exasperated. Her hand snapped up to her hip, the other still resting just where her gown met her chest. It was a more brazen posture than he'd ever seen her assume. He wished it were under any other circumstance. Maybe he'd left his socks on the floor again, or he'd forgotten about some social occasion they had to attend.

"Do not focus on me," she huffed. "Read!"

He wished he could explain that his focus on her was not optional, nor was it anything under his control. She resumed her pacing, and he made an executive decision to do something he'd never done in her presence: look elsewhere.

My boy, the first letter began. His father had always called him that. He considered it a benefit of being an only child. His father had never had to refer to him by his given name. It was something he might've outgrown by now, if he'd been given the chance.

> *I'm writing this because it may be my last chance to protect you.*

Andrew felt his heart clench. The sense of impending doom he'd felt all day came crashing over him like a thunderstorm. Quick and bright and loud. It was no longer impending, then. He didn't want his father to have to protect him, not from this. Not from her. Della had slowed her pace. She was ambling near the door, as if she still planned to make a hasty escape.

Isaac Harris is a crooked man.

Andrew felt his brows rise up in confusion as he continued reading. He'd never heard his father refer to Viscount Morley without his title. He'd almost forgotten what his Christian name even was.

You'll find all of the proof you need in these documents. I've been collecting it for years.

He must've gasped or flinched or something. Della stopped walking, and he felt her come closer.

I could never do anything about it without jeopardizing you and your mother, but he's cheating people out of money. Overcharging his tenants. All of his accounts are fraudulent. I thought it was carelessness, or a case of misguided incompetence. The viscountcy was so recently established, just by his father, and he never had a man of business. It was a mess, son. I sorted it out, but these things kept happening. Too often to be a coincidence.

Andrew paused. He had to take a break. A breath. A moment. He chanced a look at Della. She stood at the center of the room, her hands hung loosely near her waist. She was picking at her fingers, twiddling them back and forth. A nervous habit she'd always had. He wanted to reassure her, to tell her everything would be well. He wasn't sure he could, though. Not yet.

I'm certain he knew that I was aware of his dealings. He

was so obvious. So arrogant. He knew that I couldn't turn him in without losing everything I'd ever worked for. I wanted to do the right thing, son. I did. I hope you won't think ill of me, but I couldn't let go of everything generations of our family had worked for. I know that other people suffered at his hand, and I did nothing to stop it. That is the only regret I'll take to my grave.

The letter slipped from Andrew's hands as he choked on what might have been a sob. Della rushed to his side. He thought she'd reach for the letter. She reached for him instead. Her arms came around his shoulders, and he wrapped his fingers around her fevered wrist. Della leaned against him, her hip resting on the arm of the chair he sat in. Her head came to rest on top of his.

He'd never had the opportunity to hold her like this, and her swollen hands were the only thing capable of piecing his heart back together. He picked the letter back up and kept reading. He had to, for both of them.

I know you adore that girl, Andrew. That's why I have to tell you all of this. If you decide that she's what you want out of this life, you have to get her away from her family.

Do you remember that snake we found out in the garden once when you were just a lad? Your mother was so worried it would swallow her little boy right up. You asked me if it was poisonous, and I told you no. It was venomous. I taught you the difference. Now, I'm telling you all of this because you need to know that Isaac and Esther Harris are venomous.

No matter what, do not let them sink their teeth into you or anyone you love.

That was the end. Of that letter, anyway. Andrew sat up straighter, and Della moved with him. Her skin slipped through his fingers once again and it made him want to howl. She stood up, leaning her hips against the desk and turning to face him. Her palms found his shoulders. Her skin was burning, as usual. He was never sure if that was actually the temperature of her skin or just his body's fervent reaction to feeling her touch.

"What is it?" she asked. Her eyelids were heavy, dark lashes brushing her flushed cheeks.

"You haven't been reading?" Andrew asked. He hadn't been sure if she could, the way she'd left her cheek pillowed against the crown of his head.

"No." She shook her head. "I was quite busy trying to comfort you."

He smiled. Always, with Della, he smiled.

"I'm not sure," he said, finally. His fingers sought out her wrist again, rubbing circles over her skin. "But I think . . ." He took a deep, heaving breath. "I think it might be exactly what we need."

CHAPTER TWENTY-FIVE

DELLA SLEPT FITFULLY.

She and Clara had shared the lovely guest room, while Harry was across the hall and she assumed Andrew and Mrs. Lockhart were in their usual chambers. All of that would've been well and good had Clara not been so violent in her sleep. She'd relaxed into slumber immediately, and Della had lay awake, staring at the ceiling and absorbing repeated kicks to her shins underneath the blankets. In the middle of the night, she realized if she cared to confirm that Clara and Harry were intimately involved, all she had to do was check Harry's calves for heel-shaped bruises.

When she awoke, she was stiff and aching. That was not unusual, especially after all she'd put her poor, fragile body through in the past few days. She spent long moments stretching, ultimately rendering her body mobile again while Clara snored. Once she could stand, she paced slow laps about the room. Della dressed quietly, only running her warm fingers through her hair in an effort to tame it. Clara was the only one capable of such a feat, and Della didn't want to wake her. She figured she could see to herself for one morning. Clara more than deserved her rest.

It was nice, actually, to walk down the hallway of the Lockharts' home with her hair flowing freely down her back. Even if she looked a fright, the breeze fluttering about her neck was calming. She tried to walk on the tips of her toes to be quiet, but her feet were tragically unable to sustain that effort. She quickly realized that she hadn't the faintest idea where she was going. Everything about the house looked different in the light of day, and all she knew to do was head toward the front room she'd been in the day before. Within a few steps, she began to smell something. This was another pleasant sensation, walking through a house small enough for the aromas of breakfast to waft throughout all the rooms.

Della followed the scent, thinking that she'd at least find someone to direct her elsewhere. Instead, she found Andrew. He appeared to be cooking, creating those very smells that had led her there. She didn't think she'd ever seen a man cook before. Della didn't even know how to do so herself. Her body froze for a moment, as if she couldn't process what she saw. Her stomach grumbled. Her mouth ran dry. She had the oddest urge to lick her lips.

She didn't. She wouldn't. She had the sense that it was inappropriate, somehow. Even if she didn't know exactly how or why. Della cleared her throat, making herself known.

He didn't hear her. He was too busy humming a strange tune as he worked.

"Good morning," she said finally. Her voice was overly loud, and he dropped whatever he'd been holding. A tea towel, it seemed. It was charming, how his penchant for disorder extended into the kitchen. There were potato peelings everywhere. Scraps of vegetables lined the counter he worked on. It seemed he'd taken every utensil from its place along the wall in front of him. They all lay scattered about in a path between him and the hearth.

A natural born mess, her Andrew.

If she thought she'd enjoyed the simple pleasure of walking around with her hair unkempt, she vastly underestimated the impact the rest of the morning would have. Even watching the expanse of his shoulders flex under a flowing navy shirt was a wonder. The way he moved held her in rapt attention, and when he turned around to face her, he did the most dangerous thing in the world. He smiled.

His curls were falling all over the face that his grin absolutely took over. Since they'd become reacquainted, Della had thought most of Andrew's smiles to be shy. They were gentle expressions of feeling. Little gifts he'd bestow upon everyone. This wasn't that. This was the smile she remembered from her childhood. There was no shyness there, only an open and free kind of joy that she'd been missing for so long. It wasn't gentle, either. Della's heart raced away from her. It was such a swift departure that she nearly fell over. She felt like she could almost see it, beating out of her chest in an effort to be closer to him.

"Good morning," he said.

There was a silence as Della tried to collect herself. She didn't know why it all felt so important, she was just seeing the man occupying his own home. It was hardly revolutionary. She couldn't understand why it seemed to be.

"Something smells delicious," she finally managed to say. She was still standing awkwardly near the middle of the room. She hadn't managed to move a muscle since she'd walked in.

"I'm starting a stew for dinner," he told her, looking around as if seeing the half-destroyed kitchen for the first time. "That's the reason for all of the . . ." He gestured to the debris around him.

"Mess?" Della suggested.

"Yes," Andrew smiled. "The mess."

He turned fully from his workstation, looking her up and down as if seeing her for the first time. From her bare feet to the frizzed ends of her hair.

"You look lovely this morning," he said. There was the return of that shy smile, and Della realized she treasured that one, too. That grin and his words really were a gift. She felt her own mouth lift in return, and she looked away to stare down at her wiggling, swollen toes. Della was quite sure she'd never received such a bewildering compliment.

Della thought she might be blushing, but surely that was another symptom of her illness. It was odd for only her face to feel fevered, though.

"Please, sit," he gestured to the one wooden chair in the corner of the room. It was at that moment that she realized he was still wielding a knife. "I haven't started on breakfast yet."

"That's all right," Della sat, arranging the skirts of the gown she'd worn yesterday over her knees. "I'm not hungry. I don't usually feel my best this early in the mornings."

In fact, she was not usually awake. At Westfield Manor, she enjoyed the luxury of a late morning. It was everyone else who rose early to begin their days. The quiet and soft sunlight were peaceful, she realized. Though the scene in front of her missed Clara's vibrancy and Harry's stoic presence by the door, Della felt a staggering sense of homesickness. As if she were experiencing something for the first time that she should've experienced for years. As if she'd been robbed of thousands of tranquil mornings just like this one. With him.

"When do you feel your best?" he asked, returning to his work. Della watched him, as she always did. Though he created a monumental array of scraps and rubbish, his movements were sharp and thorough. The thinly diced vegetables he tossed into the pot to his right were in pristine, uniform shapes. It was fascinating to her, how he could be so chaotic and so precise all at the same time.

"Oh," she tried to answer him when she realized she'd spent too long staring at his hands. "When I'm lounging in the sun, I suppose. It's not particularly good for my condition, but I do enjoy it."

He turned to face her. He even put down the shearing knife.

"I'm sure you'll spend lots of time in the gardens at Kinloss, then." His face had grown so giddy, almost overly excited. Della couldn't be more confused.

"Kinloss?" she asked. She'd never heard the word before, and she had no idea what he was talking about.

"Oh, Della." His face fell. "I am so sorry, I . . ." Andrew took measured steps toward her, extending a hand out in front of him as he reached the chair where she sat. "I've been so wrapped up in all of this, I've forgotten myself. I never meant for you to be the last to know anything. I . . ." His voice halted. She wrapped her fingers around his. "I suppose it feels like you know everything I know. You're always the first person I want to talk about anything with. I forget that I don't always have that opportunity."

She wanted him to, so desperately. To always have the opportunity to talk to her, about anything that mattered and anything that didn't.

"I thought we'd discussed this. No more apologizing." Della squeezed his fingers.

That smile of his rose like the sun, and she was woefully unprepared for seeing it again so soon. She needed more time to recover.

"I promise I will tell you everything I know," he told her. He tugged on her hand, and she rose to standing, his other arm coming across her back. It was a gesture of support, she told herself. There was nothing overly important about him standing this close, where the hem of her gown brushed the toes of his boots. There was simply nothing to the warmth he brought her or the sense of eternal safety she felt in his presence. It was all friendly and relaxed, so she should be unaffected. She should remain levelheaded and not let herself get swept away in the fantasy she saw in the haven of his arms.

"Della?" he asked.

Oh, right. He'd been speaking. She managed to interrupt her own focus while he was mid-sentence, drifting off into the haze of her over-complicated thoughts and feelings.

"Could you repeat that?" she responded. He was still holding her, their collective posture almost like they were dancing.

"I said I would tell you everything I know." He suddenly looked much more serious, and she didn't welcome the shift in his expression. It didn't align with the wonderful fantasy she'd been building as they stood here so intertwined. "Everything," he emphasized. "And then there's somewhere I have to go. Would you come with me?"

"Of course," she answered instinctively.

He tugged on her hand again, leading her out of the room. She didn't care where they were going. Finally, *finally,* someone was going to tell her what was going on.

CHAPTER TWENTY-SIX

ANDREW HAD TOLD her everything. Big or small, he spilled every detail he'd come to know since he'd returned to London. He hadn't been sure how she'd react. It was so much information, and it must be an overwhelming rush of emotion. He thought there might be tears, whether they were an expression of hurt or sadness or rage. He'd stood close by the entire time in case she'd swooned. He told himself that was why, at least. Whether she raised her voice or tore at her hair or collapsed to the floor, he thought he'd been prepared for everything.

He hadn't expected the silence.

Even now, as they stood in the grand hall of Morley House, she was eerily quiet. She'd said hardly a word as they left his home for what used to be hers. The carriage ride had been uncomfortable, and he hadn't thought it possible to feel so tense around her. She was such a calming presence, a balm to his soul, and he hardly knew what to do in the absence of that comfort, especially as she'd been sitting right in front of him. It was as if her entire spirit had disappeared and left nothing but her physical form behind.

"Everything will be all right," he whispered. They were pitiful words, nothing but verbal fluff in comparison to the seriousness of the moment, but they were all he had.

Della looked up at him, and there was a hint of sparkle in her eyes. A twinkle. Just a flash, but enough to make him think the rest of her was still in there somewhere. Perhaps trapped beneath a landslide of emotions, but still there nonetheless.

There was a commotion, something that sounded like a gasp and an angry hiss of unintelligible words. Andrew didn't despair, he could tell by the tone that those sentiments likely weren't for repeating in polite company, anyway.

As he felt the tension in the grand manor home rise to a crescendo, Andrew once again questioned whether he should have brought Della with him. The last thing he wanted was for her to feel more of her family's ire, but she'd been cast aside and looked over far too much in her life. If there was one thing Andrew could do, it was give her a choice. She'd chosen to come with him. To stand at his side as he either secured her future or tore both of their worlds apart.

Andrew realized that this could very well be the last time he stood here at Morley House. The thought made him oddly sad, as the place held such nostalgia for him. Memories of his childhood and his father and the woman standing next to him—the girl he'd grown up with here. Beyond that nostalgia, there was a sense of peace.

If he walked out of here today with her by his side, he'd be more than happy to never see this house again.

"Adelaide!" a voice hissed. Andrew knew who it was. No one else would attempt such dramatics. It wasn't traditionally how a viscountess greeted guests in her home, but they weren't guests, and she wasn't a traditional viscountess.

"Hello, Mother," Della uttered. Her voice was soft. Almost kind, even though quite possibly no one in the world had ever hurt her the way the woman standing in front of her had.

Andrew had always found it strange how much Della and her mother looked alike. When he'd learned she was actually Della's stepmother, he'd struggled to believe it. They possessed the same features. Thick, dark hair. Strong brows. Long lashes.

He'd never truly *seen* Esther in Della, though. Della's beauty was so much more than her features. It was the light in her eyes and the innate kindness that seemed to radiate from her smile. Esther's face held nothing but misery. Even now, standing in front of a daughter she rarely had the opportunity to see, there was nothing but hostility in her gaze.

"I cannot believe you," the viscountess hissed again. Andrew had come across a rattlesnake once in his travels through America. He'd never forget the danger he'd heard in the noise it made. That sound seemed to echo in the vitriol Lady Morley was so casually spitting. "Showing up here uninvited with this boy. Unchaperoned in a carriage like a common doxy."

"That's enough." Andrew stood up straighter as he spoke. Lady Morley could call him whatever she wanted—he'd been called worse by better people—but he took issue with the way she spoke to her own daughter.

The viscountess stepped forward, poised to spear Andrew with a scathing retort, but she was quickly silenced. By Della.

"We've come to speak with you," she told her mother. Now that she'd resumed speaking, her tone felt almost eerily calm. Though he'd been deeply unsettled by her silence, he almost preferred it to this artificial serenity. "You and Father. David as well."

"And what could you possibly have to speak to us about?" Lady Morley crossed her arms over her chest. This wasn't happening as Andrew thought it might. How he'd hoped, anyway. He wanted a private, proper conversation where they could speak reasonably. In hindsight, that was far too much to ask of them. Still, shouting at each other in the hall seemed so uncivil. They were the aristocrats, though. Not him. He supposed he should defer to their sense of etiquette.

He felt Della's eyes on him. Perhaps she was looking to him for strength or to recommend he answer the burning question in the air. Andrew couldn't take his eyes off of her mother. He'd never truly loathed someone before, and he was having trouble with the feeling. His eyes began to squint, trying to find something redeemable in her vicious gaze. There was no part of him that could imagine behaving this way. Della had just come home for the first time in eight years, and to what? An anger she'd done nothing to deserve.

Silence continued to reign, and Lady Morley's arrogant indignation floated about the room like a child's toy boat on water. Andrew wanted nothing more than to watch it sink. So, he started throwing stones.

"We're here to discuss your daughter's inheritance," he said simply. He could play the role of her solicitor if that's what it took. He could pretend this was a matter of business for him, not something that had the potential to be the most devastating kind of personal.

Lady Morley gasped, of course. The fanfare of her extravagant, overplayed emotions was beginning to get old. Through Della, Andrew had seen what real emotion looked like on a face like that. This wasn't it. This was manufactured. A display that served a manipulative purpose.

"I'm sure I've no idea what you're talking about!" Lady Morley raised a hand to her chest, the other patting her forehead. She should've been an actress. "You must be mistaken. You have no inheritance. You've a dowry, of course, but it was useless."

Andrew heard the breath heave out of his lungs. He sucked in air between his clenched teeth. It seemed an unnecessarily cruel reminder to them both, that there were foolish men who wouldn't even be paid to marry Della. It was a reminder that all those years ago, he'd have married her in a heartbeat even if neither of them had a pound to their name. He'd consider it the honor of his life even now.

"We are talking about Kinloss," Della said. Her face had gone blank, taking the lack of emotion she was exhibiting one step further.

Her mother gasped again. This one was stunningly real. He couldn't tell exactly what those feelings were flashing across her face. Shock, or disbelief, maybe, but he knew they were true.

"Perhaps we should wait for the viscount," Andrew suggested. He still didn't like the thought of airing out their grievances in the middle of the hall for all of Mayfair to walk by and observe. Not to mention the exhaustive household roaming about. Besides, Della needed a chair. It wasn't good for her to stand for so long, and he couldn't stand looking at her rigid posture any longer. He couldn't make this hurt her heart any less, but he could at least make the process easier on her body.

"Very well," Lady Morley said. She gestured to the drawing room they used for guests and led them there. Andrew watched as she walked past him, looking for any slight break in her confidence. She was like bone china, he thought. It would only take a crack in the veneer to shatter the entire piece. She whispered harshly toned words to the footman at the door, and he swiftly disappeared. Andrew felt Della tense up as she watched them interact. He knew she couldn't stand the way her mother treated others, but it was as if seeing it in the flesh caused her physical pain. He hoped not. Of that, she had plenty already.

Lady Morley delicately arranged herself on a low settee near the corner of the room. It was upholstered in an ugly striped fabric, as if it were almost intentionally made to look overdone. Andrew sat on one end of the sofa. His body wouldn't relax, and he stayed perched on the edge, his back still far from resting against the equally ugly upholstery. Della sat next to him. Closer than she needed to, given the size of the sofa. Her hand hovered near his on the cushion, and seeing her pinky so close to his own made the damask pattern beneath it so much more palatable. This wasn't a competition, but already, he felt like he'd won.

"The viscount is on a ride." Lady Morley looked at each of them. She looked between them. Andrew had always thought that odd, how those with titles referred to each other so formally. He knew it was the way things were done, but it had always felt so cold. "David is with him. They should be back soon, but I've sent a servant to fetch him."

There was disdain in her voice as she addressed them, but Andrew caught the way she fidgeted. She was wringing her hands, running her fingers over each other. He saw it for what it was. A crack. He could almost hear it, the sound of her splintering, then shattering entirely. That imaginary sound filled him with strength. It straightened his spine and his resolve.

"You know," Lady Morley looked down at the hands she now had clasped in her lap, "it is good to see you, my dear." Her gaze had recovered that manipulative veneer, and Andrew hated to see it.

"It is good to see you too, Mother," Della parroted the appropriate words back to her, but her gaze was a startlingly blank canvas.

He'd always seen her as so emotive, her face so full of life that it spilled over, but it seemed his Della had a veneer of her own.

CHAPTER TWENTY-SEVEN

DELLA FEARED SHE was about to break. All the pained words Andrew had said that afternoon swam through her mind in nauseating waves. It was too much for her to process at once. Violently closing off her thoughts and emotions was the only thing she knew to do. That door was shut and locked and barricaded, but it was that one lie that threatened to break it down entirely.

It's good to see you too, Mother. It was a simple expression, the smallest of falsehoods when her life had somehow become a mountain of them. It wasn't the lie that hurt so much as the truth. It wasn't good to see her mother, or to be home for the first time in years. Della almost wished the lies were the crux of her problems. Unfortunately, that was reality.

She prepared to say something, anything that would drown out the overwhelming silence that had befallen them, but she heard the sound of the front door opening and slamming shut. Heavy footsteps making their way toward the room. A shout that she knew had to have been directed at a footman or the butler, the tone was so lacking in respect.

"What the devil is going on here?" she heard him say, just before the door was opened for him. "Adelaide." His voice was a whisper of shock. "It really is you. I thought there must be some misunderstanding."

She'd never wanted to roll her eyes so desperately in her entire life. Was the idea so unbelievable? That she'd endured a simple carriage ride back to her family's main residence? It seemed a rather mundane thing to do. Not the sort of thing that inspired such fervent reactions.

"Hello, Father." Della remembered at that moment that many young women her age still called their fathers something more affectionate, like *papa*. She wondered if she'd ever called him anything like that. If she had, she couldn't recall, and that broke up the hurt in her soul with shards of deep sadness. It was another blow to the door holding back a flood of feelings.

"Is someone going to answer me?" the viscount bellowed. "What are you doing here?" He looked at Della and Andrew both, seeking the explanation he believed he so rightfully deserved. This was all going so badly, Della suddenly didn't want to give him one. She wanted to turn and run. This effort didn't feel worth it anymore.

"We are here about Kinloss," Andrew repeated. Della was always intensely grateful for him, but something about this moment made that gladness grow exponentially. "About Della's inheritance."

Della watched her mother as Andrew spoke. She had neither the nerve nor the decency to show any manner of guilt or regret. Della was willing to bet she wouldn't even recognize those particular emotions if she felt them.

"How do you even know about that?" Her father addressed Andrew only, increasing Della's indignant anger just that much more. He didn't try for denial as her mother had, and she could at least respect that.

"That is unimportant," Andrew started again. It seemed this was a conversation only for the men in the room. Ironic, since the property in question was passed down from one woman to the next. "We've come here as a warning. Quite frankly, we've come here out of a respect you don't deserve."

Everyone flinched at that, even Della. It was true, but that didn't make it any less devastating.

"We know that Kinloss rightfully belongs to Della. You have been mismanaging her estate as her guardians for years, and we know it's your intention to continue doing so by threatening the livelihoods of her household."

Andrew very plainly laid out the facts, and Della watched as her parents displayed starkly different reactions. Her father was livid, his face turning a shade of red she didn't think she'd ever seen before. Her mother cowered away, turning in on herself and shielding her eyes as if she could avoid the scene displayed in front of her. Della didn't wait to see anything like shame. She knew she never would.

"There is no way you—" her father began to spout. The anger was palpable in his voice, and he was spitting each word he spoke. "I am her guardian, and the estate has been entrusted to me. I have run it as I see fit."

"You've nearly run it into the ground. There is plenty of evidence," Andrew interrupted. "Ledgers my father kept from as far back as fifteen years ago, showing your large, unexplained withdrawals from accounts belonging to the estate. I suspect your estate agent is as crooked as you are, overcharging and neglecting the tenants you are supposed to serve."

Della looked to him. He seemed as calm as she hoped she appeared. She could see the strain, though, because she knew him so well. The hand next to hers on the sofa was tensed and a vein pulsed at his temple. The sharp line of his jaw seemed lethal.

"Well, then," her father scoffed, "if all you have to support your claim are the records of a dead man—"

He seemed so smug. It was staggering how quickly he'd incorporated all of that anger into the arrogance he projected now.

"I thought you might say that," Andrew interrupted again. He'd relaxed some. The corner of his mouth tipped up, and it made his profile seem oddly dangerous. It was almost thrilling, knowing that all of his threatening force was there to protect her.

She thought he might actually be the first person in her life to do that. "Which is why I spoke with your Dr. Seagle."

"You're lying," her mother gasped. Della had never seen her so outraged, and that was the emotion most often present on her face. She'd always seemed to treasure her anger the way other people appreciated their own contentment. "John would never speak against us."

Della noticed how she referred to the doctor by his given name. Something about that stuck in her mind. It was more evidence pointing toward an idea she struggled to believe.

"He did very little speaking, actually. And I didn't need him to say much of anything. All he had to do was confirm what I already knew."

Her parents looked at each other. They seemed to be communicating without words. That was astounding, Della thought, how two people who barely tolerated each other could still be so attuned.

"It's my understanding that the Morley estate hasn't been profitable in years, and you've been doing everything possible to replenish your coffers. You've been mismanaging the Kinloss estate for your own financial gain, and I'm sure it seemed like a brilliant plan. But that ends today."

"And just what do you plan to do?" her father asked, crossing his arms as if calling Andrew's bluff.

"There is little to do, from a legal perspective," Andrew admitted with a shrug. "There is much a judge would excuse under the guise of guardianship. But we must acknowledge that you favor your place in society, yes? So, if you were suddenly wrapped up in an ordeal involving questionable paternity and unethical business dealings, I don't believe a recently established title is quite enough to save you from such a scandal."

"We could lose everything," her mother whispered. It was as if she were considering the possibility for the first time.

"It might've been prudent to think of the consequences before you spent years abusing power that wasn't your own. To say nothing of how you've treated your own daughter." Andrew's voice had taken on a hard edge that Della hardly recognized. It wouldn't do for her to memorize that rumble so she could feel the resounding tremble it inspired in her. Would it?

"What do you want?" her father asked. His gaze was sharp, but he wasn't looking at her. No one was.

Then, Andrew was looking. He was nodding in her direction. He'd turned his body to face her, and she didn't know if it was an effort to lend support or to shield her from the view of her family. She would've appreciated both.

"I want what is mine," she said simply. There was so much more threatening to spill out of her. Words of the deepest hurt and the brightest anger. She couldn't speak them, though she wanted to. They felt as if they were stuck in her throat, choking her. "I want Kinloss."

"You will let her run the property, whether she'd like to live there or appoint a new estate agent of her choosing. And you will leave her—and everyone who currently works at Westfield Manor—alone. If you do not, I'm afraid that nasty rumors will begin to swirl."

There was a moment of silence, and Della held her breath until her ribs ached.

"Very well," said her father. He was slumped in defeat, and his spine curled inward. This was a man she'd never met. Downcast and just plain sad. "I must say, I didn't expect this from you, Andrew. I held your father in high esteem."

"You did." Andrew hung his head for a moment. "And while I appreciate that, I only wish he could've said the same of you."

Silence swept over them again, and Della felt the sudden, irrepressible urge to cry. She had to get out of here before she suffocated under the weight pressing against her chest. She couldn't breathe and she couldn't think, and they were talking, but she couldn't listen.

Della stood. She couldn't help it, she ran. Past their horrified faces and their vengeful words and past the footman and the butler. Out the front door, down the rocky stairs. Her ankles stabbed at her and her knees threatened to buckle, but she kept on. Until her hip caught. Always, that damned hip. Where was her walking stick? She couldn't remember. She'd brought it with her to Morley House, but where had she put it?

She'd made it to the gardens, stumbling into a corner around the back of the house. Della sank down to the ground, resting her back against the stone fountain. She tucked her feet under an overgrown bush.

She was hiding, but she knew Andrew would find her.

Della tried to make herself take long, deep breaths. This was a strategy of hers, when she was engulfed in pain. She focused on her breathing, because everything would be all right as long as she kept air flowing in and out of her body. At that moment, in her rush of pain, it was her one objective.

Andrew did find her, eventually. She'd lost track of time, her senses overwhelmed by the fountain's gentle spray raining over her and the occasional twitter of an errant bird. Down here, in the dirt, her former home almost seemed like a peaceful place.

"There you are." He was at her side in an instant, lowering himself to a squat in front of her. The sight of his face made her realize this idyllic little haven she'd created for herself wasn't real, and there was too much pain here for her to remain.

"Can we go?" she asked him before he had a chance to utter another word. She held up a hand, he took it. They rose slowly because her dramatic exit had done more damage than she'd thought. Della hissed as pain lanced down her legs as soon as they bore her weight.

"Of course," Andrew murmured, leaning into her body to support her. "But . . . is there anything else you want to say to them?" His eyes were so kind, so remarkably gentle. She got lost there for a moment, in another idyllic haven. She felt him wrap her fingers around the handle of her walking stick. She'd have to ask him where he'd found it.

Della understood what he meant, though. What he wasn't

saying. This would be the last time she would be welcome at Morley House, but it had hardly been a welcome at all. If there were any words she had left for her parents, she'd better say them now.

"No," she said, finally. "I never want to speak to them again."

✦

CHAPTER TWENTY-EIGHT

Andrew practically carried her to the carriage. Her feet remained on the ground the entire way, but he was supporting all of her weight. It would've been quite the honor if it were under any other circumstances. This wasn't what he'd wanted for her, an abrupt exit, as if she were running away in shame. He'd wanted her to be able to walk out of Morley House with her head held high, triumphant in her victory.

He helped her up into the waiting carriage, and then she broke. Her body had hardly touched the seat before she began to cry. It wasn't a tame expression of emotion, it was a complete shattering of her heart. They were loud, wracking sobs, and Andrew didn't think he'd ever seen anyone shake so hard. Her teeth had to be cracking against each other, she shook so violently.

"Oh, Della," he whispered, climbing up into the seat beside her. He'd intended to sit on the opposite side, of course, but there was no way he could sit and bear witness to her devastation like this. Andrew knocked on the roof, and they jolted into motion. He figured the quicker they got away from Morley House, the better.

She'd pressed her hands against her face, covering her eyes. She was crying so hard she couldn't breathe, and Andrew didn't know what to do. He had no idea how to help. All at once, Della pitched forward, and she fell into his arms. He felt the backs of her knuckles against his shoulder, where she still held her fingers against her face. He wrapped one arm fully around her body. His other hand found the nape of her neck. He ran his fingers through the thick hair that had escaped her pins.

"Shhh," he whispered. He didn't know why he was whispering. He didn't know if she could even hear him over the sound of her own gut-wrenching sobs. "Everything will be all right." He said it over and over, hoping his voice was an even-keeled reassurance. He hoped she couldn't hear the desperate panic he felt. "They don't deserve your tears," he told her, as he'd resorted to rambling. Anything to get her to stop feeling this way. "They're horrible. Awful people, Della. To treat you this way. I can't even imagine."

Andrew shook his head, and they were so close that his chin brushed her hair. He gave in to temptation and pressed a light kiss there, right at the crown of her head. He stayed there for long moments, savoring the feel of her hair on his lips. Eventually, he found the strength to shift back, to allow space for air between them.

"I do feel badly for their household. It must be hell to have an employer like that, so bitter and vile. I wish that your brother had been there, but he's probably drunk in a gutter somewhere. Or sleeping, getting his rest in preparation for being drunk in a gutter somewhere." He'd really run out of words by this point, but she was still crying in his arms, so he knew he had to come up with something. "You know, it was quite impolite not to offer us tea, even if we were barging in unannounced and exposing their sordid dealings. Some common decency would be nice. And did you see what your mother was wearing? I cannot decide what's more garish, her gown or the furniture."

At that, Della silenced, except for an unladylike sniffle. Her hands fell from her face, and they landed in his lap. Andrew was not going to think about that. She leaned back a bit, resting against his arm. His thumb brushed away a stray curl at the side of her face. He could see her eyes now. They were swollen and rimmed in red, two pathways of tears streaking down over her delicate features.

She laughed. He was so surprised he almost let go of her entirely. He almost fell into the floor of the carriage, he was so taken aback. Her laughter was as loud as her sobs had been, but he liked this reaction so much more. The noise made his heart feel lighter, when it had been pounding so viciously against his breastbone. Though the tears had been so unsettling, Andrew didn't particularly know how to react to this sudden, hysterical laughter either.

"You are right," she giggled. "She was dressed like the finest lady of the traveling circus."

Andrew laughed then, too. His chuckle was one of relief, now that he'd seen some color come back into her face. He realized abruptly that they were still sitting improperly close. Her hand still rested on his knee, his on the side of her neck. It was shockingly inappropriate, but he couldn't make himself pull away. He wouldn't, unless she wanted him to. Right now, he didn't think she did. Della's eyes had softened into something like longing if he wasn't mistaken.

"Thank you," she said. She reached for his hand and squeezed it with hers. "Thank you for doing all of this, for standing up for me." Her voice broke again. "For protecting me."

"Of course," he said. Of course he'd protect her. He'd be there, standing up at her side for as long as she'd let him. He'd never been able to tell her that, though. He'd never been given the chance.

They sat in silence for a moment, only the sounds of the horses between them. Della rubbed the back of his hand with her thumb, and Andrew closed his eyes. That way, he could pretend they were somewhere else. They were in his carriage on their way home, as they were now, but in his mind, she would stay. In his mind, they'd gone out shopping or to the theatre. Perhaps they'd gone to get ice cream. Della loved ice cream. She'd climb out of the coach with his assistance, and they'd walk into their home hand in hand. He would—

"What do we do now?" Della asked, interrupting his fantasy. He opened his eyes, and he realized she hadn't interrupted his daydream after all. From the strands of her frizzed hair to her reddened nose, she was precisely what his fantasy looked like.

"Whatever you'd like, love." He ran a fingertip down her cheek, brushing over the ends of her still-wet eyelashes. "Well," he tilted his head, considering his words carefully, "I had thought to say the world is yours. I suppose that isn't exactly true. The world may not be yours, but Kinloss is."

"It's all quite hard to believe," she sighed, the movement of her breath drawing his attention to the long line of her throat.

"So," he asked, "what would you like to do?"

She was silent for another moment, staring at the unoccupied other side of the carriage. They hit a bump in the road, and she was jolted out of her seat. She hiccupped, then laughed at herself. She shifted her position as she settled, taking weight off of one hip and putting it on the other. He noticed the expression on her face, as if she'd just realized how much pain she was in. Like the rush of it all had settled, leaving her aching.

"I think I'd like a nap," she said, grinning at him. "I don't think I've ever needed a nap so desperately, in fact."

WHEN DELLA AWOKE from quite possibly the most refreshing nap of her life, it was to the smell of dinner. She couldn't pinpoint exactly what that smell was, but it was glorious. She re-dressed in her lavender day gown, which she knew was both out of fashion and indicative of half mourning. She felt as if she were in mourning, anyway. She'd lost the entirety of her family today. As she stepped out of the room she'd been sharing with Clara, she heard voices and laughter. Clara's laugh, she could pinpoint. She thought she heard Harry as well. The other feminine voice must be Alice, then. When she and Andrew had returned to his home, it was to an eerie silence. There was no one else to be found, and Della had thought she ought to be worried about that. She should've been concerned for Clara and Harry's safety, as they could've been lost on the streets of London for all she knew. She couldn't concern herself then. She was just so tired. Exhaustion had dragged at her limbs, and it was all she could do to change into her nightgown before she fell into bed.

Della stood in the corridor for a moment, appreciating that noise. After the disaster with her family, she'd feared the painful silence she'd returned to would be her new normal. Perhaps her only companion.

She gravitated to the sound, her feet taking her farther down the corridor. As she walked, she tried to assess how she felt. Fatigue still weighed on her, but her heart felt a bit easier to carry around in her chest. Her knees ached, and that hip was still bothering her. She knew it simply always would. Overall, despite such an intense day, she was doing rather well.

"Della!" Clara spotted her as she walked into the front room, and she nearly attacked her in an overly secure hug. She welcomed both the exuberance and the tight embrace. Things would never be silent for her, Della realized. Not with Clara around. "Oh, I am sorry," Clara backed abruptly away, dropping her arms and settling into a dramatic curtsy. "I meant the Right Honorable Lady Kinloss."

"Stop that," Della rolled her eyes, and she swatted in Clara's general direction. "Nonsense. All of it."

"Congratulations, my dear." Alice brushed past Clara to envelop Della in a hug. She was so warm and comforting, Della almost started to cry again. That wouldn't do. All of that negative emotion was exhausting. It simply wasn't good for her to be so overwrought. "I am so deeply sorry about your parents." Alice spoke as if they were dead, and Della supposed in a way, they were. Her lavender gown seemed all too appropriate. "I cannot credit what they've done to you. As a mother, to want anything less than the best for your child . . . I simply don't understand." She shook her head. Her arms still held on to Della, and she seemed unwilling to let go.

"Supper is—" Andrew stuck his head around the corner, his voice abruptly stopping when he saw Della. "Oh, I didn't know you'd woken up. Did you sleep well, Lady Kinloss?" His grin was impish and almost shy. Della nearly swooned at the sight of those dimples. Her heart had been through too much today. She truly couldn't handle anything more.

"Not you, too," she groaned.

"Supper is ready." He smiled again, instead of answering. His mother left the room heading toward the kitchen. She patted his cheek as she passed him. Clara and Harry followed, the rhythm of conversation and laughter picking back up.

"You didn't answer me," Andrew murmured as she stepped toward him. "Did you sleep well?"

"I did." She nodded. "I cannot believe how exhausted I was."

They walked toward the kitchen. Della took a daring step to her left, sliding into a path far too close to him. She felt empowered by it. Sometime in her sleep, she'd made a decision. Rather than focus on what she'd lost, she would think only of what she'd gained. She may suddenly have a title, a home, and a new purpose, but at this moment, what she treasured most was this new closeness to the man next to her.

Everyone filled their plates, and they settled around the small kitchen table. There wasn't a formal dining room, and Della found that she liked the comfort of eating in a more casual setting. She ate quietly, absorbing the pleasant conversation happening around her. It was a relief to not be the center of attention, to have everyone discussing mundane things like the weather and how polluted the air actually was in the heart of London compared to the countryside. After a day of being spoken over and having her future decided for her, Della appreciated the uneventful dinner talk. She was so busy in her own thoughts and tucking into her delicious roasted vegetables—Andrew really was an excellent cook—that she only noticed the lack of conversation once they'd abandoned the table and retired to the front room. As she sat, she began to feel everyone's eyes on her.

"What?" Della looked around the room. They were all looking at her curiously, as if waiting for something. An answer to a question she hadn't heard anyone ask, perhaps. Maybe there was just a bit of food on her face. "What is the matter?"

Across the room, Andrew sighed. He crossed one ankle over his other knee. His mother's furniture in this room was so delicate, he seemed out of place. Like a horse lying down in a bed meant for a pampered dog.

"They were speaking to you," Andrew said. His brow was furrowed and his posture tense. She'd thought it was just the discomfort of the chair, but now she sensed the discomfort of the situation. "About a ridiculous idea of theirs, which they decided to enact without your knowledge or permission."

Della looked directly to Clara. If there were any preposterous ideas, she would always assume they came from her. Clara sat on one end of the sofa next to Harry. Her legs were crossed over one another and she wore a pair of those flowing trousers she favored and a bodice Della had never seen before. It was like the top half of a gown, fitted to her waist and highlighting her collarbones. It seemed to be made out of a damask-patterned silk in a deep midnight blue. Not dissimilar from the elegant upholstery they sat on. Now that she thought about it, Della realized she hadn't seen those trousers before, either. They were a matching navy blue in a diaphanous linen. Despite the fact that she wore trousers, Clara had never looked so ladylike.

It made Della deeply suspicious. She could feel her eyes narrow as she looked at them.

"I'm afraid it was my idea, dear," Alice spoke up, holding a glass of water she'd carried in from the kitchen to Della as if in a toast. "I took your friends on a tour of the town, and we did a bit of shopping. We stopped into the modiste's. She always saves her scraps for me, and I used to work with her mother."

Alice continued speaking, and Della listened, although she had no idea what any of this had to do with her. She spared a glance at Andrew, and he looked to be full of trepidation. He kept rubbing the skin above his eyebrows, like he was trying to soften the lines forming there.

"Did you make this, then?" Della asked, gesturing to Clara's new ensemble.

"I did," Alice smiled.

"It's beautiful," Della complimented. She'd never noticed, but the dark blue was a lovely color on Clara. "And you made it all in one afternoon? That's quite impressive."

"Well, thank you, dear." Alice smiled again. "Clara was telling me about these trousers she wears so often, and I'd been wanting to see if I could make some myself. It's not so difficult. I could make you a pair if you'd like."

"Mother," Andrew chastised. His cheeks were blushing as if she were embarrassing him. Della was unfortunately still confused. Surely this grand idea of theirs was about more than making her a pair of trousers?

"Yes, sorry." Alice leaned forward in her chair, turning her body to face Della. She placed her glass down on the side table between her and where Clara sat on the edge of the sofa. "I may have done something foolish. And you have every right to be cross with me."

Oh, dear God. Della sat her own plate and glass down, just to prevent her from dropping them in shock or outrage or whatever other emotion the next few moments were about to invoke.

"Clara and I were roaming about the milliner's, and we happened to overhear Lady Kittredge discussing her upcoming ball. She was looking for a hair ribbon to match her gown, and I stopped to offer my help. I made the gown, you see. She is the only one I make ball gowns for anymore, because the other modistes love to put her in the worst things."

Della nodded, though she still had no earthly idea where

Alice was going with this.

"She's newly married," Alice continued. "A young lady like yourself, and she's not of noble birth. This is the first event she's hosted, and she's very eager to make a good impression on society. I'm sure everyone will be in attendance in an effort to ridicule her for the crime of being born a part of the working class." Her voice took on an indignant air. Della had never known Alice to be so . . . forward.

"With all due respect, Mother, you are taking an awfully long time to get to the point." Andrew seemed agonized, and his anxiety magnified hers. It wasn't that she wasn't enjoying the story of their trip through Mayfair; Della was simply scared of the turns it would take.

"You're right, darling." Alice sighed. "I may have . . . suggested . . . that inviting a newly minted Scottish baroness who was once a debutante who disappeared from society years ago might make the Kittredge ball a bit more . . . memorable."

"Oh, no." Della gasped. "You didn't?" That was truly a ridiculous idea if she'd ever heard one. Absolutely ludicrous. There was simply no way.

"Imagine it, Della." Clara leaned so far forward she nearly fell off the sofa. "I'm sure your parents will be there, leading the charge to find fault in Lady Kittredge. Something wrong with the dinner napkins, or the waltz played before the reel. But when you walk in, everyone will be talking about *them*. About how they haven't mentioned you and why you arrived on your own. They could be the object of society's ire for once."

At Clara's impassioned speech, Della's mind flashed back over eight years, to the way her parents had spoken to her once they'd realized she wasn't going to get better. Della had hardly processed the doctor's emphatic statement that she'd be ill as long as she lived when they'd told her she had to go. They hadn't implored her to understand. They hadn't cried or expressed any sort of emotion at all. It was as if it were a foregone conclusion. Della was sick, so she couldn't stay. Her illness was not something they could subject polite society to.

Della herself could subject them to it, though. Even if Della couldn't, the Right Honorable the Baroness of Kinloss very well could. There was power in her name now, in her presence. She would make a scene as soon as she was announced, and perhaps that would make Lady Kittredge's life a bit easier. Perhaps it would allow her parents to feel some of the shame they'd put her through for years.

She hadn't wanted revenge, but now that she was being offered the opportunity on a silver platter . . .

"What would I wear?" Della asked.

"Come with me," Alice jumped out of her seat. Clara followed, clapping her hands and emitting a sound of excitement that didn't sound quite human.

They each grabbed one of Della's hands, pulling her to her feet and sweeping her out of the room. She chanced a glance over her shoulder at Andrew. His gaze caught hers.

He appeared oddly devastated.

CHAPTER TWENTY-NINE

THE NEXT DAY was devoted to preparing for the ball, something that Della hadn't done in nearly a decade. She hadn't remembered it being so fun. With her mother, it had always been about rigid posture and impromptu quizzes on how to handle increasingly ridiculous hypothetical social situations. With Clara and Alice, it was a much louder affair. They selected fabrics for her gown, they debated on the most comfortable footwear, they contemplated the merits of floral embroidery versus intricate lace for the trim.

It was quite the whirlwind. Della couldn't believe how fast Alice worked. She thought people must slow down as they age, but Alice was a master of her craft who only seemed to speed up. She spoke as she created, not even watching the motion of her hands. As if it were instinctive.

"Are you sure about this, dear?" she asked, looking Della in the eye. "I don't want to pressure you. It was only an idea, I can write to Lady Kittredge and—"

"I am sure," Della answered. They'd had similar conversations at least three times today, and Della said the same thing each time. "I assure you that you did nothing wrong. There's nothing to feel guilty for. You apologize far too much, as does your son."

Now that she'd mentioned him, the thought of Andrew

weighed on her. She hadn't seen him much today, outside of meals where they were immersed in the larger group. He wasn't looking at her as he had been before, and she couldn't pinpoint what was different or why it felt like such a loss. It seemed she and Alice were both thinking of him. They sat in silence for a moment.

Then Clara burst through the door. She was always so adept at breaking up any bit of lingering quiet.

"I found them!" She proclaimed, jingling a bowl of mismatched buttons. Alice collected them, and she'd sent Clara to her room to fetch some for Della's gown.

"Thank you, dear." Alice took the bowl and began sifting through the buttons.

Her evening gown was taking shape around her. She stood on an old wooden box in front of the looking glass. Her skirt draped over her waist and hips, flaring out just slightly until it fell over her feet. It was made of the most beautiful light-pink silk. Della ran her fingers over the fabric. She didn't think she'd ever felt something so soft. The bodice fell over her chest, waiting to be assembled and attached to the skirt. The neckline was wide, hitting her collarbones and sloping downward. The sleeves hadn't been formed yet, but they were short, leaving only a bare expanse of flesh above her matching white silk gloves.

"I am still quite fond of the lace," Clara said, holding up a strip of ivory bobbin lace in a floral motif. She placed it along the neckline of the gown, though it was structurally unsound and still unsewn.

Della had no jewelry, so they'd set out to make the gown a gem of its own. She could see the beauty in the lace, but it made her feel too young. As if she were a debutante again, trying to appear delicate and soft. It reminded her of her mother, and all the times she'd been told to silence herself rather than contradict a man's opinion. It was the last thing she wanted to think about.

"Oh, I know!" Alice jumped up from her seat, setting down one of Della's in-progress sleeves. "I've got just the thing. Excuse me, just one moment." She left the room in a hurry, and Della took the time to temporarily hold her bodice together, just to see how it might look.

"Are you nervous?" Clara asked. She looked at Della, met her eyes in the looking glass.

Della stepped off the rickety wooden box she'd been standing on. The uncertain ground had been dangerous to her knees and her lower back. She carefully extricated herself from her bodice, making sure not to dislodge any of Alice's hard work. She unhitched the one temporary button holding her skirt up, and the light fabric fell from her waist. It made a liquid whoosh as it pooled on the floor. Clara picked it up, laying the dress out on the bed in their guest room. Della picked up her nightgown and threw it over her head. She breathed a sigh of relief. Her new gown may be gorgeous, but the thin cotton nightshirt was so much more comfortable.

"I am nervous, yes," she finally admitted. "I cannot credit why I even want to go, if I am honest with you. I don't wish to see them or speak to them. I don't even wish to hold power over them. I have no desire to make them pay for what they've done to me."

Clara sat on the bed, facing the wooden chair they'd dragged in from the kitchen. It seemed to follow Della around the house, and she never noticed why or how, but it was undoubtedly convenient.

"Why, then?" Clara asked. "*I* want to make them pay. I do not understand why you do not."

In her mind, it was easy to explain. She couldn't accurately verbalize it, but it was about her own perspective. Her own mood. She had a short life to live, and she didn't want to waste it on negativity. She had limited energy within each day, and things like hostility and revenge would take so much of it.

"I suppose I've missed it," Della sighed. She felt vapid and shallow just saying it, admitting that this long-dead part of her life was something she felt deprived of. "I never really got to have my season . . ." She began picking at her fingernails. Her mother would be livid. "I thought it might be nice to be someone society cared about again."

Clara nodded. They sat in silence for a moment, and Della didn't know what to do. Clara was always humming or singing or talking. The quiet was overwhelming.

"Would you like to go?" Della asked her. "To the ball, I mean."

"Oh good heavens, no." Clara laughed. "Could you imagine? Me at a ball. I don't think so. You know the aristocracy makes me itch."

Della had thought as much. She did repeat that sentiment often, about being allergic to the rich. She'd just wanted to offer Clara the opportunity. Clara deserved her moment, too. In theory, she more than deserved to be introduced to the world and paraded around a ballroom. In all reality, though, she would despise every aspect of that experience.

"Very well." Della smiled. "Would you mind, then, if I asked you for a favor?"

"Of course not." Clara leaned forward to rest her elbows on her knees. Her new outfit made her look more formal, but her posture couldn't be more relaxed if she tried.

"Would you and Harry mind terribly if I sent you back to Westfield Manor ahead of me? Just to inform everyone that they are more than welcome to come with us to Kinloss? They may also stay and remain employed by my parents, of course, but I would much prefer everyone join me."

Della hoped she'd be a better employer than they were. It would be difficult to be worse.

"And you could prepare our things for the move." It was a terribly big request, she knew. "Assuming you are planning to come with me," Della stuttered. She hadn't even thought about the alternative. "You do not have to, of course, I just hoped—"

"Of course I'm coming with you." Clara said.

Della breathed a sigh of relief. "Once we make such a scene at the ball, I don't trust my parents not to descend on the manor and try to ensure we leave with nothing but the clothes on our backs. If you and Harry could go ahead—"

"Oh," Clara leaned back again, her spine straightening in what looked like surprise. "Me and Harry? Alone?"

"Is that a problem?" Della asked, gently. She wasn't sure what was going on between the two, but she didn't want to make either of them uncomfortable. "We can make other arrangements—it's no trouble at all."

"No, no," Clara insisted. She stood up and began pacing their little room. "I was just . . . surprised. Harry and I haven't discussed . . . well, we haven't discussed anything. I was always planning to go wherever you go, but I don't know . . ." She sank to the carpet at the foot of the bed. "What do I do if he doesn't want to go?"

Della heard what she wasn't saying. She didn't know how to respond.

"Just . . ." Della sighed. "Talk to him, all right? You must talk to him."

Clara nodded. The door opened, Alice walking in at a much slower pace than Clara had. She walked much slower than she sewed.

"You must do the same," Clara warned. That one brow of hers arched up in challenge.

"I found it," Alice walked to where the half-finished dress lay on the bed. She began placing little bits of beaded fabric here and there. One piece draped across the hem of the bodice like a sash, another few scattered across the sleeves. Each of the beads caught the low light they were working in, and it was dazzling. The fabric itself was a nude lace, and the beads were a dark golden bronze. "I made a wedding gown for the strangest young lady, years and years ago. She was an heiress of some kind. I don't remember. She must be old enough to have children of marrying age by now, if she were ever so blessed."

Della and Clara listened as she began to ramble. It reminded

Della of Andrew, all the seemingly random things he'd said in the carriage just to make her feel better.

"Anyway, she had more money than God himself, and she wanted this strange gown of vivid orange silk with dark beading all over. None of the modistes would make such a thing, even for her and all of her riches. But I had a young son to feed, so I took the job. The gowns were much bigger back in those days, not these slim silhouettes you young ladies are wearing now. I sewed each bead on myself, and I couldn't bear to throw away the scraps."

"They're beautiful," Della ran her fingers over the delicate beadwork. "But you cannot use them on me, surely if you've been saving them all these years you must use them for something special."

"Oh, my dear," Alice patted her cheek, as she'd seen her do to Andrew yesterday. "I promise, you are something special."

Della had only moments to absorb that statement before Clara spoke.

"And you must use them, Della. They match your walking stick!"

CHAPTER THIRTY

DELLA WAS IMMENSELY frustrated. In sending Clara and Harry back to Westfield Manor, she'd also dismissed her lady's maid. She almost never thought of Clara that way, but she was reminded of the convenience of having such a person available when dressing for a ball. She was proud of her own forethought in anticipating a less-than-positive reaction from her parents at what she was about to do. What she hadn't considered was the meantime, and how nice it would be to have Clara here. Not only for her help, but as a reasonable counter voice to drown out the sound of Della's own anxiety.

She laughed at herself as she thought of that. Clara was never reasonable.

Della stood in the corner of the guest room she now occupied on her own in just her stays, stockings, and chemise, her gown resting in front of her on the wooden chair that seemed to appear wherever she was. There were but a few laces on her stays, but her body just couldn't tighten them on her own. No matter how she tugged and pulled and twisted, her knobby hands simply weren't capable. It was so damnably irritating to be engaging in this entire night to celebrate her power when she couldn't even dress herself properly. Della almost desperately wanted to cry, and some part of her wanted to abandon the idea of going to the ball.

There was a knock at the door.

"Oh, thank goodness." She breathed a sigh of relief. That must be Alice coming to check on her. "Come in."

Her back was to the door, but she didn't need to see him to know exactly who that was. The gasp gave him away, but so did the energy that took over the room as soon as he stepped in.

"I am so sorry," he said, turning as if to leave. "I didn't realize you'd—"

"No, no," Della hurried to say. She took one step toward him, and she couldn't credit why. "I am sorry. I thought you were your mother. She said she would fix my hair, and I was having trouble, so I thought she'd come to help . . ."

Her voice trailed off as she realized the situation she was in. She was alone and nearly naked with a man. It was by far more daringly inappropriate than she'd ever been, and a particular tangle in which she thought she'd never have the opportunity to engage.

Would he ever look at her like that again? She wondered. Before he'd turned away, that flare of heat in his eyes—she wanted to see it again. She wanted to feel it.

He turned back around, and it was quite possibly the most victorious Della had ever felt.

"Having trouble with what?" he asked. As if making a final decision, Andrew released the one hand he'd kept on the doorknob and let it fall closed. The noise it made rang with irrevocability.

"Oh," Della breathed. "My stays. My hands are . . . not quite functional at the moment, and I can't get them laced and tied."

"Would you . . ." he started to ask, shifting from foot to foot, "like me to assist?" His tone was oddly formal, as if this were an act of common decency. As if he were taking her hand to help her out of a carriage or picking up the handkerchief that had fallen out of her reticule. This was not an act of decency, she hoped. In her wildest dreams, this was an act of want. Not even a particularly active decision, just a sense of need that compelled him forward toward her.

"If you wouldn't mind." And then all Della could do was nod.

Andrew let out a noise that Della couldn't quite place. It was somewhere between a groan and a bitter chuckle. He crossed the room slowly, and she realized some of his rigid posture could be attributed to his manner of dress. He was stunning. In fawn trousers with a matching waistcoat and a cravat she'd never seen before. It must be new, if he'd worn it before it would already be stained.

"You are so beautiful," he said once he reached her. She felt his words like a caress, across her cheek and underneath her jaw, down over her collarbones.

"I believe you're supposed to save the compliments for when I'm fully dressed," Della remarked. It was an attempt to bring some levity to the situation. Everything felt so heavy, even the air between them.

"I'll be sure to repeat the sentiment then." In the looking glass in front of them, he smiled. Those dimples were all the levity she needed. Della felt herself relaxing, and as her spine curved, she met the ridges of his chest. His hand came to rest at her waist, and his thumb rubbed circles over the fabric of her chemise just below her still-loose stays.

His other hand moved her unbound hair over one shoulder, and she felt a tug on the laces she'd been trying so desperately to tame. If this was what happened when she asked for help, Della would never dress herself again. The laces tightened just a bit more as he tied them off. In the mirror, she watched as his head dipped to press his lips against the nape of her neck. Della's sharp intake of breath was audible between them, and she reached for his hand where it still cradled her waist.

"What about your gown?" Andrew asked. She didn't recognize this voice of his. It was low and husky, almost a grumble that she felt beneath her ribs. "Can you do up the buttons?"

Perhaps on a good day she could. Though she reconsidered, as today was turning out to be a very good day indeed, but she had no desire to even touch those buttons.

"I am not sure," she murmured.

He seemed to take that as the invitation she'd intended it to be, and he picked up her silk gown off the chair at her side. He draped the back open and held her hand as she stepped in. The silk flowed around the bottoms of her legs and those gorgeous beaded sleeves fell over the tops of her arms. Andrew started at the bottom of her waist, lodging each button with slow precision. It was torture, to feel him so close. His breath blew across the hair at the back of her neck and Della felt the oddest sensation, a tugging in her core. An ache that she'd only read about.

"Andrew," she moaned, and she felt his entire body stiffen at her back. The hand she still held to her waist flexed against the fabric covering her skin.

She watched in the mirror as he opened his mouth to respond, but then they heard it.

"Della, dear?" His mother's voice, then a gentle knock at the door. She should've known before that it was Andrew rather than his mother. His knock had been much less soft. Perhaps she had known. "Are you ready for me to turn up your hair?"

Della met his eyes. He nodded. He was standing so close his chin brushed her temple. She wasn't ready, in fact. She would never be ready to let this moment go. She'd never be ready for him to back away, from the aching warmth of those hands to fade into cold.

"Yes," Della shouted in the direction of the door. Andrew backed away, giving the image of respectability even though they were still alone in her temporary bedchamber. She'd never felt such intense bliss evaporate so fast.

"I'm ready."

ANDREW FELT PATHETIC. He hadn't wanted to come to this godforsaken ball in the first place. He didn't belong among the rich unless he was working for them, but Della had begged. Well, perhaps begged was an overstatement. She'd asked exactly once. Her eyes had softened, and his heart had melted, and that was all it took. Hence the reason he felt pathetic.

As they rode in tense silence toward the Kittredge home, Andrew cursed his own inability to take action where she was concerned. The more time he spent around her, the more he realized it was entirely possible to be frozen in adoration for someone. He cared so much for her that he'd never been able to risk it. Except he had once, and that had ended disastrously. He could only hope that tonight would be different. For her sake, at least.

The cravat around his neck was impossibly tight, and so was every single one of his muscles. They had been since he'd touched her. Scarcely an hour ago, he'd lived out the beginnings of all of his wildest dreams. Alone with Della, standing so close. Feeling her warmth and her skin. In his mind, it went in reverse. She let him peel the clothes off of her, though he had more than enjoyed helping her dress. The sensation of that almost-liquid silk would linger on the pads of his fingers for days. He would always remember the soul-deep peace he felt when his skin touched hers.

"I will be lingering about the lemonade table," he heard his mother say. "I am a chaperone in name only. I have no plans to hinder your evening."

Andrew's stomach churned while Della laughed. This was why he hadn't wanted to come. Of course, he wanted to witness her big moment and her triumphant return to society, but he didn't think he could bear to watch her charm every man in the room the way she'd so thoroughly charmed him.

She hadn't even tried, all those years ago, just as she wasn't trying now. She'd done nothing but be herself, a gem of a person everyone in London was going to get to behold in just moments. There would be someone there bolder than himself. Stronger. With more courage. Someone who was not frozen in their enchantment with her, someone who was set aflame by it. Not a coward like him who had her in his arms and let her drift away.

"I'm not sure what kind of evening I'll have anyway." Della sighed, looking out the window at the fading light. "I have this terrible fear that no one will want to speak to me. It seems childish to be so scared of silence, but I truly am."

Andrew heard her voice break, and he would give anything to give her her confidence back.

"Well, that is why we're here." His mother grabbed one of Della's hands, sending her a warm, maternal smile. It made the tight strings around Andrew's heart loosen. He didn't think Della had ever received enough smiles like that. No one could ever have enough gestures of familial tenderness, but Della had felt so few.

"I appreciate that—" Della continued, then her words halted on a gasp. Andrew followed her gaze out the carriage's small window. It was another carriage, the one marked with the Morley crest. Her parents. They hadn't been sure they'd be here, not entirely. They'd assumed, they'd prepared, but all of that anxious forethought paled in comparison to knowing they were but a few paces ahead of them approaching the crowd of revelers filing into Kittredge House.

They sat, trapped in the heavy traffic. Andrew couldn't look out the window any longer. The sight of carriages and people and horses going every which way made him nauseous. If there was going to be an accident, he couldn't watch. Horses unsettled him to begin with, but this crush of activity in so small a space was a recipe for disaster. Some part of him feared this whole night was, actually.

His mother and Della made small talk as they spied on other partygoers. They discussed gowns and gloves and his mother gasped as she swore she saw a dowager countess's ankle as she descended from her curricle. They seemed to be having fun, at least.

They slowly neared the top of the Kittredge's drive, and Andrew began to hear the music and the voices and the laughter. It crept up on him, rising slowly until his senses were almost overwhelmed. He heard the noise, he saw flashes of people moving through the candlelight, he smelled Della's delicate perfume. He felt her skirts brush against the tops of his new, over-shined shoes.

As the voices began to blur together, he wondered if any of them would be the one to win Della's heart. He wondered if tonight would be his last night with her like this, tucked in close enough to feel her. He thought of how many more opportunities he might have left to experience the exquisite peace he felt when he touched her.

The carriage door opened before Andrew could prepare himself. He climbed out first, thanking the formally dressed footman. He helped his mother take the stairs, and she did so with an excitement in her step that Andrew hadn't seen in years. Then he reached for Della. Always, it felt like, he was reaching for Della. She tucked her walking stick under one arm and rested her palms on his shoulders. It was such a privilege to have her trust, to have her lean into him and allow herself to be swept through the air in his arms.

All too soon, she was safely on the ground. She gripped her

walking stick in her left hand. Her right hand lingered on his shoulder, sliding down his arm with a certain devastating slowness.

"Thank you, Andrew," she breathed, and her face transformed into a wide, open smile.

It was heartbreaking.

They'd discussed this part. It was better for Della to have her moment alone, to walk in and receive the entrance she deserved. Andrew and Alice would stay behind and remain unannounced. He knew this. He'd been anticipating it, but he still wanted to chase after her the second she took that first step.

Della didn't turn back. As the dazzling lights reflected off of her beaded gown, she walked forward. Her lingering hand fell away, and Andrew let her go.

CHAPTER THIRTY-TWO

"THE RIGHT HONORABLE the Baroness of Kinloss."

The footman's voice was booming, and Della wasn't sure if that was the sound itself or the way it echoed in the suddenly quiet ballroom. It was so immediately silent that Della heard her own heartbeat in her ears. She gripped her walking stick with clammy hands and she forced her face into the smile she used to practice daily. One that was demure and meek. Her mother had always said she reminded her so much of herself as a young debutante, and Della only felt like it now. That unassuming smile was so artificial it had to remind her of her mother.

Every head turned at her introduction, and all of the movement in the ballroom seemed to halt. So did Della's breath. She squared her shoulders and lifted her chin. Many of the expressions she saw were curious, open mouths and squinting eyes, trying to put a name to a face they'd likely forgotten. Other faces flashed with recognition, because despite her illness, she did still look like herself. Those who knew her as a young lady seemed to sense it was her, but they too were puzzled by the title they'd never known her to have.

After a moment, the room seemed to collectively resume speaking, and Della was finally able to breathe. She'd done it. She'd introduced herself to society, standing up in front of everyone so they knew exactly who she was. From this vantage point, she could see each and every face. Most were turned back toward their conversations. Servants floated around with champagne, and people lingered near tables spread with food.

Della felt lingering eyes on her, somewhere to her right. It wasn't the comfort of Alice or the searing warmth of Andrew. Before she even turned her head, Della felt the maliciousness hidden behind that gaze. Her mother. The only person in the world who could despise her so desperately. She wouldn't look. Not yet.

She'd only just realized why she could see everyone so clearly.

She stood at the top of the home's grand staircase. Somehow, Della had never thought of this part, and she had no idea what to do in the face of such an obstacle. She'd considered the repercussions of making such an entrance, but the mechanics behind doing so in her disabled body eluded her. Ever so slowly, Della took the first step. It seemed the only option. There was only one way forward, and it was down those stairs. It felt good to move, after long minutes trapped inside the carriage. One step, then the next. One hand on her walking stick and the other on the banister. Others were being announced and music still flowed through the room, but all eyes had resumed watching her.

Della couldn't look. She wouldn't. Her eyes were trained on her feet, making sure she didn't trip over her own hem and making sure no one saw she wore old, worn-in riding boots under her gown. She counted the stairs. There were seventeen. Entirely too many. She considered whether she'd ever counted the stairs at Westfield Manor, and how many there were. She wondered how many there'd be at Kinloss. It was something a baroness ought to know.

Finally, she made it. Her feet reached the ballroom floor, and Della wanted to cheer. It had been painful and slow and wobbly at best, but she'd made it. She finally raised her head in triumph, and she met what felt like a thousand sets of bewildered eyes.

Many had the decency to immediately look away, as if they were sparing her a passing glance instead of openly gawping. Others continued the rude staring. Some simply leered, gazing at her with pinched eyebrows and unabashed frowns.

This was not a triumph. This was not a moment of celebration. This was a reintroduction to a society that didn't want her. She'd never felt her own ostracization so acutely as she did in that moment. Perhaps this was what her parents were protecting her from all those years ago, Della thought as she continued to stare back, meeting each disapproving eye in the room. She found her mother's gaze, guarded and harsh, her eyes bracketed by fine lines. They were so full of rage, and Della couldn't recognize love in them at all. Perhaps they'd only been protecting themselves, then.

She stood in the very silence she'd so deeply feared. There was sound, but she could hear none of it. Behind her, she heard Lord Kitteridge attempt to reengage the room, and the music still played, but Della was trapped in a nightmare of her own creation. She felt Alice and Andrew come to flank her, posting themselves at either side like they were personally responsible for her safety and wellbeing. They weren't. She was, and she was doing a poor job of protecting herself at the moment. There was no reason to stay here and subject herself to this torture. If no one could bear the sight of her, she'd spare them the trouble.

Della wouldn't run. She'd done so much damage to herself the last time she had. She wanted to, though. Almost desperately. It would be almost freeing to pick up her skirts and abandon this place and this party once and for all, but Della knew she had to stop hurting herself all in the name of freedom.

With as much poise and calm as she had left, she walked toward the door she'd just seen a servant appear through. She didn't know where it led, but she assumed there would be significantly less judgment there, and that was enough for her. She followed a dark corridor, turning the opposite way each time she heard a voice. Della opened a door. There was nothing in the dimly lit room besides something covered in a sheet. She assumed it to be a pianoforte based on the shape. In the inconvenient absence of furniture, Della leaned against the wall. The dust in the air was so thick she nearly choked on it, or maybe that was a ball of her own emotions clogging her throat. Tears sprang up in her eyes and she felt the telltale burning in her nose that meant she'd long passed the point of being able to stop herself from crying.

"Damn," she cursed, realizing she had no handkerchief and no way to stop the stream of tears without staining her perfect gown or her pristine silk gloves. The door opened, and Della sniffled in an effort to appear whole.

"Adelaide," she heard a woman say. Though she couldn't see her through the barrage flooding her eyes, she almost thought she'd recognized the voice. But it couldn't be, she thought. "I'd hoped that was you."

Della furiously swiped at her eyes, her gloves be damned. As her vision cleared, she stifled a gasp.

"Mercy," she mumbled. Her voice was an unsure whisper, because as much as the lady in front of her in a resplendent vivid purple gown resembled the friend she hadn't seen in so many years, she still couldn't believe her own perception.

"It is Lady Kittredge now," Mercy grinned. "But I'm sure you do not mean any disrespect, unlike so many people we know." She rolled her eyes. "I'm so sorry I missed your introduction. A foul young lady decided to speak rudely to one of the footmen, and I had to politely ask her to leave."

"This is your house?" Della asked redundantly. She was still flabbergasted at this turn of events. She never thought she'd see Mercy again, let alone be a guest at a ball at her home.

"Yes," Mercy nodded. She was so patient, and she'd clearly been named after the right attribute. "I haven't had a chance to redecorate yet, so please don't judge based on this room alone."

"Oh, I wouldn't judge at all," Della assured her.

"You are the only one." Mercy smiled again, this one just a

tad rueful. "And I thank you for it. When Mrs. Lockhart spoke of a baroness who'd just returned to town after years in the countryside, I could not help but hope it was you. Though I had no idea how such a thing was possible."

Della understood the feeling perfectly. What had Alice said about Lady Kitteridge? That she was a young lady like herself. She hadn't thought that meant she too was ill. That she'd been cast aside as Della had been.

"I could say the same for you. What happened?" Della implored. "You've always remained in my thoughts. I spent so long hoping you weren't alone."

Mercy's eyes softened. She gripped Della's arms right above the line of her long gloves, then as if she'd thought better of it, wrapped her in a tight, warm hug. Della nearly choked on her own sudden rush of tears. Not again, she thought. Not for the first time, she questioned how much she was physically capable of crying in one bloody night.

Mercy let her go, taking her hands in her own. The door opened, and they both turned to look. It was just Andrew. Her heart swelled at the sight of him and fresh rivulets of tears poured down her face. He'd followed her.

"I am not alone," Mercy said. "And it seems neither are you." Mercy squeezed her shoulders before she left the room.

"Andrew," she breathed his name on a watery sigh, and he stepped so close that the only air she could inhale was tinged with his scent.

He did not respond. His thumbs swept away tears faster than she could release them, and suddenly Della felt a bit more like the whole version of herself she'd been trying to imitate a minute ago.

With Mercy gone, her mind swept violently back to the reason she'd ended up in this room in the first place. Fresh hurt knifed through her chest. Mercy had said she wasn't alone, but in that moment, she had been, and she'd never be able to forget it.

"I don't know why I came here," Della admitted. Her tone

was morose and miserable, and she knew she must look as bad as she felt. "I do, I mean. I know. I missed all of this, the music and the dancing and smiling at people as you pass them. I missed conversations about nothing of importance. I just don't know why it all feels so different." Della sniffled again. His fingertips were still tracing over her face, even though no tears fell any longer. "I don't know why I can't still have all of that."

For a moment, all she could hear over the faint music was the sound of her own sniffling.

"I know I shouldn't apologize, because you scold me each time I do. But I wish I could make this better for you." He hummed. "I wish I could fix it."

"You can't," she whispered. Tears began to flow again, and Della tasted the salt on her lips. "One can either be ill or out in society, and no one can be both. You cannot fix that."

She thought of Mercy again. How she'd somehow been able to defy that rule. Andrew's hands fell from her face just slightly, wrapping around her neck and cradling the back of her head, the other smoothing the skin over her cheekbone. Through the wall she leaned against, she heard the music change. She recognized the tune; it was the waltz. So early in the night for such a dance. He took one step backwards, away from her, and Della's body nearly fell forward. It would've been so easy to give in to that intractable pull she felt toward him. It would've been the easiest thing in the world.

"You can still do all of those things," Andrew said, holding out a hand in the space between them. "You can dance with me, if you'd like. Smile at me. Talk to me about nothing of im-portance."

Della did smile then. It was instinctive. So was letting go and falling toward him. Placing her hand in his.

"Are you sure?" she asked. He pulled her toward the center of the large, open room. "I'm not very light on my feet anymore."

They took the first few steps slower than the music called for. Della scarcely remembered how to do this at all.

"Darling, I'm afraid you've never been very light on your feet." He spun her away from him, pulled her gently back to his chest. "But I would sooner never dance again than dance with anyone else."

Her breath caught. On her inhale, her chest pressed against his. She didn't know whose heart was beating faster. She could feel them both pulsing in the space they shared. They'd stopped dancing entirely, stopped moving, almost. Della caught his hypnotic eyes. Her fingers flexed against the fabric of his waistcoat. She felt his hands meet at the middle of her back, right where he'd tied the laces of her stays.

Andrew's eyes left hers, and she watched as they drifted down to her mouth. Then he was moving, closing the already minute space between them and claiming her lips with his. He was reserved at first, almost shy. So much like himself. Brushing her lips once, twice, three times. Quick bursts of energy against her skin. It was so much, a rush of sensation, but it wasn't enough. She'd waited for this for so long, dreamed about it a thousand times and hardly ever dared to think it would ever become her reality. She could taste the raw edge of fear on his lips, along with a kind of devotion she'd never felt before. Her stomach pitched and her core tightened. Only when he gently tugged on her bottom lip with his teeth did she realize this was indeed happening.

At that moment, Della finally knew what it meant to be home.

Della closed her eyes and let her hands drift. They found the curls at the nape of his neck. She tugged him closer, until they truly collided. Her lips opened on a sigh and she felt his hands tighten around her waist. His tongue hit the roof of her mouth and he tipped up her chin as he swallowed the moan she couldn't voice. All of that shyness was gone, and there wasn't room between them for reservations, or anything else like rational thought.

"Della," he whispered into the air they shared. She tried pulling him back, but her hands were lazy and her vision was clouded by his closeness. His lips landed along the curve of her jaw. "Finally," he murmured, breathing slow, open-mouthed kisses down the front of her throat.

She pressed her palms to his cheeks, steering him back up to her lips. She was mesmerized. For so many years, she'd yearned for a life like this, to be this close to him. It was agony to realize this might be the only glimpse of that life she'd ever get.

The door creaked, and Della dropped her hands. They fell to her sides at the wall, and Andrew wouldn't let her go. His eyes were hazy, and he seemed to be in a fog.

"Oh, I am sorry," Alice exclaimed. "I didn't mean to interrupt."

She stepped inside the dimly lit room, closing the door behind her.

"I've been looking for you. There are so many rooms down this bloody hallway, I've just been opening doors and snooping about. I fear I must apologize to Lady Kittredge for the intrusion! I've been to the study and the library, and I thought those were one and the same. There were two rooms that were entirely empty, and look at this! So much wasted space. I cannot credit such extravagance when there are so many without—"

Della couldn't help it. She laughed. It was a boisterous and entirely inappropriate giggle, and in front of her, Andrew licked his bottom lip like he wanted to taste it. Her laughter subsided into an indulgent sigh.

"I am sorry, dear." Alice became much more subdued once she got all the rambling over with. "I shouldn't have pushed you. I suppose I never realized how . . . cruel society can be."

Oddly, Della smiled. Her left hand reached for Andrew, finding his elbow, as his arms were still wrapped around her. He was becoming bolder in his impropriety, and she couldn't be more pleased. Her right hand took hold of Alice's.

"I am only going to say this once more to each of you. You must stop apologizing, at least to me. You both mean so much to me, and I cannot thank you enough for all of your help. I would not be here without you, and I mean that in so many ways."

Andrew squeezed her hip. Alice squeezed her hand.

"Well," Alice sighed, "while I am enjoying bumping elbows with the aristocracy, do you suppose we should head home?"

CHAPTER THIRTY-THREE

A S ANDREW WALKED her to the guest room, he wondered if she considered this the worst night of her life. He certainly hoped not. Even under the circumstances, getting to dance with her made this one of the best nights of his. Getting to kiss her made it a miracle.

They stopped in front of the closed door, and Andrew wondered whether or not he should push his luck. Neither of them had scarcely said a word since their hasty departure from Kittredge House. She'd stopped to offer a remorseful goodbye to Lady Kittredge, who was mortified by the behavior of her guests. Della, of course, waved off her regrets. At least it wasn't only him that she wouldn't let apologize to her. After that, his mother had filled the carriage ride with inane chatter, and Andrew was more than grateful for the silence hovering over them now.

It meant he could divert all of his attention to her. His eyes always followed her, in a way he hoped was subtle. He was fairly sure it wasn't, but he continued to hope anyway. In this moment, though, he didn't have to be subtle. He could openly and earnestly stare like he'd always wanted to. Andrew desperately wanted to do more than stare. He wanted to feel her lips against his. He wanted the warmth of all of her skin.

"Tonight was . . . unexpected," he said. It seemed the only apt term. It had been horrible and incredible. Heartbreaking and exhilarating. It had been a bit of everything, and Andrew had no idea what was supposed to happen next. Half of him wanted to kiss her hand, bid her goodnight, and start over in the morning. The rest of him wanted to kiss her everywhere and not say goodbye until well past the morning.

"It was," she said simply, giving him no indication of how she felt or what she wanted. Her fingers gently swept over his face, cupping his cheek in her palm and sifting through the ends of the curls just above his ear. His entire body froze. He was learning that his body's reaction to soul-searing bliss was to turn to ice.

"Della," he whispered again. That was another reaction. If his body were a block of ice, her name on his breath was a smattering of snowflakes. Each a wholly unique piece of him that he could give only to her.

She didn't respond, but her fingertips continued those slow circles across his temple. He sucked in a breath that smelled just like her, vanilla and lavender and ink and paper. Like memories and longing and distance.

There was no distance between them now. Not enough to matter. Andrew turned his head, leaning into her touch. He brought his hand up to cover hers. He pressed a kiss to her palm.

"Your gown," he said, as if that was supposed to explain everything. All of his intelligence was lost on her, and he couldn't stand it. "I mean, it's beautiful. You look beautiful in it." He continued to stumble for words. "Did I say that before? I'm sure I meant to—"

"Yes," she interrupted him, holding his cheek more firmly. Her lips tilted up in the corners, as if she were fighting a pleased smile. "You mentioned that. Thank you."

"Do you . . ." he started to ask, before he choked on his own tongue. Her hand still held his face, and he wasn't sure if that was making this worse or better. "With your gown . . . would you like . . . some help taking it off?"

She fell silent. Her hand dropped from his face and the smile dropped from hers. For a moment, Andrew thought he'd made a grave mistake. He wanted to take it all back, at least assure her that he meant nothing untoward. He'd assisted her into the gown, he'd just thought he might assist her out of it. It wasn't about that, though, and he feared they both knew it. He took a deep, aching breath and prepared to admit defeat.

Then she opened the door. She did so with one hand, not even turning around or stepping away. It was rather impressive, but he was biased. Even her heartbeat was impressive to him.

Della led the way into the room and closed the door once he'd entered. Andrew swallowed so loudly she must've heard. She never did respond verbally, she simply leaned her walking stick against the wooden chair he'd been following her around with all week and walked to the looking glass in the corner of the room.

Andrew knew no matter what happened tonight, that mirror would haunt his dreams every night for the rest of his life.

"Sit down," he said. His voice sounded gruff to his own ears, and he willed his reckless attraction to her to calm. He didn't want to be anything but gentle with her. It wasn't that he thought she was fragile, as everyone else did. He thought she was precious, and that was something entirely different. "Let me take off your shoes."

Della stalled for a moment, turning so she walked toward the bed instead. He knew she had worn her usual riding boots to the ball for comfort, but he could tell she was no longer comfortable at all. She walked differently when her pain started to worsen. Her steps were smaller and her posture was slumped, like her bones were no longer able to hold her up.

She slumped onto the bed and he heard a slow hiss of pain escape her lips. He got the sense that she'd been suppressing that very noise all night. He hated she was in pain, but he felt almost honored that she'd shared it with him.

Andrew sank to his knees on the carpet. Della gasped, and he pretended not to hear it. His fingers found the laces of her right shoe. They were so bloody small he had some trouble untangling them.

"I know I've no personal experience, but the things you ladies wear seem awfully uncomfortable." He wiggled the first boot off and threw it over his shoulder. Della laughed. That always made him feel like he'd won the King's fortune.

"I don't believe the discomfort is exclusive to ladies," she told him. "I know you are yourself uncomfortable in your present state." Della tugged on his cravat, loosening it just enough for him to feel human again. "And you didn't even spill anything on yourself." She hummed. "I'm quite proud."

Andrew smiled as he worked on the other set of laces. "I'm sure if we'd stayed a bit longer I would've managed."

She giggled again, leaning forward toward him. Her thumb brushed the skin of his throat where she'd untied his cravat, and Andrew lost whatever remained of his good sense. His fingers swept up her legs, drifting over the silk stockings covering her feet, ankles, and calves. He traced circles over the backs of her knees as he raised his head to meet hers.

"May I?" he whispered against her lips. Andrew wasn't sure exactly what he was asking for, but he'd take anything she was willing to give.

"Mmhm," Della hummed again, tilting her chin until it bumped his. She kissed him with an enthusiasm that would've knocked him down had he not already been on the floor. His tongue swept against hers as his fingers tugged on her stockings, releasing her garters. Once all he could feel was warm, bare skin, he ran his hands from her feet to her thighs. Her toes and ankles were hot to the touch, and her knees felt fevered.

"Are you well?" He pulled back just enough to ask, his hands still drifting up and down her legs.

"I'm quite well," she smiled. Her eyes were heavy lidded, as if she were seeing him through a haze. "Why do you ask?"

"Your joints are . . . hot," he said, his thumbs massaging her knees again. "I know you must be in pain."

"I am always in pain." Her smile fell just a bit, and her face relaxed into something heavier and more heated. "But I don't particularly care at the moment."

Andrew tilted his head up again, capturing her lips. They were lazy, messy kisses, something to occupy his over-eager, roaming mouth while he reached around to her back to undo the buttons lining her bodice. He'd never considered himself a particularly coordinated person, but he was rather proud of himself for that effort. Her heavy beaded sleeves slipped down her shoulders and he peeled the gown down to her waist.

Della continued for him, raising up her hips to allow him to remove the dress entirely. Once it was a puddle of beads and silk on the floor, he watched as she slowly removed each of her gloves. Then she was touching him in earnest, her fevered knuckles gracing his cheek.

"May I?" she asked, those fingers scalding the skin of his neck as she tugged on the ends of his cravat.

"Of course." His breath came out in such a rush it was almost a scoff. "Always. You can always do whatever you want with me, Della."

She smiled, and he was close enough that he saw two of her. His vision blurred into a haze of nothing but Della, and Andrew swore he'd never been happier in his entire life. She began to unknot his cravat and she sank her hands underneath where his shirt draped open. He absolutely loathed formalwear, but he was developing a fondness for taking it off. His hands operated of their own accord, unlacing her stays much more efficiently than he had her boots. Freed from the confines of the garment, she seemed to breathe deeper. Her posture sagged a bit, and she fell forward more against him. Left only in her chemise, he could feel the heat of her more than ever. From her flushed cheeks to her curling toes, she was a blaze and he desperately wanted to be burned.

"Lean back," he whispered. There was no point to the hushed tone, it just felt like the slightest thing could pop the bubble of perfection around them, even the sound of his voice.

Della lay back and rested her head on the pillows. She reached for him, and he aligned his body over hers, supporting his weight with his forearms on the bed on either side of her.

"Della," he moaned, sucking a spot just below where her jaw met her ear.

For a brief moment, he just smiled against her lips. Then she was smiling, too, and she giggled into his mouth. It was an expression of unbridled joy, and Andrew couldn't believe he was somehow actually making her as happy as she made him.

CHAPTER THIRTY-FOUR

"ANDREW," SHE MOANED back. Della was awash in sensation, and somehow it still wasn't enough. Her hands wrapped around his neck, sinking into those curls she loved so much. She pulled him down on top of her more fully, letting his weight rest on her body. All the breath rushed out of her at the feel of him, firm and hard everywhere she was soft and pliable. His skin was cool compared to hers, but the heat of his breath scorched her neck.

Della wanted that heat everywhere. For once, parts of her weren't fevered enough. Andrew lifted up, his body shifting off of hers. She let out an audible groan, and he smirked. She caught a flash of those dimples in the low light, and that almost made up for it. She sat up, too, just a bit. Her shoulders were leaned against the pillows, her head against the headboard.

His mouth brushed her skin again, just over the neckline of her thin chemise. Della closed her eyes. Her hands roamed over his chest, feeling the corded muscles of his shoulders underneath his shirt. She felt him slide down her body in one fluid motion, his fingertips dragging wherever they went. He found the backs of her knees again, and something shifted. Her eyes flashed open and there he sat, on his knees on the bed in front of her, staring at the exposed skin beneath the hem of her chemise.

"Della, do you want me to—" he started.

"Yes," she interrupted. The only thing she didn't want him to do was stop.

With his hands on her calves, he shifted her legs, spreading them farther apart. Della let out a muffled hiss.

"I'm sorry," they said at the same time. He laughed, she didn't.

"I am sorry," she repeated. "That damned hip is always—"

"Della." He leaned over her again, kissing her lips and her cheeks. Her nose and her forehead. Her eyelids and the wrinkle between her brows. "What have we said about apologizing?"

She did laugh then. It barely counted as a chuckle, but it was enough to ease the tension.

"Are you certain?" Andrew asked. His tongue laved the shell of her ear and Della heard a sound, an agonized moan that she didn't even recognize had come from her own body.

"Yes," she whispered. There was little space between them now, and his hands began to roam. At first, his knuckles just brushed her skin, down her arm and back up. Then he drifted over her collarbone and followed the neckline of her chemise downward. Those knuckles grazed the swell of her breast. His thumb teased her nipple and it drew out another one of those moans. She was weighed down by the delicious pressure of his body, but she felt the need to move. Her ribs heaved and her hips jerked.

"Fuck," Andrew murmured under his breath. Della didn't know if that was good or bad. She was about to ask, but then he lowered his mouth to her breast while his hand still circled the other.

Della let out a guttural sigh, and Andrew's mouth slipped away suddenly. He slid down her body again, his left hand still stroking her skin. His right hand pushed up her chemise, and he shifted her right leg, creating space for himself between her thighs while ensuring her fragile left hip remained still.

"Andrew," she gasped. She couldn't help it. All of her natural capacity for words went out the window. All she could see, hear, and feel was him. All she could think was his name. All she could do was tug on his hair.

Della felt his breath against her core, and she let out another rib-heaving sigh. His wet, hot tongue stroked her skin and she finally gave into that compulsion to move. She shifted her hips forward, seeking more of that contact, and a stab of pain ripped through her body. That damned left hip. She must have done something, hissed or winced or tensed. Andrew stopped for a moment, and as if he knew exactly what she needed, his right hand came to rest on her left hipbone. The strong pressure eased the pain, and she tried another roll of movement. He held her steady, even as she rutted against him, and that rush of pain faded to a dull roar.

Andrew gripped her hip tighter as he sucked on her skin. His tongue speared in and out of her body, his left hand rising back up to knead her breast. Della felt a mounting pressure, increasing with each stroke of his tongue. Losing herself in the moment and being swept away in pleasure was something Della had never done before. As if realizing that fact, she decided she wasn't savoring the experience enough. Her eyes flew open and her fingers tightened in his hair. Her other hand wrapped around the wrist he still held against her hip.

He paused for a moment, withdrawing his tongue and teasing her with his fingers instead. Their eyes connected as he looked up, and Della nearly gasped at the raw need in his gaze.

"You are perfect, Della." He licked the corners of his lips, and she watched him lower his head between her thighs again. "So fucking perfect," she felt him whisper against her skin. After one long, slow lick, he returned with renewed vigor.

Della gasped. She moaned. She lost all sense of control over her own body. With each point of contact and every roll of her hips, she inched closer to a peak she'd never before reached. She heard her heartbeat in her ears and the sounds Andrew made. She was almost certain he was still mumbling, rambling words she couldn't hear, but she felt the press of them against her wet skin.

He sucked on a spot at the apex of her core that he'd previously only glanced over, and Della groaned his name. He did it again, long, steady streams of pressure on the center of her pleasure. She tugged on his hair again, and he moaned. They were lost in a sensitive awareness of each other, of themselves. Della had never felt such pure, white-hot ecstasy in her life.

Andrew moved. His right hand dug further into the skin of her hipbone. His left hand pressed into the skin of her thigh, right by his head. Della thought she might have bruises there shaped like his fingertips. She certainly wouldn't mind.

All it took was one more swirl of his tongue, and she went over that peak she'd so been anticipating. Her eyes slammed shut again, flashes lighting up behind her eyelids. She transcended her body for a moment, sparks shooting down her spinal cord until she was made of nothing but numbness and tingling.

When she regained her faculties, Andrew was right there. His hands had fallen away from their stalwart grip on her, and Della missed it already. He'd rested his head on her torso, his chin digging into her skin just above where he'd previously held her hip. That damned hip. She ran her fingers through his hair again, just because she could. He stared up at her from his perch near her waist, and he looked almost shy. His wide eyes were soft and longing, and the touch that had been bruising was now achingly gentle.

"Stay with me," she whispered. He could take that to mean whatever he liked. For the night or forever, she meant either or both.

He softened even further, and he rearranged her chemise as he stood. Della took that as a silent but polite refusal, even as she noted the hard length pressed against the trousers he still wore. He walked around to the other side of the bed and pulled back the coverlet. He climbed over toward her, enveloping her in the warmth of his arms in one swift motion. She shifted her hips to allow him to fully pull the blankets over her, and Della let out a contented sigh as her head found the solid block of his chest.

After the numbness and tingling faded, they'd left her with a soul-deep exhaustion. Her eyes fluttered closed and her hand rested under his half-buttoned shirt, just above his heart.

She heard the steady beat there, and it almost matched hers. It was strong and secure. Constant, just like him. Della thought he might be saying something. She felt his breath disrupting single strands of the hair at the crown of her head, she thought that air carried words she couldn't hear.

Andrew would tell her in the morning, she hoped.

Just before she had to leave.

Chapter Thirty-Five

DELLA AWOKE IN the pitch dark of night. The act of waking up in the middle of the night wasn't unusual for her. The pain and stiffness she dealt with on a daily basis meant that she often had to interrupt her sleep to stand up and stretch. On particularly bad nights, she'd have to pace several laps about the room.

She'd turned away from Andrew in her sleep, but his legs were still tangled with hers. She could still feel the heat of him against her back, and she so desperately wanted to remain where she was, her pain be damned. She couldn't, though, and she knew it. It was a sense of foreboding, like an opposite reaction to the sixth sense she'd always had about him. She was leaving at first light, but something about this felt more urgent.

Della stood up, loosening her limbs and rocking back and forth on her toes to pull her muscles back into place. She hoped her joints didn't make some awful, inhuman sound loud enough to wake Andrew. She didn't know what she'd say. She didn't think she'd be able to give the thoughts swimming in her head a voice. It was easier to let them drown her.

She pressed a hand to the center of her chest. Though the beat of her heart was strong and steady, all of the buoyant hope she felt just hours ago had turned to heavy dread.

A horrible thought flashed through her mind, bright and vivid and unavoidable. This was going to end, and it was going to hurt. This couldn't last forever, no matter how much she wanted it to. Andrew had never offered such a thing, and she wouldn't dare assume. But she could picture it, him with her forever. He'd be there by her side, loyal and caring and maybe even loving. He'd feel obligated to stay with her, because no one else had, and because he was that uniquely kind. And he'd grow to resent her and their quiet life in Scotland. He'd miss London and his mother and everything he'd worked so hard for.

Della could see it so clearly in her mind's eye. She'd be happy, and he'd lose himself in caring for her. Just as her mother had. Andrew wouldn't become so frigid and heartless, and he wouldn't abandon her or send her away. He'd stay and silently resent her, letting her be the source of his unhappiness as they lived out the rest of their days.

She thought of how her mother had looked at her just last night. The disdain in her gaze, the way she was only ever callous with people, how she valued wealth over all else. All of that was Della's fault, and she couldn't bear to harm Andrew the same way.

On her bare feet, Della took slow steps across the room. The farther she led herself from the bed, the easier she could breathe. Her pace quickened as her thoughts did, and she found herself chewing on her thumbnail. It was an old nervous habit, and she hadn't done it in years. She looked at Andrew's sleeping form. He lay on his stomach, sprawled over his half of the bed and part of hers. One of his hands was splayed out over the mattress, as if reaching for her.

Della stopped in her tracks.

She couldn't do this. That was why she'd woken up, it wasn't about her pain at all. It was a protective instinct. For them both, it seemed. Della cursed her own affection for him. It had gotten her in trouble again, even so many years after the first time. She should've stopped this before she was in too deep, before she was standing at the foot of the bed watching his back rise and fall as he breathed. That rhythm of his subtle movement was soothing, and Della's chest clenched with a fierce desire to protect the peace she saw in him.

He'd done so much for her. He'd tried to fix everything, and he'd stood with her to fight the most difficult battles she'd ever fought. She couldn't ask him to leave everything to be with her. He was so bloody selfless, he'd probably volunteer to stick around Kinloss just to keep fixing things for her. Della wouldn't let him. She couldn't.

Della paced another lap. She chewed on more of her fingernails. Eventually, she came to a decision. She walked one more turn about the room, just to be sure.

She could offer them a way forward, but it had to be his choice to take it. Della wouldn't allow her heart to be something else he had to fix. She had to be something he wanted. There was almost no way he would want a forever-ill Scottish baroness who had a penchant for getting herself into incredible messes, not truly. He might want to help her, but he wouldn't want to keep her.

Della slipped from the room with remarkable stealth for someone with such usually inoperable limbs. She wasn't a particularly religious person, but she sent up a silent prayer as she hugged the wall and walked down the short hallway toward the front of the home. There was so much that could go wrong. She could wake Andrew or Alice. She could stub her toe. Of all options, that one was the most likely.

Della reached the small writing desk in the great room. She fiddled around for a match and lit a slow-burning candle. With a fresh sheet of paper in front of her and a quill in hand, she took a deep, cleansing breath. That sense of foreboding settled over her again, and her stomach churned.

This was the right thing to do, she told herself. It was the only way to save him from a life he'd come to sorely regret.

My dearest, Andrew, she wrote. Already, the page was stained with tears. Della sniffled, trying to rein in her frantic emotions.

I hope you don't despise me for leaving without a proper goodbye. It was just something I couldn't say to you. There are many things I haven't been able to say, and I am so sorry for that. I want you to know that you are always welcome at Kinloss. Nothing would make me happier than if you were there by my side every day.

Images of that hypothetical future filled Della's mind and ruined all progress she'd made in trying to stop her tears. It was beyond a futile effort.

But I cannot ask that of you, to leave everything you know and the life you've built, just for me. You have already done more than enough, more than anyone else in the world has ever done for me. If this is all we ever have, I will be forever grateful.

I want so much more. I've never been able to tell you that, because I've been so desperately afraid you might not feel the same. Now, what I fear is that I am too late. There was a time, when I was nearing eighteen and my world was on the edge of falling apart, that I wanted nothing more than to be your wife. For years, I mourned the loss of that future. Now, my world has just been put back together, reshaped into something entirely new. I don't know how you fit into it anymore, but I know that I want you to. However you'd like. I hope that you'll still write me letters. I hope that you'll visit, if you don't think too ill of me after all of this. I hope I get to kiss you one more time. I don't even dare to hope for anything more than that.

Della sniffled again, but she was no match for the power of her own tears. The sheer force of her emotion was staggering, and she didn't know if she had the strength to finish writing. Her bags were packed, and transportation had been arranged. The morning light would come, but she didn't know if she had the strength to leave.

I love you so dearly, Andrew. That is my deepest hope, that you know that. I pray this isn't goodbye.

Yours always,
Della

She folded up the letter and blew out the candle.

CHAPTER THIRTY-SIX

A S HER CARRIAGE rolled the final few meters to Westfield Manor, Della was reminded of the first time she'd approached this place the very same way. She'd been on the verge of eighteen, riding across the countryside alone to a home she barely knew. She hadn't been able to cry, then. All the way from London, she'd ridden in somber silence, an icy numbness taking over her heart. This time, she'd cried nearly the entire way.

Della thought this must be what it felt like to be in mourning. A constant state of despair that had no solution and seemingly no end. She mourned the man she left behind, and she regretted doing so the farther she rode away from him. A thousand times, she'd thought about turning around. She'd thought through every word of her letter and wondered if she'd said enough. She rewrote it in her head over and over again. There was nothing else to do but listen to the horses trot and the chirp of an occasional bird.

And cry. There was crying to do. The bumpy carriage ride was time spent in grief. The trip was short as possible, and she kept a quick pace so as to minimize the unsafety and impropriety a woman risked when traveling alone.

At some point, she'd stopped wiping her tears with the handkerchief she kept tucked into the sleeve of her pelisse. Doing so was useless when the tears wouldn't stop flowing. Hour after hour. Over time, those tears were for more than Andrew. She missed him so much her chest ached, but the real mourning was for herself. Her family. The closer she got to the manor, the more she thought of that young girl who'd been sent here with only an unfamiliar maid for companionship and protection. She thought of the cruelty and the coldness and the complete disregard for her wellbeing her parents had shown. They'd cared more for their own reputations than her.

She'd mourned the lost life of a debutante long ago, but now she felt the full force of years of lies and subterfuge and casual mistreatment. It was cleansing, crying until she couldn't anymore. She felt almost renewed, a sense of freshness beneath the exhaustion weighing down her soul. She would leave the weeping and the mourning here at Westfield Manor and embark on the journey to her new home guided by that refreshed spirit.

Her carriage rolled to a stop, and she heard the muffled speech of the coachmen rattling around. The door opened, and Della breathed in a lungful of fresh, familiar air. It really was clearer in the countryside. She could only hope Scotland was just as nice.

"Harry." She smiled as her faithful butler reached a hand out to assist her. "It's so good to see you."

"Della! What a surprise! We knew you'd be back soon, but you must've raced home." He helped her down the stairs, and Della turned her face to the fading sun. It was warmer here, and brighter, even at sunset.

"A pleasant surprise, I hope," she told him.

"Of course." He nodded fervently. "I was a bit concerned, with an unmarked carriage arriving unannounced. I'm sure you were the best possible outcome. Clara will be delighted to see you."

He seemed poised to speak again, but Della was overwhelmed by an attack on her person. Her walking stick clattered to the ground as she was swept up. The motion was fast enough to be blurry in her vision, but Della would recognize that explosion of energy anywhere.

"Clara, sweetheart, you're going to break her." Harry didn't try to separate them, he only took a step to the side. Della took note of the term of endearment, too. She would inquire about that later.

"I'm not so fragile as that," Della tried to say, but it really was quite a tight hug. Her ribs might be suddenly misaligned.

"What are you doing here?" Clara asked, pulling away from the crushing embrace to look Della over from head to toe as if examining for injuries. She wore her old clothes, the trousers Gwendoline had made and a man's shirtsleeves. "I mean, I know this is your home for a while longer, but we did not expect you back so soon. You didn't write."

Clara looked around suddenly, at the coachmen loading back up to leave, then to Harry, then back to Della.

"Where is Andrew?" Clara asked. One glance into Della's tear-wrecked eyes, and she knew. "Oh, no," she said, reaching for Della's arms again. "Is that why you look so dreadful?"

"Clara," Harry huffed. Even chastising her, his voice held a particular fondness. "That's terribly rude."

"You know what I mean," she huffed back, waving a hand in his direction as if in dismissal.

They walked into the manor's front hall arm in arm, and Della gasped. It was as if the home had been abandoned. All of the furnishings had been stripped away, and trunks were stacked on top of one another in the center of the room. The furniture was covered in Holland cloths.

"What happened here?" Della asked, her eyes roaming the space like she'd never seen it before. She certainly hadn't ever seen it like this.

"You told us to pack," Clara shrugged. "So we packed."

"Yes." Della rolled her eyes, breaking away from Clara to pace the overly empty floor. "I told you to pack, but I did not ask you to take everything that wasn't attached to the home itself!"

This was absolutely not what she'd imagined when she'd sent Clara and Harry back here ahead of her. She'd simply wanted everyone to have a chance to secure their belongings. She'd never expected them to ransack the entire home.

"Actually," Clara smirked, "we might have taken some things that were attached, at one point."

"And what would that be, exactly?"

"That is not your concern." Clara had the temerity to blush. "And Harry made me promise you'd never know."

Della nodded solemnly. Her parents would be furious. She thought of all that crying she'd just done. She thought of the woman she'd grown up to be during her time at Westfield Manor. The young girl who arrived here eight years ago would've put each and every item back in its rightful place and begged her parents' forgiveness. That girl would never have left the house to begin with.

The woman Della was now—the Baroness of Kinloss—could not be bothered to care about ornamental vases and silverware. If her mother became apoplectic over her missing tableware, then so be it.

"And how are we to get all of this," Della gestured around them, "to Kinloss? The journey will be difficult enough, just getting ourselves there safely—"

"Again," Clara began with a smile, "that is not of your concern. Let me worry about that."

Della considered that for a moment. She'd followed Clara's lead thus far in terms of their move to Kinloss, and the world hadn't crumbled. Even thinking about the complicated logistics of transporting herself, her household, and all of their belongings to Scotland made her head spin. To her, it seemed an impossible task. To Clara, it seemed a challenge, one she appeared eager to undertake.

"I suppose you have everything well in hand." Della ran her hand over the corner of one trunk, feeling the leather straps that held the metal buckles.

"We were just about to have supper," Clara said, grabbing her arm once more. "Everyone will be glad to see you."

Della didn't know about that. She'd decided to uproot their lives and give them what felt like an unimaginable choice: to leave the country with her, or potentially lose their positions—or their livelihoods depending on the mercurial moods of her parents.

"Miss Della!" Gwendoline arose from her seat at the table, approaching her with significant enthusiasm, but a much gentler hug than Clara had. "How was your trip? London must be so incredible, I cannot even imagine all the adventure you've had!"

Della so often thought of Gwendoline as a much younger girl than she'd been at her age only a few years ago. With the unbridled excitement shining in her eyes at the thought of the big city, she truly looked it. She practically bounced on the tips of her toes in front of her.

"It was lovely," Della lied. She didn't have the energy to explain the kinds of *adventure* she'd been up to, but she didn't want to shatter the image of London that Gwendoline held. It wasn't her place to impart that particular dose of reality.

"Sit down," Mrs. Goldsmith said, gesturing to Della's empty seat at the table. "Everyone, sit. I did not cook all of this to sit here watching it go cold."

Della laughed. She hadn't missed this place, not the furniture or the wallpaper or even whatever fixtures that Clara had somehow unaffixed. She had missed them, though. She'd missed the sight of each of their faces and the passing of bowls of stew and chunks of bread. She even held a fondness for the way they all seemed to forget their manners and no one cared which fork or spoon anyone else used.

"Clara has told us congratulations are in order," Mrs. Goldsmith said once everyone had begun eating her delicious roast and gravy. Her smile was so kind. It reminded Della of Alice, and that sent a twinge of regret through her heart. She'd left a letter for her, too, but just as with Andrew, it no longer felt like nearly enough.

"I don't know about that." Della stared at her plate. "It is just a title. It was . . . a gift. From my late mother. I am grateful for it, but I did nothing to earn it."

"Oh, please," Clara scoffed. A bit of potato flew off her fork as she dropped it against her plate. "You did nothing? My goodness." She shook her head, and Della felt sufficiently chastised, but she had no idea what for. "You fought the people who had taken it from you. You stood up to the people who were profiting off of your estate."

She'd never seen Clara so angry, and Della felt mired in guilt that it was on her behalf. She looked at each of their faces, some tightened in anger and others in discomfort. She'd brought all of this on all of them, and once again, Della couldn't help but feel that to know her was a burden in and of itself.

"I must say"—Della set down her own fork and lay her napkin on the table next to her plate—"to all of you, I am truly sorry for all of this. I had no intention of . . . upending everything for everyone. I'm sure Clara has discussed this with each of you, but you are more than welcome to come to Kinloss with me. I certainly hope that you do, as I would be lost without you."

She tried to laugh, to inject some humor into an increasingly tense moment. There was nothing for it, though. Each face looked back at her with a shocked expression, as if they hadn't expected her to speak to them directly about this.

"But if you would like to stay in my parents' employ, I would not blame you. They are . . . unpredictable, and I would hate to see any of you suffer because of their ire toward me. If you'd like to seek positions elsewhere, please know you will receive a superb reference from me." Della heaved in a deep breath. She'd been talking so fast she'd forgotten to take in the adequate air to continue speaking. Or living, almost.

"You have nothing to apologize for, my dear." Mrs. Goldsmith reached across the table to clasp Della's hand. "I am so glad for your mother, because this gift of hers is the first show of any affection I've seen from your family since you fell ill."

Della's head dropped low, as if in shame. She couldn't meet Mrs. Goldsmith's eyes. They were too forgiving, so much more than she deserved.

"Gwendoline and I have discussed it, and we'd love to come with you to Kinloss." She squeezed Della's hand once more. "As long as you don't expect Scottish food. I'm afraid I've no idea what that is."

Della laughed, as did everyone else at the table.

"You know that I am coming with you," Clara said. Her grin was smug. "Even if you did not want me to join you, someone would have to pry me off the top of the carriage."

"I would, unfortunately, be the poor fool peeling her off the top of the carriage," Harry said, raising a hand in salute. It was a historic moment, Harold Stanton making a joke. Della hadn't known he was capable of such a thing. "So I'd really rather we just go along with everyone else."

Della smiled. Her eyes were becoming misty again, and she couldn't stand it. She'd cried enough for this life and the next. Even if these were particularly happy tears, she did not want to waste any more time crying.

"I would love to join you as well," said Silas, their quiet, overly formal jack-of-all-trades.

"You know," Della told him, "we may very well need to hire more people. I don't see a need for you to do the work of three men. You decide which position you'd best like to keep, and it's yours."

"Thank you, my lady," Silas said, ducking his head in a seated version of a bow.

"Oh, none of that." Della waved him away. "I am the same person I was when I last left this place, and I would hope you'd treat me as such."

As Della spoke those words, she realized they couldn't be further from the truth. The person who had returned to Westfield Manor was someone else. Not because of her title, those were just words. She was a different person because of Andrew.

The Della of weeks ago had been infatuated with him, nearly obsessed with his words and fascinated with extrapolating hazy childhood memories. She was in love with an idea. A very specific potential future.

Now, Della knew exactly how that future could feel, what it could look like. She knew the sensation of waking up next to him, of his lips on hers. She knew what it was to love him, and she thought she knew what it was to have him love her, too. No one had ever risked so much for her. No one had ever put her first.

Andrew was no longer a potentiality or an idea born from memory. For a fortnight, he'd been her reality. And then she'd left him. Guilt and regret and fear swam around in her chest, drowning her lungs and agitating her heart.

"Della seems . . . overwrought," she heard Clara say. "Let's give her a moment alone."

Around her, everyone began gathering dishes and discussing plans for packing up the rest of the kitchens and renting carriages for the impending journey. They were talking about important details that Della ought to know, but she couldn't speak. She couldn't think properly anymore. Della sat for long moments, trapped in her own thoughts.

"What happened?" Clara asked, coming to sit in the chair next to her at the table. Della had no idea how long she'd been sitting there since everyone else had vacated the room. It was possible they'd packed up the remainder of the house around her. Perhaps the dining table and chairs were all that remained.

"I left," Della admitted. It was a confession, an admission of but a small percentage of the guilt she felt.

"What do you mean?" Clara leaned in further, crossing her legs and leaning forward, her chin resting on an elbow she'd placed on her knee. "I know that you left, because you're here now, but—"

"No," Della huffed. Her anger at her own behavior began to

boil over. She picked up her napkin, the only thing left on the table, and threw it to the floor. "I didn't just leave London, Clara, I left *him*."

"Why?" Clara asked. Her voice was a shocked whisper, and Della didn't want to answer. There wasn't an explanation that would make any sense. She'd felt how she felt, and she'd reacted how she reacted. She'd never regretted anything more, but she didn't know how to tell anyone that.

"I was scared," Della admitted. Once her anger faded, she was left with a mortifying sadness. She'd had the only thing she'd ever wanted in this life, and she'd left him behind. "But what was I supposed to do, Clara?" Her voice was exasperated, weighed down by sleep deprivation and complete emotional depletion. "I could not ask him to leave everything for me. He is selfless enough to do just that."

Della rolled her eyes at that, like she was cursing her own words. Her own feelings.

"I had a problem, and he fixed it for me." She sighed again, looking down at the fingernails she'd picked to death along the ride back from London. "And he cannot do it anymore. I won't allow him to. He would do anything for anyone, and I cannot let him exhaust himself and . . ." She heaved an angry breath. "I cannot let him become another person who only cares for me out of obligation."

Tears streamed down her face just as they had in the carriage, and Della gave in to the rush of feeling that poured out of her. She didn't think she had anymore to give, but she should never have doubted her own ability to feel.

"I would so much rather be alone than have him tether himself to me out of a sense of duty. Or honor, or something. Because it's the right thing to do. He would lose himself in caring for me."

Clara picked up Della's napkin off the floor and handed it back to her. Della knew she needed it. She could feel tears and snot creating a disgusting trail down her face. She wiped her nose and dabbed at her eyes, awaiting Clara's response. She was waiting but a few more moments, though that response was not even remotely what she was expecting.

"My God, that's bloody ridiculous." Clara rolled her eyes. "Complete rubbish, everything you just said."

"Clara!" Della almost wanted to laugh at the absurdity of it all, of pouring out her heart and voicing her deepest fears and getting *rubbish* in return. She wouldn't, because she was mortally offended, but she did want to. "Have you no compassion?"

"I wasn't finished." Clara rolled those eyes again, but then her expression turned uncharacteristically serious. "Della, I need you to listen to me." She removed the napkin from her clenched fist, unfolding that hand and covering it with hers. "Are you listening?" she asked, one brow arched in mock gravity.

"Of course I'm listening. What else am I to do?" Della really was far too bone weary for a conversation of this magnitude, but she didn't appear to have been given a choice.

"Good." Clara patted the hand she still held, sandwiching it between both of hers. "No one could ever lose themselves in caring for you."

"But—" Della started to refute. Her parents had, she thought immediately. Her mother especially. Caring for Della had made her cold, and it had broken her heart so fully that there was simply nothing left of it anymore.

"No." Clara's voice was stern, authoritative in a way Della hadn't known she was capable of. "Listen to me," she demanded. "I know you are thinking of your stepmother, the wretch. She made you feel as if you are unlovable, as if caring for you is some exhausting chore. But I have been here with you for nearly eight years. Each and every day. In truth, we've grown up together. Have you once seen me *lose myself*, as you say Andrew is doomed to?"

Clara didn't give her time to answer. She wasn't planning to, anyway. She wasn't going to argue a moot point.

"And this sense of obligation! Whatever that means. Nonsense. What obligation would Andrew have to you, anyway? You played in the garden together as children. Do you know where the people I played with as children are now? I certainly do not. I don't remember their names, let alone have some duty to care for them."

"I understand what you're saying, but—" Della tried to interject on her own behalf, but Clara was having none of it.

"I am not finished." Clara arched a pointed brow. "Everyone who lives here has an obligation to you in some way, because you are the lady of the house in which we work. But you gave each of us a more than fair choice—to be freed of that obligation or to stay with you."

Della's eyes teared up again. She had to be defying the limits of her body's natural capabilities at this point, she'd cried so many tears.

"All of us chose you." Clara spoke so plainly, so simply. As if she weren't changing Della's entire perspective on herself. "Just because your parents weren't capable of loving you properly does not mean the rest of us suffer the same affliction. Andrew certainly has no such problem."

Della sniffled once. "Only time will tell, I suppose."

CHAPTER THIRTY-SEVEN

DELLA AWOKE AT first light yet again. She'd exhausted herself with tears and emotions and silent goodbyes to the stairs and the wallpaper and the carpets. There was but one thing she had left to do before they all left Westfield Manor forever.

She sat behind her writing desk one last time. Clara had tried to convince her to take it with them, but the packing had really become excessive. There were only a few sheets of paper left, the rest tucked safely away in one of her trunks with all of Andrew's letters. She couldn't think of him right now, though, unless she wanted to cry again.

The first letter was to her brother. They'd always been so different. He'd always been groomed to be the next viscount. She was groomed to marry well. They had so little in common. But still, she'd loved him. That he was her half brother never mattered, so it stood to reason that finding out he was not truly her brother at all shouldn't have mattered. And it hadn't, really.

Until Andrew told her about their outing to the club. What David had said about her, how he held such resentment and repressed anger. It was enough for Della to sever the last ties she had to him, however fraying and weak they'd been in the first place.

~~Dear~~ David,

~~While you will always be the brother I grew up with, you must know that you mean less to me than the dirt under my boots.~~

I fear that you haven't considered what your life might be like once Mother and Father are gone, beyond possessing the wealth that's been stolen from other far more deserving people. Andrew tells me you have all of these grand plans for your viscountcy, but I fear that you will always be miserably alone.

~~I'm sure that you'll seek a wife at some point, because Heaven knows Father will not rest until you've secured an heir. I do hope that you'll be kinder to her than you have been to me. Even so, I do fear that no one could ever truly love you.~~ I'm inclined to believe that everyone is worthy of love by virtue of their own innate humanity, but therein lies the issue. You have lost all of your humanity. Whether it was the excessive cruelty or the carelessness or the copious drinking, you've lost everything that ever made you capable of caring for others.

I hope you find some peace in this life, whatever that looks like for a spoiled aristocrat like yourself.

Della didn't sign the letter, because she'd already decided he'd never read it. It was written at a much higher level than a man who failed his way through Eton could comprehend. She tossed the paper into the fire, and she watched it turn to ash. She'd sworn to leave her family behind here, and that was exactly what she was going to do.

Her father came next.

Father,

I don't know what it means to know you any longer. To think that when I'd run into your office as a girl and sit on your knee, when you'd tug on my hair ribbon just to retie it for me, you were in that very office swindling others. Sending people to the poor house for your own gain. ~~I don't know if it matters to you that I think~~ you are despicable~~, but I very much do~~.

I've come to realize what it means to make a choice~~, and~~

~~you've made so many poor ones~~. You had a choice, what was in my best interest or what made you the most money. For years, you chose money over ~~your own family. Over~~ me, ~~at least~~.

The only child you have left is an incredible disappointment, and that may very well be punishment enough for what you've done. I hope you never feel the destitution you've put others through, because that is something no one deserves.

But David Harris being the only legacy you leave in this world? That, you do so deserve.

At that, Della actually laughed. What a gift, to be able to laugh at her own pain. It was as cleansing as the tears or the writing itself. As she watched the second letter burn, Della felt the warmth on her smiling face.

That smile only began to fade when she thought of what she must do next.

Esther,

~~Even now, my first instinct is to apologize to you. For not being the daughter you wanted, among other things. I've been trying not to do that, apologize so much. People have been telling me I do so extravagantly.~~

~~So, I've decided I owe you no apology.~~

~~I won't apologize for taking what's rightfully mine. I won't even apologize for embarrassing you and ruining the only thing you've ever truly cared about: your reputation.~~

~~I've also decided I do not want an apology from you, either. Though I know I would never receive one, anyway.~~ Your words are as meaningless to me as I have been to you these past eight years. ~~Some people are just not meant to be mothers, or to care for others at all.~~

Where my memories of Father are now forever tainted by his betrayal, my memories of you are clouded by your neglect. Finding out about your duplicity was not an additional slight, it was an explanation of the way I've felt since you abandoned me: that you never deserved to be anyone's mother.

*Please inform your beloved Dr. Seagle that his services are
no longer needed as far as I am concerned, and if he ever attempts to touch me again, I will react with the utmost violence.*

Lastly, Della began a letter to her mother. Not Esther, who
no longer held that title in her mind, but the woman who had
given birth to her. She sat for long moments, waiting for the
words to come. But they wouldn't, because she was writing to
someone she'd never known, someone who was more absent in
her memory than any stranger.

In the end, she had little to say.

*Do not worry, Mother. I will take good care of Kinloss, and
your family legacy is safe in my deformed, fevered hands.*

Della smiled again. The letter to Esther she threw with the
rest in the fire, but she ran her fingers over those few remaining
words to her mother, the only thing she truly had left to say to
her family.

She carried that piece of paper with her as they prepared to
leave, and Della finally took one last lap through the first floor.
She ended up in the sitting room, standing in front of that sofa
Esther loved so much. She'd always sit there, in that exact spot,
whenever she decided to grace the manor with her presence.

Della left the note on the side table. Whether anyone ever
saw it, she did not care. She looked over it once more, saying the
words aloud as she read.

*Do not worry, Mother. I will take good care of Kinloss, and
your family legacy is safe in my deformed, fevered hands.*

Then, for the last time, she left.

CHAPTER THIRTY-EIGHT

THE JOURNEY TOOK every bit of two weeks, and they were perhaps the single most exhausting fourteen days of Della's entire life. Her constitution was weak, her bones weary, and her joints unimaginably stiff. Still though, her spirits remained oddly high. She had indeed left all of her melancholy behind at Westfield Manor, and she enjoyed the lively conversations and unpredictable antics of traveling with the household that had become her family.

Somehow, they'd made a game of passing along a single, lonely spoon among them. They'd been just about to leave in their enormous parade of carriages when Mrs. Goldsmith nearly tripped over herself to run back into the house for a forgotten spoon. It was a favorite of hers, apparently, and she had no place to put it since the trunks were all already packed. So, she sat with it in her lap for the first day of their journey. Gwendoline took it, placing it in Harry's seat when they left the coaching inn the next morning. Harry, of course, passed it on to Clara, who managed to tuck it into the side of one of Silas's boots. He'd felt the cold metal through his socks and nearly jumped out of his skin. It gave Clara quite the thrill, until Silas convinced Harry to drop the spoon down the back of her gown.

It was all unbelievably silly, but it was something to pass the time. While Della had thought the traveling monotonous and never-ending, she did enjoy how everything seemed so exciting to everyone else. They rotated who rode in each carriage, and no matter who she was with, Della watched as they observed wide open fields of wildflowers and huge, sloping hills. Taller trees than they'd ever seen and wildlife none of them could identify.

Harry had become obsessed with pinpointing the crest on each carriage they passed. Silas had to be retrieved from the stables each morning, as he much preferred spending his time with the horses. Mrs. Goldsmith always seemed to disappear into the kitchens of each coaching inn, whether she'd been invited to or not. Gwendoline spoke fervently about the gowns everyone wore. She wouldn't go up to people and speak, as many others did in the common rooms at the inns, but she'd whisper about them to Della or Clara like the worst gossip on the traveling road. Though her gossip was usually complimentary. Gwendoline had been so inspired that Della knew she'd have them all dressed in the newest finery within weeks. Where Gwen was shy and wouldn't approach a soul, Clara spoke to everyone. At the start, Della had counted the people she watched Clara converse with, but she'd abandoned the effort during a particularly crowded dinner just outside of the border of Scotland.

They'd told stories and shared laughs. There were late nights and early mornings, quick stops in the middle of nowhere to roam about and stretch their legs. Della had never considered how an arduous journey like this, especially one that was a source of excitement for so many, could bond them together so deeply. They'd started along this road as a band of misfits, a group of people who were less than favorable in the eyes of society. Each had no other place in the world, and that sense of listlessness was exactly what brought them there. Now, more than ever, they were family. Della felt that deep down in her aching bones.

As they neared Kinloss, the energy in the carriage began to stir into something exhilarating. Della had only felt this sense of impending joy before in anticipation of one of Andrew's letters. Perhaps that's what this was, then, a sign of desperately wanted correspondence. She didn't want to get her hopes up, though. While she looked forward to her new life with her new family at Kinloss, she had to imagine it without him. Even doing so, picturing her remaining days, months, and years without him by her side, set her teeth on edge. It wasn't right. It would never be, but she was certain that would be her reality.

Della heaved out a deep sigh as she looked out the window yet again. It seemed all she'd been able to do for days, lose her sense of time and place as she watched the world pass by.

"What is the matter?" Clara asked. She gently kicked Della's shin with her bare foot. She'd taken to abandoning her shoes as soon as the carriage was in motion. "I know that sigh. One of your particularly unhappy ones, if I recall."

It was just them in the carriage at the moment. Silas sat with the coachman and Gwendoline and Mrs. Goldsmith were in the carriage behind them. Harry rode alone in the coach that was overstuffed with their belongings. He'd said he wanted to read, and he couldn't do so with Clara's constant speaking. Clara told him reading in a moving carriage would make him ill. Seeing the way they interacted with each other made Della almost sick with jealousy.

Oh well, she thought. She had always been ill anyway.

"I am not unhappy," Della responded. Her thoughts and feelings were jumbled, and she didn't think she could identify them. Still, she could confidently say she wasn't unhappy. That she had no idea what she was instead mattered little. She was sitting on the side of the carriage facing the opposite direction in which they rode. She saw things as they passed them, looking backwards instead of up ahead. Della felt that was apt.

"You could have fooled me," Clara said. She tucked her feet up underneath her on the carriage bench. "I mean that genuinely. You've seemed as pleased as the rest of us, but every so often, you get this faraway look in your eye. As if part of your heart is elsewhere and you're trying to find it."

Della hung her head. She'd resorted to picking at her fingernails again, and her cuticles were in a truly horrible state.

"I know that you miss him," Clara whispered. Della didn't like this, being spoken to in such a gentle tone. Not from Clara, anyway. She was a human explosion, and her speech reflected that. That she was treating Della so delicately made her feel as emotionally fragile as she'd always been physically.

"I do," Della admitted. There was no use in denying it. She did miss him terribly, and she was not a strong enough actor to convince Clara otherwise. "But I must make my peace with it. With him. I regret leaving, and perhaps I will write him again later on, but I suppose he'll need some time. To be hurt or angry with me or to come to a decision on what we are to be now."

"Some time, you say?" Clara spoke absently, her line of sight straying from Della's face to some point out the window. She tilted her head, seemingly straining her neck to see as far forward as she possibly could. "You think he requires time to come to a decision?"

Her words were puzzling, her expression even more so. She wouldn't meet her eyes anymore, and her lips were upturned in a strange sort of smirk. Della wasn't sure if Clara could ever be considered devious, but she did appear so at that very moment.

"Yes." Della nodded, thinking that Clara simply hadn't been listening. She hadn't been paying attention, and that must be why she required repetition. "I left, and while I hope how much I care about him was rather clear in my letter, I still should've spoken with him. I should have stayed. He's very thoughtful and intentional, and he'll need his time to think about what he wants."

"Well." Clara sat back in her seat, abandoning her intense study of the scenery ahead of them. She crossed her arms over her chest. "He has had ample time, with all of the traveling you've been doing."

"You cannot rush these things, Clara," Della sighed. It was one of her unhappy sighs, she realized now that Clara had pointed it out.

"Yes." Clara hummed in agreement. Then she giggled under her breath. "I suppose these things do work out on their own time."

"And what are you laughing about?" Della asked. The scenery they passed was different now, as if they'd entered a village. She saw homes and gardens and people. It was a wonderfully refreshing change from the sea of amorphous green they'd spent days riding through.

"Oh, nothing," Clara answered with forced nonchalance. She reached to the floor of the carriage to retrieve her shoes. She slipped them on her feet and tucked the laces in rather than tying them. She would trip over herself once those laces slipped back out, Della knew it.

Della had absolutely no idea what was going on, but she felt that sense of anticipation spike in her heart. It was a shower of sparkles within her ribs. Never had she felt that particular sensation so intensely. The carriage began to slow, and she pressed a hand against her breastbone to calm her sparking chest. It wasn't particularly helpful, but the pressure eased the ache in the joints that held her ribcage together.

"Stay here," Clara told her, looking at Della with wild, wide eyes. "Do *not* move."

She froze, quite literally, that hand still held just below her collarbone. She lacked a certain awareness, and that warm, incandescent anticipation turned to a cold fear.

"What is the matter?" Della asked. She tried to turn her body toward the window, her mind racing with all the horrid possibilities. She thought the entire barony might be ablaze. Or someone lay dead in the road. She thought of injury and death and tragedy.

"No," Clara said firmly. She stopped Della's movements, not allowing her to see anything. "I tell you not to move and you immediately move." She huffed.

The carriage stopped and Clara practically jumped out. Della heard a commotion, and she assumed it was Harry yelling at her from two coaches back. She only hoped she wouldn't trip over the laces of her boots. There was more noise, and Della couldn't decipher it. She couldn't decide what to do, whether she should obey Clara's fervent command to stay here or if she should disembark and insert herself into whatever chaos had befallen her new home.

As she was still deciding, a shadow fell over the still-open door of the carriage.

"Della," he whispered. She barely heard him, it was so faint. He wasn't smiling, but his was a face she didn't think she'd ever see again. Della felt her own smile overtake her. Behind that smile was a rising tide of relief. She had more questions than answers, but he was here. She was looking at those wayward curls and a half-untied cravat. His strong brows and those fathomless eyes.

"Andrew," she whispered back.

He stood in the light of the sun, she still hid in the dark of the carriage. Andrew extended a hand in her direction.

Well, that was her decision made.

CHAPTER THIRTY-NINE

ANDREW ALL BUT ran outside when he'd heard the carriages approaching. It could've been anyone, but he'd hoped it was her. Them, he should say. But all of his hope was for her. Before they'd come, he'd been roaming about the house unpacking trunks and pulling sheets off of dusty furniture. The Harrises' crooked estate agent was long gone, and they were clearly rather lax in keeping up with their duties, given the fact that the house was in a beyond neglected state.

Andrew felt odd being here alone, like he was lingering somewhere he shouldn't be. This was Della's property, and he didn't know if Della wanted him here. He didn't know if Della wanted him at all. He was here for an explanation, nothing else. Preparing rooms for their arrival was just something to pass the time, he told himself.

It had only been several hours since his own arrival, and he heard the crunch of gravel as he explored the wide, open pantry in the over-large kitchen. Kinloss was an overwhelming estate, and he'd scarcely learned to find his way around. He took several wrong turns on the way to the front hall, ending up in one of the parlors. He didn't know why there were so many parlors.

When he reached the front door, he nearly tripped down the stone staircase. There were so many carriages, and Silas waved from his perch atop the first coach. Andrew couldn't remember if he'd waved back.

Then Clara sprawled out of that very same carriage, and it was a true display of athleticism that she managed to land on her feet. Her smile was beaming, and she rushed to Andrew with the force she'd used to catapult herself out of the vehicle.

"I knew you didn't need time," Clara said, squeezing his arm as she walked by.

He opened his mouth to respond with an expression of his confusion, but she was already moving swiftly toward the house behind him. She pointed in the direction of the carriage from whence she'd come. He took that bit of direction for what it was—an order—and marched to the carriage's open door.

"Della," he'd whispered. It was all he'd been able to say. Through all of his traveling here, he'd planned out so much he wanted to tell her, and all of that conscious thought and eloquent speech abandoned him at the sight of her.

He reached for her, as he could do nothing but. Her hand clasped his, and finally, she smiled. He was completely shattered or melted or burned. He felt as if he'd left the world of the living behind for weeks, and now he'd just become something new. Something that was entirely hers, if she'd have him.

"Andrew." Her voice barely reached his ears, but her hand squeezed his, and that was so much more than enough.

Della stood as far upright as she could in the dark confines of the carriage, and he hesitated to move. He wasn't sure how to proceed. He'd touched every inch of her skin, but he had no idea if she'd want him to touch her at all now. Eventually, as she struggled to lower herself to the ground, his free hand rested at her waist. That damned hip. She didn't say it aloud, but he could tell she was thinking it. It was such a gift to be able to look at her and know the line of her thoughts. It was such a privilege to look at her at all.

Her right hand gripped his shoulder, her left still entwined with his. She found her footing, and he reached into the carriage to find her walking stick. Andrew had to extricate himself from her to do so, and it was more painful than that morning he'd woken up alone. Then, she'd been long gone. Like smoke in the wind. Now, she was right in front of him. Close enough to touch, and he didn't know if he could.

He didn't know if showing up here was a grave mistake.

"Andrew," she whispered again as he passed her walking stick along, "I believe we need to talk."

Those words were terror inducing on their own, but the downtrodden expression on her face confirmed that he was indeed in the midst of a horrible reality of his own making. He'd come here for an explanation. One more chance, he'd told himself. He'd give them one more chance before he left her alone forever. It seemed she was eager to take that one chance and use it to break him.

"Of course." He nodded, his hands behind his back. He didn't trust those hands or his own ability to control them.

Around them, he eventually realized, the carriages had become hives of activity. There were trunks everywhere, more than he'd ever seen in any one place. The coachmen helped everyone disembark and unload. Clara ran the entire length of the drive. Mrs. Goldsmith waved Harry away from several of the trunks. Andrew assumed those were her kitchen implements and she was trying to ensure their safety. Harry began directing the coachmen, which was admirable as none of them, Andrew included, had any clue where to put anything. Gwendoline stood in front of one of the large bay windows, staring up at the height of the turrets. Her neck was bent back as far as it would go, and she seemed frozen in awe.

Andrew knew that feeling. He found comfort in it, actually. Freezing in the face of a chance at happiness had been easier. He'd forced himself to take action now, just this one last time, and now he was certain the fragments of his heart would be handed to him on an old, rusted silver platter.

They should talk, she'd said.

He wasn't sure he was capable of that, of listening to her

dismiss him and responding in a polite, respectable way.

"Should you not settle in first?" Andrew said. It was one last effort to postpone the inevitable. It wouldn't make it easier, but he wouldn't have to face it now, either. It was an opportunity to freeze once more. "You've only just arrived after such a long journey."

He looked at her in earnest, now that she was in the vast sunlight. Her hair was escaping its pins, and her gown was terribly wrinkled from all that time spent in such a confined space. Her eyes were clear, though. There was none of the exhaustion he expected to see. Rather, there seemed to be a sense of peace. He thought she'd appear softened, as if almost asleep. Instead, she was softened in just the opposite way—as if she'd just woken up.

"Oh, yes," she agreed, looking down at her feet. She wore those riding boots again. The sight of them was so endearing that Andrew's chest ached. "I suppose we should. Everyone is"—she looked around them at the flurry of motion—"rather excited to be here."

"I see," he chuckled. Despite the tension between them, the rest of the traveling party seemed to feel no such apprehension. Their thrill was palpable, even in the warm Scottish air that surrounded the estate. "Please, don't let me stop you. Go and see your new home."

At that, Della smiled. It was so overly bright, his eyes almost couldn't stand it. His body warned him to turn away, to protect himself, as if he'd been staring right into a raging fire and waiting there for it to consume him.

"Would you . . ." Della took a deep breath in the middle of her sentence. She looked down at her feet again for a moment, then met his eyes once more. There was a certain vulnerability there he'd never seen. Immediately, he understood that she'd never before let him see it. "Would you come with me?"

"Of course," he answered reflectively. Of course he'd go with her. Of course he'd stay for a while, or for all of his remaining days. It was always his instinct when it came to her, to any question she had, to offer a certain, unrestrained affirmative. Whatever she asked of him, it would always be yes. Even if, at the end of the day, she asked him to leave.

Della turned away from him to begin her very first walk into Kinloss, into the home she now rightfully owned.

Without warning, her hand wandered over the sleeve of his coat, slipping her arm through his and resting her hand at the crook of his elbow. Her doe eyes looked up at him once more in uncertainty, as if she were asking for permission or anticipating a refusal of her touch.

Somehow, she still didn't know his answer would always be *yes*.

He didn't voice that, not yet. Now wasn't the time. With her fingers tucked into his left arm, his right hand covered hers. He squeezed gently, just as she had a few long moments ago. Her face softened. There was that newly awakened peace again. He would do anything to keep that look on her face, to give her that tranquility forever.

Della leaned on him the entire way up the stone stairs, and some reckless part of Andrew hoped she wasn't just in need of help, but she was also in want of him.

CHAPTER FORTY

DELLA HAD NEVER been so overwhelmed in all her life. Kinloss was a massive, sprawling estate, and she was suddenly its owner. Clara had worked miracles assuring all of their belongings made the journey safely, and she continued to work them as they unpacked it all. Where Clara and Harry were methodically sorting everything out and Mrs. Goldsmith had already taken off to assemble the kitchen, Della stood in the hall in a daze. It felt as if the home spun around her, so awash with activity, and she stayed stagnant. She wasn't necessarily immobile in a physical sense. She *could* move, she supposed. She simply had no notion of where to go.

"I took the liberty of . . . preparing some things. Just dusting off the furniture and airing out the rooms. Perhaps I should not have, but I arrived—" Andrew spoke lowly, as if he didn't want to be overheard.

"Andrew." Despite the sinking discomfort in her chest, Della smirked. "Do not apologize. Please do not make me say it again."

He smiled, too, and some of the weight fell off of her shoulders. She didn't know how to do this—to talk to him. Even the confrontation with her parents hadn't felt so high stakes. Nothing had ever been as important as this moment, this second chance with him, and she had no idea where to start. She could tell him not to apologize, though, so that's what she did.

"How did you arrive so early?" she asked him. It was the shock of her life to find him standing there right outside her coach, but she hadn't stopped long enough to think how such a thing was even possible.

"I left shortly after you did." He chuckled, a dark, self-deprecating sound. "As soon as I could, really. Nearly ran out of the house without my trousers on."

Della shook her head. While the mental image was undoubtedly funny, she was puzzled. Her letter had made it clear that whatever they were to be, it was up to him. She'd told him in no uncertain terms that she was his, and she didn't see a reason for him to rush across the country to find her.

"Why?" Della asked finally. She felt her brows knit up in confusion. Behind her, up the stairs, she heard Clara and Harry shouting something unintelligible back and forth. She heard a laugh, so she assumed it wasn't something too serious.

"What do you mean, why?" His own brows met in the middle of his face, and he leaned in closer, as if they were whispering secrets in the middle of the grand hall. "I . . . I needed an explanation. You left, without saying goodbye, and I needed to know why. And I had these plans to bring flowers and call on you, ask to begin a courtship with the lady of the house." Andrew rolled his eyes. She didn't know if that bit of rudeness was for her or himself. "But that felt so forward, to turn up to the home of a baroness uninvited and attempt to court her. I am not nearly that bold, but I wanted to do this properly, Della. Everything except asking for your father's permission. I would sooner fall on my own sword. And I don't even have a sword—"

"Wait," Della interrupted. She put her hands up in front of her as if in defense. He was speaking too fast. Her calm, staid man had become intensely frazzled. She almost didn't recognize him, and she hadn't the faintest idea what was happening here. What was he talking about? "I did leave without a goodbye, and for that I am so dearly sorry."

Andrew tried to protest. She knew it was about their rule

against apologizing, but this one was warranted. She'd never needed to apologize more for anything else in her life.

"I left, but I did give you an explanation." Della felt her own brows knit up in confusion. "Or at least, I thought I did. I thought it was an explanation. I thought it was enough. And you must know by now, Andrew, that I do not require courtship . . . or even propriety."

Andrew stood in silence for long moments, and Della knew there were things happening around them, but neither moved. She was stagnant again, but this time, he was with her. Right in front of her, staring with a quizzical, perplexed expression that she didn't often see. He was such a deeply intelligent man. He could predict novels' dramatic endings and anticipate the outcomes of court proceedings. She always felt he was one step ahead of everyone else. Now, he was at her side, both literally and figuratively, and they were both dumbfounded.

"I believe we need to sit," he said, taking her arm and steering her in a direction she'd yet to go within the house. They came to a large sitting room outfitted in dated but classic damask wallpaper in a light rose gold. It was distinctly feminine, and Della took a moment to appreciate her late mother's taste. It was an odd thing to do, to come to appreciate someone she'd never truly had a chance to meet. Sitting in this room, Della had a feeling she and the former baroness were somewhat alike. She had a feeling that she would've liked her very much.

"This is a room for sitting, yes?" Andrew asked.

Della nodded. There was nothing else to do. He continued to steer her in the direction of a large settee covered in a light-pink silk. She sat. He paced. It was interesting for Della, watching someone else move about a room in an effort to calm themselves, in the way she and Clara so often did. If she weren't so exhausted, she'd stand back up and join him. It would soothe her, matching his steps and tracing patterns in the carpet with their feet. Mentally, it would calm her. Physically, it would further destroy an already-debilitated body. She'd done too much of that already lately.

"I do not know what you are speaking of," Andrew finally said. He marched laps around the room with one hand on his hip and the other chewing on the back of his thumbnail. Even though Della sat, she picked at her own nails in a similar motion.

"Well, about that at least, we have an understanding." Della let out an almost rueful chuckle. "But how is it that neither you nor I know anything about a matter that's exclusively between the two of us?"

Andrew sat, finally. He placed himself on the sofa opposite her, leaning forward to rest his elbows on his knees and his head in his hands.

"I've no idea," he muttered. His voice was muffled by those hands, and they drew Della's line of sight. It wouldn't do for her to be thinking about them. It wasn't helpful or productive, but she couldn't stop.

They sat in silence for what must have been half an eternity. Besides the building tension between them, it was quite comfortable. Della felt that overwhelming peace again, and she found that she liked the sight of him in this setting. This was home—in a room and a person and a feeling.

"So." Andrew stood up again abruptly. He began to pace, walking closer and closer to her with each lap he took. "Here is what I cannot grasp." He took a deep breath, and he looked over at her in a quick, fleeting glance, as if to make sure she was paying attention. That made Della want to laugh, the idea that he could ever be right in front of her and she wouldn't be paying attention.

"You left." He stopped walking. That fleeting glance turned into a soul-baring stare. "But you mentioned an explanation."

"Yes," Della nodded. "In my letter, I wrote—"

"Letter?" Andrew's face tightened up even more as he interrupted her, and Della hadn't thought that possible. "What letter? I know we've exchanged many, but—"

"Oh, no," Della gasped. She stood up. Where he'd now stopped his frantic walking, she resumed hers. "You did not get my letter." It wasn't a question, it was a statement of fact. Della had never felt such guilt or shame, even though those emotions were prevalent enough in her upbringing to symbolize them as part of the Morley crest.

"I don't suppose I did." Andrew leaned back, then he let himself slump against the sofa again. "You wrote me a letter? Before you left?" His voice had gone soft, almost broken.

"Oh no," she repeated, just realizing all that this meant. "Your mother must think so little of me, to have left her home without a word."

"You wrote *my mother* a letter too?" he asked, his brows shooting up nearly to his hairline.

"Of course!" Della despaired. She resumed her pacing. "I had to thank her for her hospitality and her support and her compassion. I would not have left without doing so. And I left the letters right on the writing desk. I assumed you'd see them. Someone would see them, anyway."

"Ah." Andrew's head fell. Della couldn't tell if he was blushing or if that was simply a shadow over his face. "That explains it. I'm sure she did find them, then. I simply did not . . . stop to look. I told you, my departure from the house was rather hasty."

Oh. So he was blushing, then. He looked almost embarrassed. There was no reason for that. No reason at all.

"Wait." Della halted her movements as soon as she realized. "So you . . . you thought I'd left without a goodbye, and you still came chasing after me?" Now her voice was broken, her eyes once again on the verge of tears.

"Of course," he answered quietly. "Would you . . . would you tell me what you wrote? In the letter?"

She took one step closer to the window, away from him. She turned her head to face the fading sun. Somehow, all of that had been so much easier to write than to say. Her heart was so much better at expressing itself in writing. But all she'd wanted for weeks was one more chance to actually speak to him this way. He was giving her an opportunity she felt she did not deserve, but she would absolutely take it.

"I do not remember word for word . . ." She turned to face him again. Took back that step she'd used to distance herself. She took another one toward him, just for good luck. "But I told you that I was leaving because I could not ask you to abandon your life for me."

He started to move, to stand up or speak or something, but she held up a hand. If she were interrupted, she'd never get through this.

"You have worked so hard for the life you've built, and I couldn't ask you to leave all of that behind. I thought that you'd come to resent me if you did. I told you that I wanted to be with you, and that you'd always be welcome here. That we could be friends again or we could be . . . more, but it had to be because you truly wanted that. It was up to you, I said."

Della heaved out a breath. For a moment, she felt so much lighter. Keeping her affection for him such a secret for so long was a heavy burden, and it was amazing to be free of it. That was, until she realized how life-changing what she'd just said was. It was even more of a risk than her unreceived letter. She'd spoken it into the air between them, and now nothing would ever be the same.

"Della," he breathed. His hands came up to cover his face once more. "If it were up to me, I'd have married you eight years ago."

She gasped. Her legs carried her to the settee and promptly gave out, leaving her sitting there in a heap. That was impossible. She didn't think he'd lie to her, not after everything, but she knew it could not be true.

"You . . ." He looked at her again, his expression agonized. "You said that you don't require courtship. Why?"

It seemed an odd change of subject, but Della could almost see his train of thought. He had a list of questions in his mind, and he was ticking them off as he went. The first question was why she'd left without warning. This was the second. Della wondered how many there'd be, but she'd answer them all just the same.

"I do not require courtship," she sighed, "because I would marry you tomorrow. Or today, if I weren't so exhausted."

Now he gasped. They were finally beginning to understand each other. Apparently, they were two people who'd wanted to marry each other for years. Knowing that was like falling into a deep sea of relief, but once Della saw the remaining despair in his face, she felt they were starting to drown in it.

"Now that we are . . . speaking," Andrew said. He stood up, waving an arm out in front of him and speaking with his hands. It was rather animated for such a docile man. "There is something I have nearly always wanted to ask you."

Della's breath caught. She might've thought her heart stopped beating, but she could hear it pounding in her ears.

"Why did you leave that night?" His voice broke, and his face fell, and the gut-wrenching hurt he felt was nearly palpable between them.

"What do you mean? What night?" She'd thought they were coming to an understanding, but now she was back to an uncomfortable confusion.

"The night that you left London. Eight years ago. Why did you leave in the middle of the night? You said you were leaving in the morning, David told me you were to leave in the morning, but by then you were . . . gone."

Della wanted to speak, to respond, but there was a clump of shame in her throat. She considered her words for a moment. They had come to a fragile understanding, but she did not want to break it.

"I was not happy about being sent away, as I'm sure you remember." Della rolled her watery eyes at her own teenage stubbornness. When it came to him, though, she was afraid she'd always be stubborn. That had nothing to do with her age.

"I . . . I wanted to see you. One last time. To say goodbye. I begged and begged Esther to let me. She denied me over and over, and eventually she told me how you really felt. That the best thing I could do was free you of the burden I'd become. That you wouldn't want me as I got sicker, and I should want someone better for you, someone whole."

Della's voice broke, and she heard an agonized groan that was not her own.

"All I wanted was you," she sobbed. "But she convinced me you could never love me, and I fled before I could wait around for you not to come. And I did it again, when I left London after the ball. My mother became a different person—a deeply unhappy person—after she spent so much time trying to fix me. I couldn't let that happen to you. She sent me away eventually. I knew you'd never do that. You'd stay, and you'd just grow to hate me."

She'd thought that if she never saw that London morning, it would never have to be over. She'd never have to feel the defeat of his absence, and she'd always get to remember him as the one person who smiled when she walked into a room. For years, all she'd had to remember him by were flashes of curls and dimples and a bunch of letters tied together with twine. Now, she had so much more.

"I did come, Della," he whispered. Her eyes were still misty, so much so that he was only a hazy silhouette in her vision. She couldn't see him properly, but she heard his tortured voice, and she felt those words in her soul. "That morning. I came to say goodbye, and she told me you were already gone. I could never resent you, let alone hate you. Being with you would never make me unhappy. It would be the pleasure of my life to care for you, if you'd let me."

Strong, heavy sobs wracked Della's body. It all rushed over her at once. That what she thought would always be her greatest mistake had in fact been another aspect of her life orchestrated and perpetrated by the person she'd called her mother.

She didn't know what to say, or if there was anything she could do to fix this. Some part of her wanted to apologize, to beg his forgiveness for the way life had managed to ruin them so fully. Della remembered their rule, though. Instead of this apology feeling warranted enough to break it, it instead felt woefully insufficient.

Della looked up at him, just once. She'd never seen that face so despondent. It was as if she could see the pieces of his broken heart lying on the plush carpet between them. She started to speak, to utter that apology, no matter how inadequate it would be.

Andrew shook his head.

CHAPTER FORTY-ONE

A S ANDREW TOOK slow, measured steps across the room, he
was surprised there was still ground underneath him on
which to walk. The entire foundation of his world had been
rocked. His entire perspective, upended.

Every decision he'd made in the last eight years, he'd chosen
based on the fact that Della didn't love him. That she didn't want
him. That she'd rather be banished to the countryside alone than
be with him. He'd fled the country, roamed all over the world,
and eaten up scraps of her attention, all because he thought he
couldn't have her.

To know that he could've . . . that every day of the eight
years they'd spent apart, she was thinking of him the way he'd
been thinking of her . . . nothing had ever made him so angry. It
wasn't her fault, and it wasn't his, but he couldn't let her see him
like this. He felt poised to explode, and he wouldn't have her hit
by shrapnel.

The room was largely empty but lit by giant, west-facing
windows. The furniture wasn't much to look at, but those
windows were a vision. For a moment, Andrew was startled by
the beauty before him. Rolling hills and verdant trees, an over-
bright sunset in splashes of the brightest orange and the lightest
purple.

He walked toward the window, mesmerized by those colors.

His gaze caught on the tallest tree he could see. It was skinny and unstable looking, and he'd almost bet it was half dead and in danger of falling. It brought him back to childhood, to the version of Della he'd done nothing but lose. If their younger selves were out there right now in those fields, he'd be climbing that sickly, half-dead tree just to impress her.

As if watching it play out in front of him, Andrew continued to imagine them there. He'd be overdressed, wearing one of his father's cravats and old boots he'd still shined. She would have a ribbon in her hair, and she'd be carrying a book around with her at all times like a beloved pet.

He would start to climb that tree, and she would gasp. He'd always treasured those gasps of surprise. Back then, he'd thought they were expressions of unexpected amazement. He thought she couldn't believe how daring he'd been. Now, even in his own mind, he saw that version of her differently. He saw her, on the ground, looking up at him with widened eyes. He thought she might be nervous, terrified of him falling.

As he watched his younger self climb back down to safety, he remembered how she'd sigh. He'd always interpreted that as something wistful or longing. That was naive of him. Now, he could see it for what it was: relief. It was that sense of peace he always felt around her. Had she really always felt it, too?

Andrew had climbed all of those trees because she always smiled at him when he came back down to the ground. Perhaps he'd never had to impress her at all. Perhaps all he'd ever needed to do was stay on the grass by her side. If he had, maybe the past eight years would've been full of those never-ending smiles. None of those terrified gasps, and none of those gut-wrenching sobs he'd heard today.

As darkness began to take over, he tried to imagine the future instead of the past. He tried to forget about the possibilities of which they were robbed. Eight years' worth of smiles and laughter and kisses and dreams. Thousands of mornings they'd both woken up alone, silently wishing for each other. All of those letters. Though they'd been a sacred connection between them, they seemed so shallow now. So many missives back and forth about the minutiae of their daily lives, all while they hadn't been able to say a word of what they truly meant to each other.

With the sun, his anger faded. His heartbeat slowed as he overthought each and every one of his feelings. Once he worked through the immediate, surface-level rage, there was a deep well of grief for all of that lost time. The worst thing about grief, though, is its longevity. There's no cure for it, no remedy for relief. There was no way to get all of those years back.

At some point, once he started counting stars, he realized he'd already missed entirely too many sunsets he could've spent with Della. It had all been out of their control, those years they'd spent apart. Now, though, they were sitting in the same room, looking up at the same inky black sky.

Andrew counted the stars in his field of vision one more time, just for good luck. Then he prayed that would be the last of Della's sunsets he'd spent with her so close but still so far away.

CHAPTER FORTY-TWO

"A NDREW," DELLA WHISPERED, finally.

He turned around. Far away from her still, but somehow, he felt closer than he'd ever been.

"You and I, we keep passing each other by like ships in the night. So close but so far away, and I do not think I can bear another near miss."

Oddly, he smiled. All she could see was the flash of his teeth in the barely there light, and he was alarmingly beautiful. That grin was something alive, the way the moonlight fell over him was almost otherworldly. Almost tinted blue, he seemed like some kind of apparition. A spirit here to haunt her with dreams of nights like this she'd missed.

"I have been on many ships," he said, rolling up onto his toes and then lowering himself back down to his heels. He was trying not to pace, Della knew. Despite his uncanny appearance, it was that familiar motion that made Della realize he was indeed real. He was here, again. "And maybe you do not see other ships when you pass by them in the night. But you hear them. You feel them. Even if you miss them, you know they have been there."

He took a breath so deep Della thought she felt it displace the air around her, and she knew, with that sixth sense she had about him, that her life was about to change forever.

"I am trying to say that I have been devoted to you for years.

And I should not have left. Even if I thought that you felt no affection for me—"

"Oh, Andrew." Della stood up abruptly, launching to her feet from the settee in an impressive show of force. "You cannot possibly continue acting as if I do not love you."

Andrew froze. Della watched it happen, from head to toe, as his blood turned to ice. She wondered if his heart was still beating below all that frigidity.

"Are you so surprised?" Della mused. His reaction was quite ridiculous. "I'm sure I have at least alluded to falling for you. For God's sake, Andrew, you are the one person from my old life I wanted to keep. I wrote to you, I worried about you, I . . ." She was so overwhelmed by it all that her words wouldn't come. They refused to manifest themselves, and her lungs emitted a frustrated breath instead.

All at once, though, Della realized that some things were beyond words. As she took each creaking step toward him, it was as if she were the fire needed to melt the sheet of ice he'd become. She'd watched him freeze, and right before her eyes, he was melting.

He reached for her as soon as she was close enough, and Della let out a blissful sigh. The hand against her cheek wasn't frigid or even cool. It was the exact warmth her life had been missing for eight years. His other hand swept locks of her thick, unbound hair off of her shoulder.

Della had forgotten about that, what she looked like. With her swollen, red eyes and hair that hadn't been brushed since they'd left the last coaching inn. She was certain she made a disastrous picture in front of him. It was not the ideal time to be declaring oneself, she realized entirely too late. The pads of his fingers traced up her neck, and all thoughts, both rational and otherwise, made a swift exit from her mind. Both his hands came to hold her face, his thumbs moving over the highpoints of her cheekbones. Della breathed in his scent. She leaned in close enough to feel his heartbeat against her own chest. That radiant sense of peace fell over her like the warmth of her favorite blanket, the one that lay somewhere in this house, having yet to be unpacked.

"I love you so much," Andrew said. His lips hovered over hers. One of his hands gripped her waist and the other twined through the strands of already tangled hair at the nape of her neck.

Della kissed him. All she had to do was tilt her head up, just enough to bump her chin against his. He reacted swiftly, pulling her closer in every way that he could. With his hands, with his lips, with his heart.

She opened her mouth once she tasted the mint on his tongue, and she sank her fingers into those untamed curls. Della heard a melting sigh, and she couldn't place who it'd come from. They were sharing breath, so she supposed it didn't matter.

Andrew broke away from her mouth, raining hot, open-mouthed kisses across her face and down her jaw. She felt him suck on the delicate skin just below her chin. She felt the brush of his teeth and the swipe of his tongue.

Della moaned something that sounded vaguely like his name. As soon as she spoke, even one broken, unintelligible word, she realized what she hadn't actually said. She stopped him with her hands on either side of his face. She tilted his head back so she could look at him. She'd never get tired of those kind, fathomless eyes turned so darkened and hungry. His pupils were blown, and he was still supernaturally lit by the moon.

"I love you," she said. He needed to hear it, and she needed to say it. Not out of exasperation or a sense of urgency, but because it was the truest thing she knew. One of the most basic things she knew about herself. She would always be ill. She would always be a baroness. She would always be in love with Andrew Lockhart.

"I know, love." He kissed her, brief, fleeting presses of his still-smiling lips. "It's all right. I know." He held her shoulders for a moment, his hands sliding down her arms until he intertwined their fingers.

Andrew steered her toward the settee she'd just abandoned, and Della let out an inelegant giggle.

"What is so funny?" Andrew asked as he spun her around to lower her body to the cushions.

"You said it was much too forward to walk into the home of a baroness and ask to court her, but here you are now in a baroness's sitting room in the middle of the night, making all sorts of propositions."

He grinned, and Della left a thumbprint in the hollow of one of his dimples.

"Della, you told me that you wanted to marry me years ago. What else was I to do?" He crawled across the divan, leaning his body over hers. Close, but not nearly close enough.

"Nothing," Della said. She hooked her right leg around his waist and used all the strength she possessed to pull him down on top of her. "Nothing at all."

His eyes drifted down between them. His hand ran up her leg, from where her knee rested at his hip up to where her thigh disappeared under her gown. Della arched her back, her neck stretching in search of his mouth. She bit his bottom lip, and she felt a guttural moan leave his chest. She responded in kind, letting her body do what it wanted and rolling her hips against his. Before she could even emit the hiss of pain she'd anticipated, he rested his palm flat on the flare of her hip bone. Just as he had the first time. The pressure eased her pain, but his fingers splayed out so close to where she wanted them only ignited a pressure of an entirely different kind.

Della let her hips slide against his once more, this time she felt only the press of his hardness against her core. Her hands sought him out, gripping wherever she could reach. The back of his neck. The curve of his shoulder. The space where his shirt was coming untucked from his trousers. That drew her focus, and she tugged at his clothes with all the dexterity she had left in her near-destroyed hands.

As she grabbed at him, Andrew began to understand her

intentions. She pulled at the buttons of his waistcoat. He tugged at his cravat. Della wondered why she hadn't started there. She loved that hollow at the bottom of his throat so much. She ran her tongue over it as soon as he tossed his cravat away, and that little slice of exposed skin made her want to burn all of the cravats he owned.

He rose to his knees to strip his shirt off, and while Della whimpered at the loss of his weight, she had to admit she did enjoy the view. Within moments, he was back, slowly pushing her gown up her thighs. Della met him halfway, peeling the thin fabric off of her in a show of the kind of boldness only he inspired. His mouth grazed over her collarbone, his teeth gently dragging down toward the valley between her breasts as he loosened her stays and pulled at her chemise.

"Della," he moaned her name against the skin above her sternum. Her back arched again, wanting more of his mouth.

He continued his path down her body with the faintest licks of his tongue, tugging clothing off as he went. He sucked on a spot next to her left hip, right beside where his hand still rested. Her hips thrust against him again, and he seemed to get the message. She felt the heat of him on her core, his fingers dancing over her flesh where she was wet and wanting. There was the press of his tongue again, those slow swipes through her folds.

"Tell me to stop if I hurt you." He looked up at her from between her thighs, and she was nearly too captivated to respond. "Della?" he asked, when she'd been staring for a moment too long.

"Yes?" she responded. She was still half dazed, even though he'd stopped the movement of those talented fingers and his mouth was otherwise occupied. Della ran her fingers through his unruly curls. She realized they were particularly disheveled because she'd been tugging on them.

"If something causes you pain, you have to stop me. Promise me." He looked so suddenly serious that Della had no choice but to nod.

Andrew squeezed her hip, and then he was back to where she wanted him. As much as she loved this, as much as she needed the pleasure he brought her, she did miss the feel of those eyes already. His deft fingers worked over her again, and fire spread down Della's spine. He thrust two fingers inside her body, and Della gasped. He stopped for a moment, as if trying to make sure she was well. He must have seen the bliss on her face, because he moved those fingers again, crooking them to hit a perfect place that made Della's eyes roll back in her head.

Pleasure mounted like nothing she'd ever felt before, and every roll of her hips pressed the heel of his hand against the apex of her sex. Between her legs, he was frantic. His fingers moved and his hand flexed against her hip and he pressed hot, lazy kisses against whatever skin he could reach. Her hip, the underside of her breast, her shoulder.

Della reached for his neck, pulling him up to her lips. Her tongue swept into his mouth and she came undone. She gasped into the air he breathed, and she shuddered as white-hot sparks exploded across her vision. All of her muscles went lax, and Andrew's weight came over her. Her hands still gripped his face, and she swept her thumb over one of his eyebrows.

"I love you," he murmured, "so much, Della."

"So much," she echoed.

Andrew moved to pull away, to lean back or climb off of her or extricate himself from the cramped settee that was not made for this kind of activity. Automatically, without her permission, even, her arms tightened around him. It was a paltry attempt to keep him there, as her grip was weak at best. Once again, Andrew froze.

Her legs were still tingling, but she wrapped them around his waist. Her thighs pulled his hips toward hers, and she felt the hard press of him against her center. Just a brush of him against her, and she wanted so much more.

"Andrew," she moaned, and she'd never heard herself sound so desperate. So needy.

"Are you sure?" he asked, his hands running all over her. Up and down her sides, over her face, through her hair. He was everywhere except where she needed him.

"Yes," she nodded. Della leaned up and kissed him. She used her mouth on his and her legs around him to pull him closer.

"I . . ." Andrew broke away from her kiss just enough to speak. At his hesitation, Della froze. She tried to let him go, but her hip was locked into place.

"What is the matter? Do you not want to—"

"No, no," he assured her, "I do." His hand fell to her hip again, massaging that spot. By the time her muscles loosened, she didn't want to let him go anymore. "It's just . . . I have not . . . I have never done this before," he admitted.

"Oh," Della breathed. He was still so close that she'd felt those words pressed against her cheek. She pulled back, locking her fingers around the back of his neck. "Neither have I."

"Really?" His eyes looked strange, pupils still darkened with hunger but blown wide with surprise.

Della didn't think it was such a shock. She'd been banished to the countryside alone since before her debut. There'd been little opportunity to entertain a gentleman. Besides, there'd never been anyone she wanted. No one except Andrew.

"Yes," she nodded. Her thumb moved over his cupid's bow. "There's never been anyone for me but you."

His hands slipped away, but his mouth found hers. For someone who was so consistently a mess, he was remarkably coordinated. He bit the inside of her bottom lip and tugged. His tongue met hers as she heard him working open the fall of his trousers.

Della broke away and Andrew groaned in protest. She'd just wanted to see him. Her hands felt the expanse of his chest, warm and solid and covered in a thin layer of crisp, wiry hair. Her eyes lowered to the hardness straining toward her, and she wrapped her fingers around him. His hips jerked against her, and his eyes closed.

"God, Della," he moaned. She hadn't known what power was until that moment. Until she made him make that half-broken sound.

She slid her hips against his, finally feeling the burn of his skin against hers. Her hands touched him and herself, stroking the length of him and the tight center of her own pleasure. His hand pressed into her hip more firmly, and she thrust herself against him with renewed vigor.

He hovered above her, his forehead dropping to rest against hers as he guided himself toward her. He pressed into her body slowly, gently, and Della took in a heaving, gasping breath. There was an initial burst of pain, unfamiliar and fleeting. He wasn't moving, and she didn't know how to convince him to. Words might have been helpful, but she couldn't manage them.

Her body felt tight and unforgiving, but she moved anyway. Her legs pulled him closer, her inner muscles pulled him deeper. She found a rhythm that had pleasure building at the base of her spine in minutes, but still, he barely moved.

"Andrew," she said finally, "look at me, love."

His eyes opened, and she saw the tension there. She saw how much he was holding back.

"Don't want to hurt you," he murmured through gritted teeth.

Della's head fell back against the cushions. She saw him from a new angle. She'd never noticed just how sharp his jawline was.

"You will not hurt me," she told him. "You cannot hurt someone who wants you so much. Not like this."

She punctuated her statement with another thrust of her hips, this one completely relentless.

"I love you," she murmured, "so much." It was as if her words triggered something feral in him. He rested his head against her shoulder, his free hand wrapping around the back of her neck. He ground his body into hers and filled her up in one smooth, quick motion. Della gasped at the sensation, at the pressure of him both on top of and inside her body.

Wordlessly, they established an agonizing rhythm of quick thrusts and long, slow glides. He bit at the side of her neck. He sucked on her ear lobe. His fingers left imprints on the skin of her hip.

"So much," she said, again and again. It was mindless repetition, those barely there, gasped words.

"Della," he breathed against the crown of her head. She knew what he meant, sensed it in the complete loss of his control. Their rhythm became staccato, completely wild and unpredictable.

She kissed him again. She sucked his lip into her mouth and bit. She swept her tongue against his teeth. This time, pleasure didn't build into a crescendo. It cracked through her in an instant, like a bolt of lightning. There was no thunder, no warning. Della simply came apart, whimpering and holding on to every piece of him she could reach.

He moaned her name again—this time it was more of a growl. His hands tightened, and she felt his heartbeat inside her. She was filled with liquid heat, and then he was gone. He slipped from her body and collapsed into a heap next to her, as much as the furniture would allow.

Della was cold. So suddenly cold. She fought off a whine and she turned her head to face him.

His hand came to rest against her cheek. So tame, so gentle compared to what they'd just done, but it was just what she needed. She raised her hand over his, pressing his skin into hers and holding him there. Her eyes drifted closed. She'd felt the lightning and the absence of thunder, and this sense of overwhelming, drenching peace was the rain. Her storm was over.

"Love you," she heard him mumble again, like he couldn't stop saying it. Like it was a reflex.

The storm had washed away all her thoughts. As she fell asleep, there were only two words left in her mind.

So much.

CHAPTER FORTY-THREE

NDREW AWOKE SLOWLY, and he almost thought himself delirious with fever. That was, until he realized all the warmth he felt across his chest was Della. He was delirious with satisfaction, then.

She lay on her stomach, tucked underneath his arm. Her own arm was draped over him, and their legs were tangled beneath the blanket he'd tossed over them at some point in the night. His free hand had found her waist, and Andrew closed his eyes because he just had to take a moment to commit this exact scene to memory.

He'd woken up alone the last time they'd been together like this, and he'd thought that was his lowest point. Now that he knew the bliss of waking up holding her, he'd only ever feel his truly lowest point if he never got to experience this breathtaking contentment again.

He didn't want to wake her. His fingertips memorized the feel of her skin, running over her shoulder blade and down her back. He attempted to untangle the knots in her hair, but he wasn't so good at it. He may have made them worse. For long minutes, he watched the sun come up, but his eyes never left her face. The light drifted over her features slowly but surely, until it reflected off the strands of hair at the crown of her head. She seemed so serene like this, but still so vibrant. Like she was both peace and joy personified.

Her breathing quickened against his neck and her limbs tightened against his. Della's fingers flexed against his chest, and her wide, startled eyes jerked up to look at him.

"Andrew," she whispered. Then she smiled. That half of a grin had him breathing out a contented sigh so significant the motion shifted Della off of his chest.

"Good morning, love." He gripped the back of her neck again, his hand knotting even more of her hair, and he kissed her.

It was the greatest privilege of his life to kiss her like this, casually, and whenever he wanted. Simply because she smiled and he melted and he could. Simply because for the first time, she was truly within reach.

Her fingertips danced over his chest, sweeping up his neck and over his face in the softest touch he'd ever felt. She seemed to be doing the same thing, cataloging him. Her eyes were looking too close and seeing too much.

"What is it you want to do with this place?" Andrew asked her, once breath became necessary and they broke apart. Her pointer finger fell over his lips and he kissed it. "Now that it is yours."

"I've an idea," she said. She rolled her wrist and cracked her knuckles. Mornings were hard for her, he remembered. She was always stiff and achy. He was also hard, stiff, and achy this morning, but in an entirely different way. "I have had so much support since I fell ill."

Andrew felt his brows knit up. To him, it seemed a ridiculous thing to say. After all her parents and brother had done, to think she'd still had the support she deserved. It was preposterous.

"I have always had a home, and I found an alternate family. Not all are so lucky." Della raised her head up, looking back and forth to stretch her neck. "I want to make Kinloss a place for other young women whom society has cast aside. To give them the support they need and the love they deserve."

Andrew nodded. It seemed like such a Della thing to do, to

inherit property and immediately want to give it to other people. It was inherently Della, to see a problem that wasn't hers and offer a solution that was.

"Clara is quite sold on the idea already. She was ill herself when she came to Westfield Manor. She gets these horrible headaches, they're debilitating. That is why she doesn't wear hairpins, because they cause her pain."

She was rambling, but she was staring at him with this half-grinning, bemused expression on her face, and he'd never seen her so exuberant. Her excitement was contagious. Andrew felt himself smiling, too. He supposed that was just his body's reaction to seeing her like this. To seeing her at all, really.

"We're going to start with Gwen, I believe. She is still hiding, pretending she isn't ill at all. I do not blame her. I did the same. We all do, to some degree, I think. We're going to have to work on that."

Della nodded, as if to herself. Andrew nodded back anyway.

"I . . ." Della hesitated, and she suddenly wasn't looking at him anymore. "I could use some assistance, you know. With the running of the estate, the business of it all. I'm sure there will be an excess of paperwork."

"Darling." He tucked a fraying strand of hair behind her ear. Her eyes drifted back up to his. "I happen to love paperwork."

She smiled, a grin so wide and open and free that he thought it might split her sweet face in half.

"Where do you think we would be?" he asked her, sobering for a moment. "Now. If things had gone differently? If your mother hadn't intervened. If you hadn't been sent away too soon."

He'd been thinking about it on and off all night, when he wasn't thinking of the Della of the present that he held in his arms. He thought of the past. It still occupied entirely too much of his mind. Something about this morning had made him deeply reflective.

Della smiled again. She leaned forward to press a kiss against his shoulder.

"I suppose we'd still be right here," she said. "Together."

With the hand still woven into her hair, Andrew guided her lips to his. She melted against him, and she was all soft sighs and slow glides of her tongue. Her hand came to rest against his heart, and he hummed. He licked into her mouth. Her teeth snagged the corner of his top lip and slowly, so slowly, pulled.

"Della," he nearly moaned. In his admittedly foggy mind, he remembered this was an important conversation. Perhaps the most important.

With all of the strength he possessed, Andrew pulled away. Della let out a whiny little whimper, and Andrew cursed himself for ever moving away from her.

"Della," he repeated. His other hand came to cradle her cheek, and she leaned into him. She pressed the lightest kiss against the pulse point in his wrist, and Andrew's heart beat so fast he thought he must be on the edge of death, because he thought only heaven could be better than this. "Yesterday, you said you would've married me all those years ago."

It was a very simple statement of fact, Andrew didn't know why it felt like such a life-changing declaration. But he did—he knew. It was Della, that was why. Everything about her was life-changing.

"I did." She nodded, and the motion let his thumb drift over her lips. "And you said you would marry me tomorrow."

"I did," Andrew repeated. His entire soul smiled. "I would marry you yesterday, today, and any tomorrow you'd like, my love."

There was a flash of something in her eyes, a reflection of the unbridled happiness he felt blooming in him, but then she guarded herself. She came down from the clouds and back to the ground.

"What about London?" she asked. Her voice was oddly protective, as if she were preparing herself to be hurt. Eventually, he'd get her to see that wouldn't be necessary. It would take time, and they had plenty, he hoped.

"I've no place in London. Not without you." At his words, her eyelids lowered, and he brushed his thumb against her lashes.

"What about your mother?" she asked, in that same guarded tone.

That was a question he didn't particularly know how to answer. He was silent for a moment. He couldn't pretend that he wouldn't miss her, but there were letters and carriages. They'd been apart for long periods of time before, separated by oceans, even.

"Do you think she'd like to live here?" Della murmured. "With us?"

Andrew's poor, battered heart finally settled somewhere deep in his chest, where it would always live, right next to hers.

"I think she would love that." He smiled, and so did she, and for the millionth time since he'd seen her that first day, Andrew wanted to pinch himself.

Della lay back down on his chest, and Andrew took in a deep, soothing breath that smelled exactly like her. He kissed the crown of her head.

"There are other chambers, you know," she said, tilting her chin to look up at him. "I haven't seen them, but I'm sure there are. We needn't sleep in the sitting room again. As much as I've enjoyed it, it would likely be better for my pain if we didn't." As if to illustrate her point, she cracked her knuckles. "And we needn't sleep together at all, I suppose." She frowned at the idea, even as she said it. He watched as a line formed between her brows. "There should be separate chambers. For the man of the house. If you want them."

"I've missed too much of this." His arms squeezed around her, tight enough that she actually giggled. "If the choice is between a bed with you and one without, then there isn't a choice at all. Though I am in agreement that a bed would be preferable to our current arrangement."

Della hummed, and then they lay in silence for a while. Her

fingernails drifted up and down his forearm. Back and forth. The motion was oddly soothing, and his eyes started to drift closed again.

"Do you suppose we should get up?" Della asked after a bit, her voice betraying her own sleepiness. He thought the sentence might have ended on a yawn.

"What did I say, Della?" He shifted her until she lay on her back and he rolled on top of her. His head came to rest on her chest, and he sighed into her collarbone when her fingers slipped into his hair. "That isn't a choice at all," he murmured.

"You know," she said after a few moments of contented silence, "while I love you dearly, and I will always be more than happy here with you like this, I will miss our letters."

"Why would you stop writing to me?" Andrew asked. He didn't even raise his head. He hoped she could understand him, because he wasn't fond of the idea of moving.

"Well, what am I to do? I believe the post would be quite confused if I sent a letter to my husband addressed to my own home."

Andrew nearly died at the use of the word. His heart seemed to malfunction, skipping a beat and soaring and falling all at the same time. Her husband. That's what he'd be, as long as he lived. So there could be no more malfunctions of the heart, then.

"You don't have to send them, darling." He did pick his head up then, lazily drawing his lips over her neck and up to her cheek. "But you can still write them. Hand them to me. Or put them on my pillow, or in my coat pocket, or the drawer where I'll keep my socks. Just because you can speak to me whenever you'd like does not mean you cannot still write. Hide the letters if you want. I'll find them this time, I promise."

Her face relaxed into something pleased and serene, and her arms tightened around him. That exact expression was so precious to him. He wanted to keep her looking at him like that forever. It would be his life's work from now on.

"And you will write back?" she asked. Her fingers tugged on

his curls again, and Andrew's eyes nearly rolled back into his head.

"Of course, love," he managed to mutter. He was half asleep and also deeply aroused. It was an odd combination. That was Della, though. Just like she was peace and joy personified, she was both restfulness and attraction.

"I know you will find them," she mumbled. Her voice was as sleepy as his. Della wiggled her body around underneath him to get comfortable, and the movement of her skin against his sent a bolt of pleasure down his spine. Her body felt lax and pliable and his hands roamed down her waist, over her fevered hips toward her thighs. "You always find me."

EPILOGUE

D ELLA REACHED FOR her other ivory silk glove. She'd put the right one on already, because she considered that her bad hand. The left she'd need to use to finish getting ready. It was an odd thing, leaving that one glove until the end of her routine, but it worked for her.

As she picked up the glove, something drifted to the floor. Della smiled. She hadn't received a note from Andrew in a few days. They'd been so busy preparing to host their first party they'd hardly had time for writing, but he'd known she was nervous for this evening. It was her first event as the host, and they'd all spent so much time and effort introducing themselves to the community near Kinloss that her parents had so horribly neglected.

Della bent down as best she could with her fitted gown and minimally mobile body to retrieve the note.

If you're reading this, you are probably late for your own party.
I love you.

—Andrew

It was possible he was correct. She tended to lose track of time in her own head, because things like punctuality were nothing in the face of her worries.

"Della!" she heard Clara yell. She did knock now, in most cases, since the chambers now belonged to her and Andrew both.

"Yes?" Della shouted back. She slipped on her glove and walked toward the door. It burst open, and she was glad she hadn't been any closer or she'd have been knocked to the floor.

"You must get down there," Clara huffed. "Guests are starting to arrive, and your husband is greeting them."

"Andrew is greeting the guests?" Della asked, confusion evident in her tone.

"No, your other husband." Clara rolled her eyes. "Yes, Andrew. Harry was going to welcome everyone, but Andrew said he would do it, and Harry listened because Andrew is the man of the house, whatever that means." Her voice took on a mocking tone there toward the end.

With a sigh, Della strolled out of their rooms and into the hallway. She and Clara took the stairs arm in arm.

"Who made this?" Della asked, admiring the beading on the navy-blue sleeves attached to Clara's fitted bodice. "Alice or Gwen?"

"Both of them, I believe," Clara answered. "They are quite good at what they do together."

"Are they in the ballroom already?" Della took each step slowly. She wore her riding boots again with her light-pink gown, and she didn't particularly care if anyone saw. Her feet were killing her today, so everyone would just have to bear witness to the fashion offense.

"Everyone but you," Clara remarked. Della pinched the inside of her elbow, and Clara swatted at her in retaliation.

"There she is!" Andrew smiled when his eyes caught hers, and he patted Harry on the shoulder as he left their combined post and marched toward Della. "You look lovely."

"Thank you." She tugged his cravat straight. He must not have eaten yet—he hadn't spilled anything on it. His waistcoat was ivory, made to match her gloves and the shoes she would've worn had her feet been kinder to her. "Oh, no," Della mumbled.

She looked over Andrew's shoulder at Clara and Harry. They were standing too close together, whispering intently in the shadow behind the door Harry still held open for no one. "What are we to do about that?" she asked him.

He hummed, pressing a kiss to her temple. "I don't know, darling." He used her shoulders to turn her in the other direction, toward where their guests waited. "It is your house; I am just the husband."

Della laughed, but she followed his lead. They entered the ballroom to no grand announcement. No heads turned in their direction, and they naturally joined conversations already in progress. It was not customary to invite one's household to a ball like this, nor was it traditional to invite one's tenants. Della had never been traditional, though, and she found her party in progress to be a roaring success.

In the corner, Alice tried to convince Gwen to speak to the other young ladies her age. Those two were a positive influence on each other with their mutual interest in sewing, and they'd made half of the garments everyone in the room wore.

Harry and Clara entered behind them, walking arm in arm. Della wondered what the frantic whispering had been about, but she knew she'd hear of it later if it were anything important.

"Wait a moment," Andrew stopped them as they proceeded through the room. It was her intention to speak to everyone, and he was halting her progress. "Where is your walking stick?"

"I do not need it this evening." She patted his arm where it was connected to hers. "I have you."

"Oh, I see," he chuckled. "So, I am supposed to stay by your side all evening for support?" he asked in jest, but they both knew he would. She wouldn't have even had to ask.

"If you wouldn't mind terribly," she replied with a grin. In addition to their other changes, they were also pivoting away from the traditional schedule a ball kept to. There would be a bit of dancing and then dinner, and everyone would be home in time to retire as they normally would. They were a group comprised of mostly sick people and farmers, not those who needed to be out at all hours of the night at a party.

Music began to play from the corner of the room, and Clara brushed by them pulling Harry into the open space they'd designated as a dance floor. It wasn't even the music for any particular dance, but no one could tell Clara that.

Della began gesturing to everyone around her, couples and friends and children filling up the space in the middle of the room. Alice even pulled Gwen off of the wall. It was less dancing and more conversing to music in close proximity to one another. She looked around, and she spotted nearly everyone. Silas still preferred to be out of doors, but he would come in for dinner. Mrs. Goldsmith was finishing up the cooking, which she'd insisted she do all herself, despite Della's offer to hire several more kitchen maids to help her.

Andrew pulled her to the outside of the circle the party had formed. They stood under the portrait of Della's mother that was painted when she'd been about Della's age. At that point, her mother had been married for a couple of years and had given birth to Della, and she hadn't lived much longer past that point. Since she'd been at Kinloss, Della had felt the inkling of a connection to her mother, something that hadn't existed before. As she looked at that painting, Della tried to find some visible representation of it there. The jut of their chin was the same, maybe. Or the sharp bridge of their diminutive noses. Perhaps it was the straightening of their shoulders, or the way their brows seemed to smile more than their mouths.

"I did not know her, but I think she would be proud of you." Andrew turned her by the shoulders again, clearing a spot for them in the crush of revelry.

Della hoped so. She hoped that somewhere out there, even in the beyond, there was some piece of her born family that was proud of her.

"This is the legacy I want to leave for our children," Della said, gesturing behind her to the lively crowd with her chin. "This happiness. This sense of home."

Andrew swept her into his arms, guiding them in a dance of their own creation. Della barely moved. She didn't need to.

"We do not have children, as far as I am aware," Andrew smirked.

"Stop teasing." She smacked at his chest, but it was really more of a pat. "You know what I mean. Our future children, should we have them. I never thought I'd have the opportunity. But I quite like the thought."

"So do I," he smiled. He spun her, just like he'd done the last time they danced, but her leg caught. Pain flared through her locked-up joints, all the way from her knee to her spine. That damned hip.

"That damned hip, I know," Andrew said. He rested his hand there, massaging until the rigid muscles gave way. "It's quite irritating for you, I'm sure, but I do love this hip. It's where I rest my hand while my mouth is—"

"Andrew!" Della gasped. She looked around her, trying to determine if anyone had heard. Everyone else seemed so caught up in their own merriment, she doubted it. That was a relief.

"Sorry, love." Andrew grinned unrepentantly.

"You do not have to apologize, and you know it." Della moved her feet slowly, resuming their dance. "And that is the kind of inappropriate remark you would usually make in a letter."

Their letters were increasingly erotic, and those notes would not be a part of the legacy they left for their children. She'd keep all of their chaste, longing letters from before they were lovers forever, but she'd made him promise that those more explicit letters from the early days of their marriage would stay between them.

"You are exactly right." He spun her again, and her hip decided to cooperate this time. "Let me go get a pen." Andrew moved to step away from her, and she hooked her arms around him even tighter.

"No," she whined. It was a tad embarrassing, the petulant

tone she used. She was an adult and a baroness and a wife, and that tone was not becoming of any of those roles.

"Don't worry." He turned back to her with an easy smile and those dimples. "You know I will always be right here."

Della smiled back. She pressed her hand to his cheek and he kissed the inside of her wrist, just above her gloves. He bit at the edge of that glove, like he wanted to peel it off with his teeth. She wondered when she'd become so permitting of such impropriety in public. Probably several hundred letters ago, she supposed.

She arched a brow, either in challenge or in reprimand. She'd decide which based on his response.

"I am at your service," Andrew promised.

Acknowledgements

For me, this series represents a sharp curve in my career trajectory. It was a blip of an idea, absolutely not on my radar, let alone my five-year plan, when it grew into something seismic that rattled the foundation of who I am as a reader and a writer. This series, in a new genre, age range, and voice, with a new agent and publisher, was completely inconceivable to me just a couple of years ago. Allowing this earthquake to shake me to my core was the best thing I could ever have done for myself, and I am so fiercely proud that this is the end product.

I want to thank my agents, Katie Thomas and Josi Beck at Beck Literary, for their support through this publication journey. I'd also love to thank Kathyrn Le Veque, Shawn Morrison, Amelia Hester, Natalie Sowa, and everyone at Dragonblade Publishing for showing me how incredible and collaborative the publishing process can be. I want to especially thank my editor, Courtney Brown, for her invaluable contributions to all three of these books, into which she put her heart and soul into making such thoughtful suggestions for improvements. Her efforts to legitimize my flailing attempts at historical accuracy are incredibly appreciated!

To Daniele Hunter, thanks for having such unshakable belief in me and always being willing to help in any way possible. I couldn't be more grateful that you have my back in this business!

To Marissa Spear, thank you endlessly for your willingness to dive headfirst into whatever potentially unhinged idea I throw your way and your enthusiasm specifically for this project. I had absolutely no confidence in it at first, but you always did. I hope you know that it was such a privilege that I got such an early opportunity to discover similar confidence in your work.

To Alexandra Vasti, thank you for changing my life with your stories and supporting me in every way as I fought to tell mine. I also want to thank every author who I consider part of my own historical romance canon—Felicity Niven, Eva Devon, Erin Langston, Scarlett Scott, Elizabeth Everett, Mary Lancaster, Stacy Reid, and many others. Some of these inspiring authors offered kind words in public support of my books, and I can't thank them enough for that.

To all of my bookish friends and family members who are always cheering me on—Eliza Engram, Erin Baldwin, Kade Dishmon, Cara Leibowitz, Melissa See, Lillie Lainoff, Nicole Zelniker, Sabina Nordqvist, Gretchen Schreiber, Sydney Langford, Jessica Burkhart, Cammi Stillwell, Jonathan Honeycutt.

To my grandmothers and the legacy they've both left behind in me.

To my incomparable parents, who have had to ask, "Which book is this?" every time I share some kind of update, because four books in one year is kind of a lot, and there are so many updates, but they've been right beside me every chaotic, overwhelming step of the way. I have never been anything but relentlessly supported, simply because I was born theirs, and I am both so lucky and so grateful.

To my sister Jamie and my best friend Ashley, who have nurtured my neuroses, my belief in myself, and my stories from the ground up all over again throughout this process. It's such a shame that my Regency characters don't know the joys of the three-person group chat, but ours really is the backbone of my world. I couldn't live without either of you, and I wouldn't want to.

To my cat Boots, who I hope follows me everywhere forever.

Lastly, I want to thank all of my readers, past, present, and future, because by writing these books, I've learned that there are some things that time can't change, and one of them is that community is forever.

About the Author

Jade Hendren writes historical romance with flare—of the chronic illness variety, to be specific. Jade is the alter ego of young adult novelist Marissa Eller, and in both genres, her work explores chronic illness, mental health, and the wide-spanning impacts of disability. She spends her days in a niche corner of academia, and she lives in North Carolina with her family and her beloved chaos demon cat. She shares many hobbies with her regency-era heroines, like listening to music, afternoon tea, and conversing with friends. But her music is on Spotify, her tea is iced, and her talks with friends happen through a phone she's arguably too attached to. With low angst and a heavy dose of humor, she puts a sick spin on the historical romance genre. She is represented by Katie Thomas at Beck Literary Agency. For all media inquiries, please reach out to katie@beckliterary.com.

www.jadehendren.com
IG: jade.hendren
Facebook: Jade Hendren

www.ingramcontent.com/pod-product-compliance
Lightning Source LLC
Chambersburg PA
CBHW050658070726
47595CB00014B/372